GALVEST

INDIG

Book 3

The Atonement

N.E. BROWN
S.L. JENKINS

Galveston: 1900 – Indignities
Book 3: The Atonement

Published by Mindstir Media
1931 Woodbury Ave. #182 | Portsmouth, NH 03801 | USA
1.800.767.0531 | www.mindstirmedia.com

Printed in the United States of America

ISBN-13: 978-0-9898820-4-0

The Atonement

CHAPTER 1

It was a cool, cloudy day in early November, 1902, and the loud, high pitched whistle from the passenger train woke Alex Cooper from a deep sleep. It took him a moment to remember where he was and what he was doing on the train. Then he remembered; he was headed to Beaumont, Texas, in hopes of finding his past. The head injury he had sustained by the two bandits who shot him, and left him for dead, left his mind empty of the last five years of his life. All he knew now was what the people surrounding him had told him. He was married; he had one four-month-old stepson, a fifteen-month-old stepson and a mistress on an Indian reservation. He closed his eyes and tried to remember what he could and the last three months were clearly visible to him. Other than that, he had no memory.

Mary Windsong and the medicine man on an Indian reservation outside of Kountze, Texas, had nurtured and cared for him the first two months after he woke up from a four-day coma. Mary had fallen in love with him, and feeling gratitude for her caring, he thought he loved her, too. They had been intimate before he found out from a fellow employee who had come looking for him, that he was married to a woman named Catherine Eastman Merit Cooper. It was an unbelievable story, and he felt that before he could make decisions about his future, he had to find out about his past.

Alex got off the train in Beaumont and instinctively walked to the livery stable where his one and only friend, Pilgrim, his horse, was waiting for him. Pilgrim slobbered when he saw Alex coming and pawed at the dirt.

"How ya doing, boy?" Alex asked Pilgrim, as he scratched his head.

Alex had been an oil scout for Glacier Oil Company out of Dallas, Texas, and had been working in Beaumont, Texas, after oil had been discovered at Spindletop. While on a scouting expedition near Kountze, Texas, he was shot by two bandits; once in the shoulder and another caught him in the side of his head. The bandits chased Pilgrim, trying to catch him, but Pilgrim led them away from Alex and then doubled back and found Alex, nearly dead. Pilgrim had knelt down and Alex pulled himself up on the saddle. Pilgrim took Alex into the nearest town four miles away and waited for help at the train depot. Alex was taken to the medicine man on a nearby reservation and stayed there until he was found by Clarence Henry, a fellow employee. Alex refused to go with him the first time, but Clarence returned a few days later with Alex's wife, Catherine. Alex did not remember her, but agreed to leave anyway and go back with Catherine to Galveston. After a couple of days of trying to be a man he knew nothing about, he decided to leave in hopes of finding his past in Beaumont, Texas, where he first met Catherine.

Alex stayed at the livery stable and fed Pilgrim his oats and hugged him before he left to find the office he used to work out of.

"Alex Cooper," the man at the desk said as he got up to shake his hand. "Man, we all thought you were dead. It's a relief to see you."

"I'm glad to be back and I was wondering if there were any job openings left?" Alex said teasingly.

"Heck, man, what do you mean? You're still on the payroll," Clarence Henry said as he came out of one of the offices. "It's good to see you back, and looking so well."

"I've decided to come back here and try to sort things out before I make any hasty decisions," Alex told him.

"Good idea," Clarence answered and asked where Alex was staying.

"I haven't looked for a room yet. Got any suggestions? Alex asked.

"How about the old Billings place?" Clarence asked. "The company probably won't start drilling for oil there until later next year. The house is boarded up and we posted No Trespassing signs, but the place is broken into all the time. You could live there, free, and keep an eye on it."

Alex thought for a moment and then said, "Sure." Alex knew that Clarence was one of the few people who knew anything about his past and there were plenty of skeletons in the closet on the Billings farm. "I think I can find it," Alex said.

"Come back in the morning and I'll have some work for you. You can talk to Charlotte at the home office then. She's been holding your back pay and she needs to know where to send it," Clarence said.

"Thanks, I'll see you then." Alex left and remembered he had not had breakfast and he was hungry. He had planned to get something on the train, but he had fallen asleep instead. Without thinking, he walked a couple of blocks to a café that seemed vaguely familiar.

"Mr. Alex, it's so good to see you. Is Catherine with you?" the young Mexican girl asked. When she saw Alex looking strangely at her she said, "It's me, Consuelo, from Billings' undertaking."

"Yes, how are, Consuelo?" Alex asked as he sat down in his usual spot at the counter. Consuelo poured Alex some coffee and asked for his order.

"Just the usual breakfast special," he answered, surprising himself that he had ordered something without looking at the menu. When Consuelo came back with his food, Alex told her that Catherine was still in Galveston and he was there on a short work assignment.

"Tell her that I asked about her, and that I am still working part-time at the new funeral home and part-time here. I hope she is well," Consuelo said as she left to refill the cups of the other patrons.

After breakfast, Alex left and went to the general store to get some oats for Pilgrim and supplies to take to the farm. He bought a blanket, some soap, a few canned goods, and some beef jerky, and decided to wait and see what was in the house before he bought anything else.

Pilgrim was anxious as Alex saddled him up and mounted him. Alex thought it felt good to be riding again and he instinctively rode in the direction of the farm. He decided to take his time. Oil rigs were now gracing the pastures of the once barren land. He vaguely remembered that oil had been discovered two years earlier at a place now known as Spindletop. The discovery of the huge well on January 10, 1901, brought the sleepy town of Beaumont, Texas, from a small town of 10,000 people to over 30,000 people the first year. Many had already left to find the black gold in other parts of the country, but Beaumont was still striving as oil refineries were being constructed nearby.

Alex approached the old farm house and made sure his rifle was loaded. He didn't want to take a chance that someone might be trespassing and now living in the house. The place looked empty and the boards were still nailed across the windows and doors. He walked over to the well and pumped some water into the metal tub underneath it. He pumped it several times to remove any grit and dirt that might have accumulated, and then he poured the water out on the ground. He refilled it and then took Pilgrim over to it and tied him to the handle of the pump.

There was a broken-down corral with a small shed that had been attached to a burned down barn. He took a step back, as his memory brought back a vision of a fire blazing while Alex watched. He must have been here when it burned, he thought. Alex walked over to where he figured the barn door had once been and walked into it about ten feet. The sun was reflecting off something on the ground around some charred wood. He stooped down and used his hand to dust away the particles that were partially covering it. It was a ladies gold locket. He opened it and there were a man's and woman's picture inside. The woman looked like Catherine and he felt an aching pain in his gut. It must be her parents, he thought. He put it in his vest pocket where he carried the envelopes with pictures of his family. It was his hope that if he looked at the photographs long enough, something would come back to him.

He looked closer at the ground and then his eyes focused on a pulley attached to a chain, and fragments of Alex's memory gave him a clear picture of him and Catherine standing in the barn. It only lasted a second, but Alex was encouraged that things were beginning to come into focus. Alex saw a crowbar lying close to the chain and he picked it up. He would need it to pry off the boards over the door going into the house.

Alex pried off the wooden planks with the crowbar and after he obtained entry into the house, he went back to Pilgrim and retrieved the small sack of supplies and his bedroll from his saddle and took them into the house. The inside was musty and layers of dust blanketed all the counters and meager furnishings. Alex walked into what he thought was a bedroom and he stopped and gasp at the bloody mattress. Visions of Catherine came into focus and he saw himself trying to wake her. His next vision was of him delivering a baby. Alex shook his head and left the room. He went out on the porch to take a deep breath and then he hurriedly walked back in and rolled up the soiled mattress. He walked past the barn and carried the soiled mattress to an old burn pile. Alex took out some matches and struck one. He cupped it in his hand and lowered it to the mattress. It caught fire immediately, and he stepped back. He looked around the yard and saw a rope that had been cut and another that had a noose with blood on it. He picked the rope up and threw it on the fire and watched. Visions of the burning barn faded in and out of his mind and then he saw a dead man on the ground with the noose around his neck.

When Alex turned and walked back toward the house, he had

to side-step a large sink hole in the ground. Again, another brief encounter with his past came into his vision. He saw himself digging a grave and rolling a man into it. It was a cool day, but Alex was sweating and he walked over to the well and pumped some water on to his handkerchief. He put it over his face and closed his eyes, wiping it over his brow. Everything seemed confusing to him and none of it made sense. The easy decision would be to just go back to the reservation and make a new life with Mary. A life that would be less complicated, but Alex never was one that looked for the easy way out. He was a planner and he relied on his good instincts to get him where he was. If he was married to Catherine, his sleeping with Mary on the Indian reservation was a sin. The thieves had taken his wedding ring along with his past, and now he had to figure out a way to make things right.

He wasn't sure what had happened at this place, but he knew it wasn't good. Maybe he should forget the whole idea about finding his past. Alex looked at the cavity in the ground. It had been a grave, he thought, but the cavity was so great, he figured that the body had been dug up. It was overwhelming, so he went back in the house.

Not many things spooked Alex. He had spent many lonely nights on the trail sleeping under the stars, but that wasn't what was bothering him. It wasn't clear to him yet, but he knew one thing, he wasn't leaving until he did.

CHAPTER 2

The morning that Alex left Galveston, Texas, was difficult for Catherine Merit. John Merit, her first husband, had given her up for dead, when she was abducted and she spent almost two years with a madman, who had taken her to Beaumont as his mail-order bride. After trying to find her for almost a year, John Merit decided to move on with his life. He had Catherine legally declared dead so he could marry a Galveston socialite by the name of Carla Beranger. Catherine's first son, Daniel, had been John's son. Adam was not the love child his brother was. Catherine's abductor, David Billings, tormented and violated Catherine for almost two years and Adam was his son. Catherine loved them both the equally.

Her story was complicated. Catherine had given up Daniel when Billings threatened to kill him after he was born because he suspected that Daniel was John's son. She left Daniel in a basket at a nun's convent in Beaumont, Texas, with instructions to send him to St. Mary's Church in Galveston. Father Jonathan and the sisters there took care of Daniel until his father, John Merit, finally claimed him as his own.

When David Billings was hung by a vigilante group on his farm, Alex Cooper came to Catherine's aide. Alex had watched her from a distance as David Billings abused Catherine in public. Billings' dreadful past of murder and rape forced him to hide in plain sight as the undertaker in Beaumont and he forced Catherine to work in the business, telling everyone she was a deaf mute. When he abducted her, she had been going to medical school in Galveston and working part time at the hospital while married to John Merit. It was her desire to become a doctor.

Catherine thought back to the day she was abducted. She was leaving work at St. Mary's Hospital late one evening when David Brooks abducted her. He had used a rag soaked in chloroform and placed it over her face causing her to become unconscious. She spent a day and a half tied up inside a coffin in a hearse. David Brooks had changed his name to David Billings and had begun a new career in Beaumont, Texas, as the undertaker. It was all behind her now.

Alex had been easy to fall in love with, thought Catherine. When she first met him, he was like no man she had ever been with. Not only was he tall and handsome, but he was also gentle, kind hearted and he had fallen in love with her long before she felt the same about him. They were married and Alex loved Adam, Catherine's second child. Two months later Alex was shot, while on a scouting expedition for his company, and the bullet went through the right side of his head erasing part of his life and leaving him with only the memory of the present.

When her first husband, John, found out Catherine had survived and had come back to Galveston, he was bitter and only allowed her two days of visitation with her son, Daniel. It was Catherine's day to visit Daniel now, and that was what she was trying to focus on. The past was too painful, and she made every effort to keep herself focused on the present and hope for a future. She found herself pregnant again with Alex's child and she wondered how she would explain to her children that all three of them had a different father. Oh well, she thought. There would be time to figure that out later on.

Before Catherine left to visit Daniel, she heard the phone ringing downstairs. Minnie Wyman, the landlord, answered it and called Catherine downstairs.

"Hi, Catherine, it's Amelia, I was hoping you might be able to stay for supper this evening."

"I would be delighted, and thanks for the invitation," she answered.

Amelia Merit was John's invalid sister and loved Catherine like a sister. Catherine gathered up her things and picked up Adam. He had an enormous amount of energy and she was glad when she sat him in his baby carriage. He began crying and she handed him one of his toys. It was difficult taking the trolley with the carriage, but someone always offered to help her off and on, and she couldn't make the trip without it.

Daniel was up and in a good mood when she got there. Catherine had just missed Daniel's first birthday in August and she vowed to never miss another. Daniel crawled over and pulled up on the stroller. He started jabbering at Adam and Adam began jabbering back. They seem to have a language of their own. It was fun watching the two brothers interact. Daniel wanted to climb into the carriage but Catherine pulled him away and took Adam out of the carriage. There was not enough room for both of them. Adam was barely sitting up on his own and Catherine propped a couple of pillows behind him. Daniel crawled to the corner of the room and pushed his ball in Adam's direction. Adam tried to lunge for it and fell over, but he didn't cry. Catherine was right there picking him back up and pushing the pillows behind him again.

"You have your work cut out for you," Amelia said, and they both laughed.

"Hmmm, something smells good," Catherine said.

"I've got a roast in the oven; John's going to join us for dinner. I hope you don't mind," she said.

"No, not at all," Catherine answered. "Does he know you invited me?"

"Of course, and he's delighted," she answered.

Amelia hesitated for a few minutes, thinking. "I don't think John looks well. Ever since he married Carla, he's lost weight and he seems to be tired all the time. Has he said anything to you?"

Catherine wasn't sure how to answer. John had previously confided in Catherine that he had a deadly blood disease and he had not told Amelia about it. John's prognosis was not good. After that, John's bitterness towards Catherine disappeared and they were now friends.

"Honestly, Amelia, I've only seen John a few times and I've noticed the weight loss, but I don't know if he wanted to lose it or if Carla's not a good cook."

Amelia laughed, and said. "I think you are right. Carla is a terrible cook."

Catherine was relieved that Amelia did not pursue the conversation about John's health any more.

"That's why I'm cooking one of his favorite meals, and now that Daniel is getting bigger, it's his favorite, too," Amelia said.

John rang the doorbell at 5:20 p.m.and Daniel screamed as he crawled to the door. John walked in and picked up Daniel. He had some flowers and a big smile on his face. Amelia thanked him for the flowers and Catherine smiled as she remembered that John used to bring her flowers all the time, too. The first time he visited Catherine, when she was at the orphanage, he had brought her flowers. She was fifteen at the time. It seemed a century ago, she thought.

The meal was scrumptious. Daniel made a huge mess in his high chair and Adam was on Catherine's lap trying to pick peas off her plate. It was the first time he had experienced real food, and he loved it.

"Amelia, after we do the dishes, would you mind watching the boys for about thirty minutes while Catherine and I go upstairs and talk?" John asked.

"Sure. But if I get down on the floor with the boys, you'll both have to help me up," Amelia answered. "My back and knees get weaker every day."

Catherine looked at him inquisitively. John smiled back and

told her that he needed to discuss some personal things with her. She smiled and shook her head like she understood.

After dinner, Catherine and John did the dishes while Amelia entertained the boys on the floor in the living room. "What do you want to talk to me about?" she whispered.

"I'll tell you when we get upstairs. I don't want Amelia to hear," he answered.

Catherine gave him a look and he reached over and kissed her on the cheek.

"You aren't trying to get me in bed, are you?" she asked teasingly.

John laughed and said, "I wish. That part of me is already dead."

John looked away and Catherine knew what he meant. He was impotent now and the disease was spreading.

They finished the dishes and John followed Catherine upstairs to John's old room which had been turned into Daniel's room. Martha, the nanny, who was out for the evening, stayed in the adjoining room.

John walked over and picked up the dresser jar he had put Catherine's father's watch in and he took it out.

"I wanted to make sure this got back to its rightful owner," he said.

He took Catherine's hand and placed the gold watch in it. Catherine looked at it, not knowing what to say.

"You need to give it to Alex," he said. "It survived the flood because I had it in my pocket and I had it repaired."

The watch had been a gift from Catherine to John while they were still married.

Catherine bit her lip, hesitating, then said, "Thank you."

She wanted to hear what John had to say before she told him about Alex's leaving.

"I've made you the executrix of my will, Catherine. Hear me

out before you say anything. My wife, Carla, has no sense of money and I wanted to find some way that I could help you with Daniel. As the executrix, you'll be able to take a monthly fee, and it would secure the fact that Daniel would get his small inheritance. Also, I've included a monthly allowance to help Amelia with the house, and her needs. If I make Carla the executrix she'll spend it all and Daniel and Amelia will end up with nothing. I want you to understand that she will try and make your life a living hell, but you are strong and I am comfortable with the fact that you can handle her. Please do this for me, Catherine. I have a great friend who's a lawyer, whom you have already met, Clay Segal, and he agrees this is the best way to do it and he assures me that he will help you with Carla."

Catherine took in a deep breath and looked at John. He looked so frail and she put her arms around him, hugging him tightly.

"I guess that's the least I can do," she said. She couldn't imagine what he might be feeling now. It was bad enough that he was in a loveless marriage, but now he was facing death.

"I've decided to tell Amelia tonight about my disease, and it is going to be hard on her. I dread the next couple of months. I probably will only be able to work a few more weeks. The doctor says that it's a disease that creeps up on you, and then it attacks you with a vengeance. I'll probably be heavily sedated at the end. Don't let them keep me alive, Catherine, not for Carla or Amelia. I just need to go when it's time. There is one more thing," John said. "Amelia's days are numbered, too. She doesn't know it, though. Her last episode was tough on her and the doctor said the next one would probably be her last. If that happens, the trust dissolves and what's left over will be split between Carla and Daniel. Hang in there with me, Catherine, I need you," John finished saying.

John got up and took her hand as they walked downstairs together. They walked over and helped Amelia up and John sat beside her on the sofa, holding her hand. Catherine picked up Adam, who had started getting fussy. She opened her blouse and nursed him while

John, softly and tenderly, gave Amelia the news. Daniel crawled over to Catherine and she lifted him up and sat him on the overstuffed chair beside her. Five minutes later he had fallen asleep and so had Adam.

Amelia started crying and asking a lot of questions. Catherine had never seen John so patient and kind. He loved Amelia so much and Catherine was happy that she had once been married to this sweet man. After an hour of questions and answers, John helped Amelia back to her bedroom and made sure she took her medicine.

Catherine was still sitting in the chair, unable to move with both boys curled around her. John smiled and stood over them savoring the beautiful moment.

"You're a great mom, Catherine, and I'm at peace leaving Daniel in your care. It's too late for you to go home, so you can stay in Daniel's room."

"Where will you sleep?" Catherine asked.

"The third bedroom has a full bed in it, now. It's comfortable," John said as he gently picked up Daniel and carried him upstairs.

Catherine grabbed her bag and followed with Adam in her arms. Both babies slept through the diaper change and they shared the crib.

"It wouldn't bother me, if you wanted to share the bed with me," she said.

"What would Alex say?" he asked.

"I wasn't going to tell you, but if you don't mind, after we get in bed, I'll tell you the rest of the story," she answered.

John handed Catherine one of his long nightshirts to wear and they both changed and crawled into bed together. It felt so natural spending the night with John. She had never stopped loving him. Catherine began telling John about Alex's accident and his loss of memory.

"He walked out on you?" John asked.

"When you say it that way, it does sound horrible. But it

wasn't like that. I was a stranger to him. His whole life, as he knew it, was taken away from him when he got shot. He did the right thing. I couldn't have been happy knowing that he felt trapped in a loveless marriage. I had to let him go. At least then, one of us would be happy that way," Catherine said.

John sat up in bed and looked at her. "Do you mind if I ask you another question?"

"What?" she asked.

"I noticed when I picked up Daniel that you have a small baby bump. Are you pregnant?"

Catherine looked down at her stomach and then looked at John. "Yes, I am."

"I wish it were mine," he said, as he leaned over and kissed her.

"So do I," Catherine answered. "I'm going to have three children, all with different fathers. I never told you, but Adam's last name is Merit. I didn't want it to be Brooks or Billings and at that time, I was hoping you and I would reconcile. Alex took me to the hospital the day after Adam was born. I had almost died when he came to the farm and found me. He took us to the hospital and stayed with me until I recovered. When the hospital asked if he had a birth certificate, he told them, no, since he was born at home. I had already told Alex what name I was giving him. I hope you don't mind."

"If Alex doesn't come back, why you don't have your marriage to him annulled? You can name your unborn child and give him my last name. They would all share the Merit name," John suggested. "You two had only been married a couple of months. He left you, and I bet he'll agree to the annulment."

"What would Carla say?" Catherine asked.

"I'm not worried about her. I'm worried about you and our children," he said.

"I guess that makes sense. It would be nice if they all shared the same last name," Catherine said.

She reached over to give John a kiss on his cheek and he pulled her to his face, gently kissing her on the lips at first. The passion began escalating and their kisses grew more intense. Catherine pulled away and they were both breathless. John placed her head to his chest and kissed her on her head.

"I've never stopped loving you, Catherine and I'm glad you came back."

CHAPTER 3

Alex had slept on his bedroll and woke up in a sweat the next morning. He couldn't remember what the dreams were about, but he knew they were all over the place. He was breathing hard and he had a headache. He got up and walked into the kitchen and put on some coffee. He turned on the makeshift shower in the bathtub and the cold water hit him like an avalanche. He grimaced from the cold, but stayed under it hoping it would get his blood flowing. When he couldn't stand it anymore he got out and dried off. He dressed quickly and made a mental list of the things he needed to do. The coffee tasted good, and he drank it quickly and then poured another cup. His headache was beginning to subside and he took his cup of coffee and walked out to the coral. He had pieced the corral together the night before to have a place for Pilgrim. He wasn't worried that Pilgrim would run off, but that something might come in. Pilgrim walked up to Alex; he put his cup of coffee on the post then poured Pilgrim some oats. He scratched Pilgrim's head then went back inside.

Alex looked around the battered shack that Billings had called home, and he wondered how Catherine had stayed here for two years. He went back into the bedroom and his eyes became transfixed on the springs of the bed. He would need to buy a new mattress, he thought. He noticed something through the springs that must have been under the bed. He reached down and pulled out a pair of leg chains. His jaw dropped open and for a moment he was dumb founded. No wonder

Catherine couldn't leave, he thought. She was a prisoner. His hatred for David Billings escalated and he cursed to himself.

Alex saddled Pilgrim and rode into town. He was early, so he walked to the café for his usual breakfast. Consuelo was there and took his order.

"What time do you get off work?" Alex asked.

Consuelo looked at him suspiciously and asked, "Why do you ask?"

"I'm looking for some information and I think you might know the answer. Would you have dinner with me tonight?" Alex asked.

"I'm not a prostitute anymore, Mr. Alex. I'm trying to be a respectable girl now," she said.

Alex laughed. "I didn't know you were a prostitute. I was in a bad accident and I am having difficulty remembering some things. I had hoped you could fill in some of the blanks."

"All right," she said. "May I bring a friend?" she asked.

"Sure, but I might ask some pretty personal questions about David Billings, and I want you to be honest with me," Alex said. "How about the Road House Café at 7:00 p.m.?"

"I'll see you then," she said.

Alex finished his breakfast and walked down to his office. Clarence was already there and asked Alex to come into his office.

"You look like you are back to your old self. Has your memory improved?" Clarence asked.

"Some," Alex said. "There are a lot of things I do because of reflex. My math and educational skills don't seem to be affected. I remembered about Spindletop and scouting the range. I don't mind doing whatever you think I can handle; filing, mapping, running to the rig. I'll tell you if I don't understand."

"Tell you what I've got for now. The old Patterson farm is still waiting on some mapping. I know you lost your tools in the robbery, but I'll give you another set. Think you can still read a map?" Clarence asked.

Alex laughed. “It doesn’t sound too hard.”

“It shouldn’t take you more than two or three hours at the most. I don’t want to have to come looking for you. There’s a satchel with the tools over there,” Clearance said and pointed to the table. “Oh, by the way, you need to call Charlotte in Dallas.”

Alex grabbed the satchel and map and left Clarence’s office. Everything seemed easy except the part about calling Charlotte in Dallas. The name rang a bell, but he figured the number would be somewhere on the main desk. Alex started looking and then found a card with his name on it. He picked it up and saw his calling card with the Dallas address and phone number. He sat down and placed the call. Charlotte answered on the first ring and was happy to hear Alex was back at work. Alex told Charlotte to please deposit his back pay checks into his account at The Texas State Bank in Dallas. They had a branch in Galveston and he and Catherine had a joint checking account there. Alex had memorized the account number and gave it to Charlotte.

“All of the checks?” she asked?

“Yes,” he answered and hung up the phone.

Alex carefully studied the map, and it looked familiar. He took a look at the bag of instruments and he automatically knew how to use them. He grabbed everything and went to the livery stable.

Alex stopped first at the hardware store and bought a hammer and some nails. The Patterson farm adjoined the Billings land and he would drop them off on his way. The day went better than he had expected. He found it interesting that part of his memory was still intact. Alex had finished by 1:00 p.m. and he headed back into town. He decided to check in with his office before he grabbed some lunch. He didn’t want Clarence to be worried about him.

Alex opened the front door and stopped dead in his tracks. Dr. Windsong and Mary were sitting in the waiting room. Clarence was sitting at the front desk and looked up when Alex came in.

"Glad you made it back all right. I guess you know these people," said Clarence and he went into his private office, leaving the three of them alone.

Alex walked over to Dr. Windsong, who was standing up now, and they shook hands. Mary stood up and Alex kissed her on the cheek.

"Could we go somewhere in private and talk?" the doctor asked.

"Sure, have you had lunch?" he asked.

Dr. Windsong shook his head no.

The three walked the two blocks to the Road House Café with Alex in the lead. After they sat down and gave the waitress their order, Alex looked at Dr. Windsong. He wanted to tell Mary how beautiful she looked, but thought better of it. He knew they were both angry because he had not tried to contact them. He figured they had a right to be angry.

"You made a promise to Mary that you would only stay in Galveston a month. I heard you came back to Beaumont a few days after you got here. Mary is now with child and she needs a husband. You are the father of her unborn baby. Maybe your head injury has also affected your mental character and you feel you have no responsibility, but I am here to ask you to do the right thing," Dr. Windsong said.

Alex was stunned and when he looked at Mary, she looked away. After Alex gathered his thoughts, he finally said, "I've been here less than a week. I came back here to see if I could sort through my past. I didn't stay in Galveston, because I didn't think it fair to my wife or to Mary. Believe me, I am an honorable man and I will do the right thing, but I am already married. I would have to get a divorce, and that might take some time."

"How much time?" Dr. Windsong asked.

"Maybe a couple of months," he answered.

"The baby will come in seven moons. Do whatever you have

to do and after you talk to your wife, I will expect you to get back with me. The sooner, the better," Dr. Windsong said.

The waitress brought their food and after eating a few bites, Dr. Windsong said, "I took you in and treated you like a son. I warned Mary not to get involved with you, but her heart did not listen. She tells me she is in love with you, and wants to spend the rest of her life with you. I need to know if you feel the same way."

"I am very fond of Mary and I am sorry for taking advantage of her affections for me. She invited me into her bed and I accepted. I take full responsibility. At this time, I can't tell you who I love. I barely know who I am. Perhaps in time I will grow to love her as much as she loves me," Alex said and he smiled at Mary.

They finished eating and Alex walked them to their buckboard. "I will go back to Galveston this weekend and ask my wife to divorce me. I'll get back with you as soon as I know something, I promise," he said.

Alex watched as they rode away. He took a deep breath. The whole time he had been in Beaumont his thoughts were mostly on Catherine. Yes, he cared about Mary, but he wasn't sure he wanted to spend the rest of his life on an Indian reservation. He walked over to his office and slumped into a chair.

Clarence came back from lunch and Alex told him he needed to see him. After Alex confided his problems to Clarence, the two men sat and talked for over an hour.

"You can't blame yourself, Alex," Clarence said. "You were not well the first time I saw you after your accident. Mary's a lovely woman and there's not a man alive who wouldn't have done the same thing you did. You didn't know you had a wife. Before you make any quick decisions, go to Galveston and talk to Catherine. She has a good head on her shoulders and she will listen," he said. "Here, use my telephone to call your wife."

Alex called the boarding house and Minnie told him Catherine was visiting her son and wouldn't be home until late that evening and that she would let Catherine know he had called. In a way, Alex was relieved to have more time to think about everything.

Clarence looked over the maps Alex had completed and he told Alex he had not lost his touch. The two rode out to a couple of rigs and it was 6:30 PM when they finally finished. Alex looked at his watch and saw he had just enough time to clean up in the washroom and meet Consuelo.

He was glad Consuelo was alone. He didn't feel the need to ask Consuelo the questions he had about the last two years now. He really didn't have to ask her anything. After they got their food, Consuelo started at the beginning and told Alex the whole story. He felt guilty that Catherine's entire miserable life in Beaumont was being spread out on the table like dirty laundry. Consuelo had actually been jealous of Catherine and there were times she had wished Catherine dead.

"I think I've heard enough," Alex said as he paid the bill and thanked Consuelo for the information.

Alex rode back out to the farm in dread. Things were beginning to happen to him that he felt he had no control over. He wasn't sure he was ever meant to be married and now it looked like he would at least have two wives in his lifetime. The thought struck him for the first time that he was going to be a father, and that was the only bright thing he could see in the future at this moment.

Alex lay in bed looking at the ceiling. He tried to will himself to remember. It was like a door had closed and locked inside his head. Other doors were open, but the door to the last few years of his life was closed and he wondered if he would ever remember. Maybe he was trying too hard, he thought. He did have feelings for Mary and she was every man's dream, but so was Catherine.

CHAPTER 4

Catherine woke up on Wednesday morning and put on her robe. She peeked in at the two sleeping boys and she smiled at them. John had already gotten out of bed and Catherine thought he might be downstairs. The door to the bathroom was partially closed and when she pushed on it, something was blocking it.

"John, John, are you in there?" she whispered. She pushed a little harder and she saw John on the floor. "John, wake up, John," she pleaded. Catherine reached inside and pushed John's legs over enough so she could squeeze through the small opening. She got down on the floor and lifted his head up. He moaned. Catherine saw blood on the toilet seat and also on John's pyjama top. She looked further and then flushed the toilet. Catherine got up and wet a wash-cloth and bent down to wipe John's face.

"John, please wake up," she pleaded. She heard the boys jabbering in the crib and ignored them. She rushed downstairs and to the telephone to call for help. Next, she went to the kitchen and got a glass of water.

As she came out of the kitchen, Amelia saw Catherine's face. "What's wrong?" she asked.

"John has passed out in the bathroom. I've called the hospital to send an ambulance," Catherine said. "You need to get dressed. I'll look after John."

Catherine sat on the floor and pulled John's head into her lap.

She tapped his face lightly with her hand and held up the glass to his mouth. After she poured a few drops in his mouth, he coughed and woke up.

"Oh God, Catherine, my insides are burning up," he said.

"Try and drink some more water," Catherine said as she coaxed him to take a sip. "Help is on the way."

"I didn't have my medicine with me for the nausea and I couldn't stop vomiting," John said.

"Shhh, try not to talk. Take some deep breaths," she said. Catherine sat on the floor with John while she waited for help.

Martha, Amelia's nanny, had already gotten the boys changed and had carried them downstairs. Adam was crying and he wanted his mother. When Catherine packed her things the day before, she did not see the need to bring an extra baby bottle, and she knew he needed to be nursed. After a while, he stopped crying and she was relieved.

Two men from the hospital carried John downstairs on a stretcher and into the waiting ambulance. Amelia had called Carla in the meantime, and told her to meet her at the hospital.

After they left, Catherine walked into the kitchen. Martha was feeding both boys, alternating from one to the other, some mush for Adam and oatmeal for Daniel.

"You're a lifesaver." Catherine told Martha. Catherine picked up Adam and sat down at the table to nurse him. "Will you be all right here by yourself with Daniel?" Catherine asked. "I want to go to the hospital as soon as I get dressed."

"I'll be fine," she said, "and you can leave Adam if you want."

"It's not that I don't think you could take care of both boys, but I didn't bring a baby bottle and he would be a handful if he couldn't nurse, but thank you anyway," Catherine said.

When she finished nursing, she gave Adam back to Martha and asked her to entertain him until she could get dressed. After Catherine dressed, she took Adam's bib off and wiped his face. After she gathered up her things, she put Adam in the baby carriage and gave

Daniel a kiss, goodbye. He held up his hands for her to take him and cried when she and Adam left. Catherine walked to the trolley stop and was glad she did not have to wait too long.

Carla scowled when Catherine walked into the waiting room of the hospital. "What's she doing here?" she asked Amelia. Amelia didn't answer.

"Any news from the doctor, yet?" Catherine asked. When Amelia shook her head, no, Catherine asked her to keep an eye on Adam while she talked to one of the nurses.

"Just who does she think she is? John is my husband, not hers," Carla ranted.

"Catherine used to work here and everyone knows her, let her see what she can find out," Amelia said to Carla.

Catherine had walked through a door that said staff only, and was gone about fifteen minutes. When she came out, Dr. Copeland followed her out.

"John is a very sick man, Mrs. Merit. We will get him through this today, but he is going to require a lot of care. Is there someone at your home who can look after him?" he asked.

"What kind of care?" Carla demanded.

"He needs to stay in bed for two or three days and someone needs to make sure he drinks a lot of fluids and takes his medication. He needs to be on a liquid diet the first day, and the second day, if his stomach settles some clear soup would be fine. He should start feeling better by the third day, but there are no guarantees."

"Couldn't he just stay here in the hospital?" Carla asked.

"He could, and I was going to suggest that he stay here through tomorrow, but this is just the first in a series of episodes John will have. He may linger for several months and the hospital bill could be astronomical," Dr. Copeland said. "It's your choice, just let me know."

"I don't know anything about taking care of sick people," Carla said. "John said he had an insurance policy, but I don't know what kind. I could check with my uncle."

Amelia looked at Catherine. Catherine knew immediately what Amelia was thinking so Catherine made a suggestion. "Why don't we arrange for John to come to your house, Amelia. "We'll have him brought home in the ambulance and once they get him upstairs he can stay in the third bedroom. I'll move into the boy's room and sleep there and I can get up during the night with John, if he needs me. Perhaps Martha could help manage both boys and, Amelia, you can take care of the cooking." Both women looked at Carla.

"Why, that would be wonderful. It would be dreadful for my two teenage girls to see John so sick, and I could come visit him," Carla said.

Amelia rolled her eyes at Catherine.

"I need to get home and take care of some things," Catherine said. "I'll check with you later, Amelia, and if it's all right with you, Carla, I'd like to come back later this evening and visit John after he's rested." Carla didn't answer.

When Catherine got home, Minnie met her at the door and told her Alex had called. Catherine filled Minnie in on John's illness and that he was at the hospital now. Once he got home, she would be staying over at Amelia's house until he got back on his feet.

"Will he recover from this?" Minnie asked.

"No, I'm afraid there is no cure," Catherine answered.

Adam was still asleep so she pushed him into the parlor and dug through her purse for Alex's number.

"Will you be staying for dinner?" Minnie asked.

"No, I'm sorry I won't. Don't plan on me having dinner for awhile. Everything centers on John's well-being, and I want to be there for him," Catherine said.

"Will Alex be coming back?" she asked.

Catherine walked over and hugged Minnie. "I'm afraid not," she said. "It's a complicated story, much like my whole life. I'm not really up to talking about him right now. I will tell you when it's more bearable."

"I understand," Minnie said. "I'm a good listener, and you just let me know when you need my shoulder."

Catherine kissed her and picked up the phone. Catherine looked at the clock on the mantel; it was 11:00 a.m. She dialed Alex's office number.

"Glacier Oil Company," Alex answered.

"Alex? It's Catherine, how are you?"

"I'm well, and you?" he asked.

"I'm fine. You're still in Beaumont?" she said, more as a question.

"Yes," he said. "Did you get the note I left you?"

"Yes," Catherine lied because she did but she had not read it. "It's nice to hear from you."

"I had some things I needed to talk to you about and I thought I would come in Friday night. I'd like to see you," Alex said.

"Now's not really a good time," she answered.

"What's wrong, Catherine? Are you all right?" he asked.

"Yes, I'm fine. It's John, my first husband. He's dying and he needs help. I'm going to be at his sister's house taking care of him for a few days. What did you need to talk to me about?" she asked.

"I really didn't want to talk about it on the phone," he said.

"Alex, I'm sure whatever you have to tell me couldn't be any worse than hearing the news about John's impending death," Catherine said.

"Are you sure?" he asked.

Catherine didn't answer.

"I wanted to talk to you about getting a divorce," Alex said.

Catherine sank to the floor with the receiver in her hand and didn't say anything.

"Are you there, Catherine?" he asked.

Catherine took a deep breath and said, "Yes, just a little surprised that you came to that decision so quickly."

"I just found out that Mary Windsong is pregnant and I feel I need to do the right thing," Alex said.

"Well, I can do better than that. I spoke to a lawyer and he says we can get our marriage annulled. He's already prepared the papers and I was going to mail them to you. You'll be free to marry her in less than two weeks," she said.

It was Alex who was taken by surprise this time. He hesitated and then said, "Wouldn't it be faster if I came to Galveston and signed the papers?"

"I suppose it would," Catherine said. "I'll call my attorney and see if he can meet you on Saturday, and let you know."

Catherine hung up the phone without saying goodbye. She sat on the floor and cried. She finally got up and wiped her eyes and searched through her purse for John's attorney's card. She dialed the number and asked to speak to Clay Segal.

She told him of the nature of her call and explained that both she and Alex were in agreement to get an annulment and they had only been married a little over two months. He told her he would have the papers ready for her to sign the next day and to come in at 10:00 a.m. He asked Catherine a few more questions, and then they hung up.

Catherine picked up Adam and went upstairs. She walked over to her dresser and took out her Bible. The unopened envelope from Alex was still inside the book of Hosea. What difference does it make now? His mistress is having a baby and he wants to marry her. It's over, she thought. The letter was history now. She decided to read it anyway.

Dear Catherine,

I don't like goodbyes and I did not want it to be difficult for you, so, I thought it best if I left now. I borrowed 10 dollars to buy a ticket to Beaumont and I have to pay for

Pilgrim's care. I know I should have asked you first, but, again, I wanted to leave you in peace. I've decided to stay in Beaumont and start there. If I can figure out the last two years, I think I would be able to make a better decision. It would not be fair to Mary either, if I went back to her, and I am sorry she has made things more complicated. I can't ask you to wait, but I want you know that I won't rest until I find out the truth.

Alex

Catherine put the letter back and then put the Bible back in the drawer. When Alex left to go back to Beaumont, he left in the middle of the night while she was asleep. It didn't make it any easier. He was gone and most likely, forever.

After Catherine nursed Adam, she laid him on the bed beside her. Adam Merit, she thought. He looked to whole lot like David Brooks, but he was sweet and she loved him. She looked at her small bump and rubbed it with her hand. I wonder what your daddy would have said, had I told him about you, my sweet child. She whispered as she fought back tears. She lay there watching Adam wiggle and coo. It was a reminder to her that there were more important things in the world than her happiness. Catherine freshened up and put on clean clothes. It was too depressing being there by herself, so she decided to go back to the hospital and check on John's condition.

She put a light jacket on, hoping it would hide her bump, and left for the hospital. The waiting room was empty, and as she made her way to John's room, she heard a familiar voice. It was Father Jonathan and he was talking to John. She didn't want to disturb them so she turned and went back to the waiting area. When she saw Father Jonathan come out of John's room she got up.

"It's good to see you Father. How's our patient?" Catherine asked.

"Much better than when he came in," he said as he took a closer look at Adam. "He looks a lot like his brother," Father Jonathan said.

"I think so, too," Catherine agreed.

"I'm glad you and John have mended your relationship. He's a fine man. You let me know if you need to talk. I haven't seen you at mass and I'd love for you to come."

"I will, thank you, Father," Catherine said.

She quietly knocked on John's door and went in with Adam in the baby carriage. John was sitting up in bed, but still looked frail. She walked over and kissed his cheek. John smiled and sighed, "I'm afraid I don't have the energy to talk anymore." Catherine carefully took the pillows from behind his head and helped him get more comfortable.

"You need rest and sleep," she said.

John smiled and grabbed her hand. He closed his eyes and Catherine sat down on the chair beside his bed still holding his hand. She looked over and saw Adam sleeping. Catherine laid her head on her arm on the bed and fell asleep, too.

Later, Catherine heard girls' voices in the hall and she stood up. Carla walked in with her two daughters and told Catherine she wasn't needed anymore. John had also awakened. "Carla, you didn't introduce your daughters to Catherine," he said. Carla made the introductions.

Catherine took Adam's carriage and started to leave. "You don't have to go, Catherine," John said.

"It's getting late and I need to get Adam home. I'll come back tomorrow," she said.

That evening Alex was sitting on his porch. He kept going over the conversation he had had earlier that day with Catherine. He couldn't blame her for talking to an attorney and the annulment was the smartest and quickest way to end it, but she seemed so cold. He guessed he couldn't blame her. He had spoken first when he told her he wanted a divorce. Darn, he thought, why did she make me tell her on the phone? He was hoping to at least see her. He had her picture in his hand and there was just enough light coming from his lantern so he could see her beautiful smile and long curls. He looked up when he thought he heard her say, "I love you, Alex, and I want to spend the rest of my life with you." He wished he had more time to figure things out. He felt emptiness in the bottom of his gut. He replayed some of the stories in his mind that Consuelo had told him about David Billings and how he liked to hit her and Catherine. He remembered Catherine's black eye in the restaurant. No, he thought, Consuelo didn't tell him that. He had seen it and he remembered.

CHAPTER 5

Catherine arrived at Clay Segal's office a few minutes early the next day, so she waited until he came out and showed her into his office.

"I heard John is in the hospital," he said.

"Yes, I saw him yesterday afternoon and he's improving. He may come home this afternoon," Catherine said.

"I owe you an apology, Catherine," Clay said. Catherine didn't say anything. "I was the one who kept pushing John to give up the search for you. He was a broken man when you disappeared, I hated that he was so miserable. I thought if somehow, he could have closure, he would get over you. He never did, but I guess you know that now."

"Why are you telling me this?" she asked.

"Because I feel like I had something to do with John's quick rebound and marriage to Carla. I didn't really think he would marry her. They were like night and day; total opposites. You mentioned that Alex had an accident and couldn't remember your marriage. Are you sure you want to do this?" he asked her.

"Yes," she answered, not wanting to go into any more detail.

Clay pushed the one-page document over to Catherine and she read it thoroughly. She stared at the sentence that read, "Declarant states that no children were conceived during this marriage."

"You can sign here," Clay said as he handed her a pen and

pointed to a line.

Catherine signed the paper and pushed it back. “If there is nothing else, I’ll give you Alex’s phone number so you can call him. He wants to come in Saturday morning and sign.” Catherine took out her checkbook and asked Clay what his fee was.

“Oh, you’re paying?” he asked.

“We have a joint account,” Catherine said.

Clay told her the fee and she finished writing the check

“Good day, Mr. Segal,” Catherine said and left the check on his desk. She stopped before she got to the door and asked, “Is there some place private I could nurse my son? I don’t think he’ll be very happy if I make him wait too much longer.”

Clay Segal showed her into a small conference room and closed the door.

Clay had gone through high school with John Merit. They both went to the University of Texas and John majored in business. Clay went on to law school, but they kept in touch with each other. They were both groomsmen in each other’s wedding. Like John, Clay had lost his wife, too, shortly after John lost his first wife and child. They were still close friends and knew a lot about each other’s private lives. Clay thought John was nuts when he told him he was going to rescue Catherine Eastman from her life at the orphanage by marrying her when she turned sixteen. John was ten years older than Catherine.

In the few minutes Clay had spent with Catherine, he finally understood why. She was smart, intelligent and beautiful. Clay did not have any children and he didn’t mind Catherine having two. He knew Catherine had been through a lot with the abduction and all, and even though one of her children had been born out of wedlock, it was all right with him. Maybe after John’s death he could get her to go out with him. There weren’t too many men out there who would marry a woman with her history, so he didn’t think he would have much competition. John had told Clay in private that Catherine was an angel of endearment in the bedroom and she was very passionate. Clay smiled as he envisioned himself in bed with Catherine and the more he thought about it, the more he decided to pursue her.

He heard the door to the conference room open so he walked out to tell Catherine goodbye.

"Catherine. I know you must be going through a difficult time right now, with John's illness and your annulment, but I want you to know that I'm here if you need me. Please call me anytime," Clay said.

"Thank you, Clay, I really appreciate that."

Catherine had missed the trolley and it was a clear, cool day with the sun peeking through the clouds, so she decided to walk to the hospital. She tucked an extra blanket around Adam and she buttoned her coat. Clay watched through the curtains as she walked off.

John was sitting up in bed and Amelia was sitting in a chair beside him when Catherine walked into the room. She walked over and kissed Amelia on the forehead and John said, "What about me?"

Catherine laughed and walked over and started to kiss him on the forehead, but he pulled her face to his and kissed her on the mouth. It surprised her and she said, "Well, I can see you must be feeling better." They laughed.

"I came up with another idea that I hope you'll be open to," John said.

Catherine looked intent and listened.

"After I'm gone, Amelia and I want you to move into the house. It would be easier on Amelia. That way she would still be able to see Daniel every day and she and Martha will be able to help you with the boys, especially when you have the baby. The boarding house is just so small and the boys will need a yard eventually," John said as he looked at Amelia approvingly.

"I'd like to think about that before I give you an answer. Amelia, you don't think the boys will be too rambunctious? As they get older they'll probably tear up the house," Catherine teased.

"It was my idea," Amelia told Catherine. "It would be too

lonely without my nephews and I love you as a sister. Please do this for me. At least give it a try. If it doesn't work out, you can always find another place."

Catherine thought for a moment but before she could say anything, Carla walked in. Catherine started to leave and John took her hand and shook his head, no. Catherine could see the anger and hatred in Carla's face.

"Good news," she said. "I saw the doctor in the hall and he says you can leave this afternoon and I've worked it out for you to be cared for in a nursing home for the duration of your illness. That way you'll have round-the-clock-care, and we won't have to put Catherine out."

"Carla, I'm not going to a nursing home. I want to die at my own home. I'm not some old man you can just drop off at a nursing home and forget about and I can't believe…., yes I can believe you would do something like this. Now leave," John said and started coughing.

Catherine reached for a towel and put it over John's mouth and started caring for him. Carla stormed out in anger and they could hear her crying all the way down the hall.

"Breathe," Catherine said, "Try and breathe. John had begun hyperventilating and it was obvious that Carla had struck a nerve.

"I don't ever want to see that woman again," John said and he started crying. Catherine put her arms around him and pushed the nurse's button.

"Could you please ask Dr. Copeland to prescribe something to calm Mr. Merit's nerves? He's very upset right now," Catherine said to the nurse.

After John got a shot, he fell asleep. Catherine took Adam to the waiting area to nurse him and Amelia followed her.

"I'll come," Catherine said, "but only on one condition. Three children can be a handful and I don't want to run Martha off with the additional work. You need her."

"I need you more, Catherine. I know I only have a few years left, at best, and the house will go to you and your children when I die. That's what John and I both want," she told Catherine as she took her hand and kissed it. "We love you and the boys and I know if John weren't dying, he would divorce Carla and marry you again tomorrow."

The ambulance attendants took John on a stretcher up to his room that afternoon and Catherine was there waiting. She had gone by her house and packed a small suitcase for her and Adam and was unpacking when John came home. Daniel crawled over to Amelia's legs and tried to pull up. She wasn't able to pick him up, so Martha picked him up and he watched as his daddy was carefully taken up the stairs. "Da, Da," he said.

Catherine was watching from the top of the stairs and after John was settled she went down and picked up Daniel and took him upstairs to John. "Say it again," Catherine coaxed Daniel, "Come on, Da, Da," she said.

"Da, Da," Daniel said.

John had tears in his eyes and he reached for him and kissed him. "Daddy loves you, Daniel," he said. "You go play with your little brother, now."

Catherine took Daniel downstairs and put him on the floor by Adam. Martha was watching and motioned for Catherine to go on. Catherine went in the kitchen and began making some hot tea. When it was ready, she put it on a tray along with a glass of water and took it upstairs. She poured each of them a cup and added some sugar the way John liked his.

"Will you sleep with me tonight?" John asked. "I sleep better when you are beside me."

Catherine smiled at him and shook her head yes.

Alex was about to leave his office after lunch when he got the phone call just before noon on Friday. He had been waiting to hear from Catherine, and he had been anxious ever since they had talked.

The call was short. Clay Segal, Catherine's attorney, would see Alex on Saturday morning at 9:00. Catherine had already signed the papers and once Alex signed, they would no longer be married. Technically, to be legal, the judge would have to sign it on Monday, but Clay would take care of that part. Clay gave Alex his address and told him it was on the Strand.

When Alex hung up, he was disappointed that Catherine was not going to be there. He went into Clarence's office and told him about the annulment.

"I'm sorry to hear that, but I guess it does solve part of the problem," Clarence said. "You need to prepare yourself, though. Someday you might wake up and realize you're married to the wrong woman."

"I'm well aware of that," Alex said and he left to pack his bag for his trip.

He decided just to put a few things in a small brief case. He didn't think he would spend the night but better to have it than not. He put on his vest, tie and business suit. It was the same one he had gotten married in and it surprised him that he knew that. The mirror he was looking into was cloudy and it was hard to get a full view. He brushed his hair back with his fingers, and picked up the locket off the table beside his bed and put it in his vest pocket. He carefully took Catherine's small picture and put it in his vest pocket so it would be handy. Catherine may not want to see him, but he was certainly going to see her before he left Galveston.

Alex waited to catch a midnight train to Houston and then after a two-hour wait in Houston he would be in Galveston by 5:00 a.m. He purchased a private room in a Pullman car and hoped he might be able to sleep a bit. Alex fell asleep shortly after leaving Beaumont; it wasn't long before the dreams began flashing through his head. He was in bed with Catherine and he was tracing the permanent scars on her back from the whippings she had endured from David Billings. Another flash showed him making love to Mary in her room. The last one made its biggest impact, when he saw himself delivering Adam at the farm house. Alex woke up in a sweat and he was breathing heavily. His past was coming back in bits and pieces and he was still just as confused as ever.

He got off the train in Houston and decided to walk around before he caught the red-eye to Galveston. He stopped at a café and ate a sandwich and then went back to the depot.

When he boarded, he went straight to the dining car. He was the only one in there except for the bartender and Alex ordered a double shot of whiskey. He needed something to calm his nerves. He sat at a table and watched out the window. The moonlit Texas landscape passed by and then darkness as they went through a tunnel. He tried to gather his thoughts and he thought about what Clarence said. What would he do if his memory came back and he was married to Mary? He figured he must have loved Catherine a lot to have waited until he was older to marry. It meant he had not fallen in love with anyone else but her. He thought about Mary and other than feeling gratitude for her taking care of him, he didn't think he was in love with her. Maybe he'd feel differently about her once they got married. He knew one thing, if he did marry Mary, he'd be a good husband and a good father to their child. He hoped she would allow him to continue to work. He would go crazy being isolated on an Indian reservation. He knew he liked being around intelligent people and he wasn't sure he would find that in Kountze, Texas.

After Alex finished his drink, he went back to find his compartment to try and get some sleep. He woke up when he heard the Galveston stop called, and he looked at his watch. It was 5:30 a.m. and his appointment was not until 9:00. Alex looked at the address of Clay Segal's office and decided to find a place to eat. He had three and a half hours to kill so he stopped at a diner to have coffee and breakfast. When he walked in the café, he saw a phone on the wall along with a telephone book attached to it with a string. He ordered his breakfast and then walked over and looked up Merit. There were two listings with two different numbers and addresses. One was for John Merit and the other for Amelia Merit. He vaguely remembered the street Catherine said she used lived on and when he saw Amelia's address he made a mental note. He also memorized the phone number. The street sounded familiar so Alex assumed that was John's sister's place. He might have time to go by Minnie Wyman's boarding house where they stayed after they were married, so he ate a quick breakfast and caught a trolley.

He found his way back to Minnie's and he looked down the side of the house to see if there was a light on. It was barely 7:15 a.m. and Alex didn't want to wake anyone. He stood there watching for a few minutes and a light suddenly appeared in a window at the back of the house. Alex knocked on the door and a few minutes later, Minnie came to the door with curlers in her hair.

"Why Alex," she said surprised. "Catherine's not here but you are welcome to come in. I just put some coffee on."

Alex followed her to the rear of the house where the kitchen was.

"Catherine has temporarily moved into hers and John's old house, but I bet you know that," she said.

"How's Catherine?" he asked. "She won't see me?" Alex said.

"Well I figured you and her got into some kind of disagreement when you called the other day. She hasn't been the same since. She's been crying off and on for several days now. I know she's upset about John, but I don't think that's why she is crying. What's going on with you two anyway? You seemed so in loved with each other," Minnie said.

Alex told her about the accident and about the Indian reservation and Minnie listened quietly as they sipped their coffee.

"The call the other day was about me wanting to get a divorce. She said she had already talked to a lawyer, and that we could get an annulment and that's why I'm here; to sign the papers this morning," Alex told her. "Catherine's lawyer said she had already signed the papers. I'm at a total loss of what to do." Alex ran his fingers through his hair. "I don't want to lose her."

"Well it seems to me you've got some thinking to do. You can't have 'em both," Minnie said. "You've got a bit of a mess on your hands and I don't envy you. You know, its sad how tragedy seems to follow her around."

Alex looked like he didn't understand.

"That David Brooks killed her mother two months after they got here from England. Then a year and a half later he abducts Catherine and keeps her in chains, and then she comes home and finds she's been declared dead, and her husband remarried. Now you're leaving her. I'd say she's had her share of hardship in her young twenty years."

Alex had not put all this together until now. He vaguely remembered Catherine telling him about the death of her mother. It's amazing that she ever fell in love with me, he thought.

Alex got up from the table and thanked Minnie. "I'm going to go now and I can't thank you enough for the information." Alex kissed Minnie on the cheek and left.

He was running out of time, and he felt like he was drowning and couldn't come up for air. He wanted more than anything to talk to Catherine, but he knew she wouldn't talk to him. He had no idea what to do. If only he could think. Everything seemed so twisted and he was beginning to get one of his headaches. The more Alex thought about it, the more he decided Catherine would be better off without him. If he couldn't figure out who he was, then how could he and Catherine have a life together? The annulment was the right thing to do, he convinced himself.

"Just sign right here, and you'll be a free man," Clay Segal said. Alex read the paper twice and he looked down where Catherine had signed below where his signature would go. He finally picked up the pen and signed his name.

"That's all?" Alex asked.

"Yep, once the judge signs on Monday, you are free to find someone else. But I am curious about one thing." Alex looked at him. "Why after only two months would you leave a beautiful little thing like her?"

"The only thing Alex said was, "How much do I owe you?"

"Nothing, absolutely nothing. Catherine took care of it," Clay said.

Alex had an immediate dislike for Clay and he could hardly wait to leave. The brisk wind coming off the bay slapped Alex in the face and he grimaced. He had not brought an overcoat, but he decided to walk in the cold air anyway. He had picked up a map at the depot when he got in, and he looked to find the street where Catherine's sister-in-law's house was. It was just ten blocks away. When he got there, he stood outside and looked at the house for a while trying to get up his nerve. He didn't want to make it hard for Catherine, but he wanted to give her the locket in person. A few seconds later he rang the buzzer. Martha answered the door.

"I'd like to speak with Catherine, please. Tell her it's Alex and I have something for her."

Catherine was at the top of the stairs and heard every word. She whispered to Martha that she would be down in a minute and to tell him to wait outside. Catherine went to Daniel's room and took out her long coat. She buttoned it and looked in the mirror to make sure her belly was covered.

Alex was standing outside the door when she went out and closed the door behind her."I just wanted to tell you that I've signed the papers and I really appreciate your being so understanding," he said.

Catherine cleared her throat. "Martha said you had something for me," and she looked away.

"Yes, I do," and he took the locket out of his vest pocket and put it in Catherine's hand.

"Where did you find it?" she asked.

"I was walking through the burned out barn at your old farm and found it on the ground," Alex answered. "You look a lot like your mother. She was beautiful, like you."

"Thank you," Catherine said. "Was there anything else you needed to talk to me about?"

Alex hesitated a few seconds and then grabbed her and kissed her passionately. Catherine stood frozen for a minute and then she pulled away. She stared at him, and then flew into his arms and kissed him back. They were both lost in the moment and when they pulled apart, they were breathing heavily. She turned and went into the house, closing the door behind her. Alex wanted to follow her in, but he stopped. He stood there for a moment and then turned and walked toward the train depot. Catherine ran upstairs and closed the door behind her. She walked over and looked at the two boys napping in the crib and then walked over to the closet and opened the door and went in, closing the door behind her. She sat on the floor in the dark closet for a while crying. She didn't want anyone to see her falling apart.

There was a knock on the bedroom door and she heard it open.

"Catherine?" John asked softly. He heard a sniffle and he walked over to the closet and opened it. Catherine didn't look up. John sat down on the floor beside her. "Was that Alex?" he asked.

Catherine shook her head, yes. "He signed the papers for the annulment."

"I'm sorry you're taking this so hard. I know you love him. It'll get better in time," John said as he kissed her forehead. He put his arms around her and cradled her. "I'm glad I can be here for you, too." They sat on the floor in the closet not saying anything.

"Da, Da," they heard Daniel say as they looked up and saw him standing in the crib watching them. They both laughed. John was still weak and he asked Catherine if she could help him get up. They both walked over to the crib and Daniel reached for John. Catherine took him because she knew John would be too weak.

"Can you make it back to your room?" she asked John, and

she watched him slowly make his way out the door. She changed Daniel's diaper and took him downstairs to Martha. When she heard Adam, she went back upstairs and changed his diaper and took him into John's room. She nursed Adam as John watched.

"I'll be fine," she assured John and smiled at him.

After John began to feel better, he asked Catherine to help him to his study.

"I need to show you where everything is. All my personal things, including the mortgage on this house, are in this file folder."

He went over his ledger with Catherine and she caught on quickly when he showed his bookkeeping entries. She would be responsible for making the house payments and all household expenses. He showed her his separate checking account for Amelia and that she had the right to sign the checks. Catherine just needed to prepare the checks for her to sign.

"I know you'll be there for her, and I can't even begin to tell you what it means to me, that you will be looking after her. There is no one else," John said.

CHAPTER 6

When Alex took Catherine in his arms and kissed her on the front porch, he wondered what she might do to him when he finished kissing her. He was afraid she might slap him. He was not expecting her to jump into his arms and kiss him back, not the way she did. It was hungry, sexy and passionate and it turned him on. He felt his blood race through his body and he had a brief moment of remembering. They were in bed together at the Tremont and she had kissed him the same way there. She was beautiful, sultry, smart and caring and he knew he would regret forever that he had let her go.

Alex boarded the train and began making his way to a seat in the back and changed his mind. He turned to go to the dining car for a drink. The train began moving, but stopped abruptly like the engineer had hit the brake. Alex lost his footing and fell, hitting his head on the side of the door frame. It stunned him for a moment, but he managed to get his bearings. He turned around and made his way back to a seat at the back.

He was sitting alone in the corner of the train when the conductor asked for his ticket. Alex was lost in thought and the conductor had to ask again for his ticket. He pulled it out of his vest pocket and gave it to him. He glared out the window, watching the scenery pass by and he looked hard trying to find something that would arouse his memory from the cobwebs. It was not his nature to be anxious, but since his accident, he felt like he had unfinished business and he couldn't figure out what it was. He must have fallen asleep.

"Houston, next stop," said the conductor.

The words woke him and for a moment, he had to think hard as to why he was on the train. His head was throbbing and he felt like it was going to explode, so he moved his neck, stretching it from side to side. Alex got off the train, forgetting about his bag, and looked up and down the tracks. He wasn't sure where he was, so he walked over to sit on a bench and get his bearings. He watched as the train pulled away from the station and he felt confused. He had a horrible headache and he felt like his brain was mush. A young Negro boy about fourteen years of age came over and asked if Alex wanted his shoes shined for ten cents. Alex just looked at him and shook his head no.

Thirty minutes later, a clerk from the depot saw Alex sitting on the bench and decided to ask him if he could assist him. "You look like you've lost something or somebody. Are you waiting for another train?" he asked Alex.

"I don't think so. Actually I don't know where I am," Alex answered.

"Did you come in on the last train from Galveston?" the clerk asked. Alex didn't know what to say, so he sat silent.

"Are you all right? You don't look like you feel well," the man asked. "What's your name?"

Alex shook his head and said, "I don't know."

"Well, check your pockets and see if you have some identification on you," the clerk suggested.

Alex stood up and put his hand in his pants pockets. They were empty, except for Catherine's picture. He had no idea where his wallet was or if he ever had one. He pulled out a five dollar bill and some coins and found nothing else. He began feeling dizzy and he put his hands up to his head. A second later he blacked out and fell to the ground.

When Alex woke up he was lying on a table in a sterile-looking room with a sheet covering him. A man in a white coat approached him. "You are in a hospital, sir. Can you tell me your name?"

Alex didn't answer.

"I see you had a head injury, maybe a gunshot wound. Do you remember anything about that?" the doctor asked.

"I don't know," Alex said.

"We have a new machine that takes pictures of things inside your body. It's called X-ray photography. It was discovered by a doctor in Germany about six years ago and it helps us see things we couldn't see otherwise. It won't hurt and there is no pain, but I need your permission to take some pictures. By the way, my name is Dr. Ryan Peterson."

"If it will help me figure out who I am, then let's do it," Alex said.

Another man in a white coat came in and moved his rolling bed around and up to a strange looking machine that looked like a door on a pulley that was pulled over his head parallel to his body.

He was told to lie extremely still for several minutes. Alex complied and waited for more instructions. An hour later he was wheeled into a ward with rows of beds, and curtains were pulled around him. He had no idea how long he had been there, and after awhile, he fell asleep.

He woke up when a nurse came in and turned a crank, slowly lifting his upper torso. She set a tray of food over him and he was told to eat. Alex cleaned the plate. He had no idea how long it had been since he had eaten.

After a while, a doctor came in and told Alex they had the results of his x-ray and wanted to go over it with him. The doctor asked him again if he knew who he was, or if he had any relatives in Houston. Alex shook his head, no.

"Apparently a few months ago, I'm assuming, you suffered a bullet wound to your head. The bullet went through your scalp, just brushing your skull. The wound has healed nicely, except for one thing. A fragment of the bullet stayed in your head and that is what is causing your memory loss," the doctor said. "Since you have no idea who you are or where you came from, we can't help you. We need a next-of-kin and also, the surgery is very expensive. I'm afraid we will have to send you over to a mental sanatorium until someone finds you. Otherwise, you are healthy as a horse."

"What if I say no and just walk out of here?" he asked.

"That is your choice, but you came in with nothing, and you don't know who you are. Without money or a place to stay, I'd say your chances out there aren't as good as your chances at the sanatorium. Perhaps some therapy at the sanatorium could at least help you come up with an identity. Your wound is about two months old and obviously someone has been looking after you. You're clean, you have nice clothes, and by the way, we found a picture of a woman in your inside vest pocket. Does she look familiar?" the doctor asked, as he showed Alex the picture.

Alex looked, even straining his eyes. "She's beautiful, but I can't be sure. I might know her. Why can't I remember?"

"There is a fragment piece of the bullet lying around one of your nerves that send signals to the brain. It's like a roadblock. I'm afraid the human brain can be fickle sometimes, especially if you mess with it. What do you want to do?" the doctor asked.

"What if I change my mind after I get to the sanatorium?" Alex asked.

"You'll have to be willing to commit yourself, and I am not sure what their policy is. You'll have to ask them," the doctor said. "I have a friend who works at a small, privately-funded sanatorium southwest of Houston and they are doing some experimental treatments there. He might be able to fit you in for a few weeks or so." The doctor left Alex's room and said he would be back later.

Alex was unsure of what he should do. He closed his eyes and tried to see a picture of something that might jog his memory, but it was just a vacuum. That evening, he had a visitor.

"My name is Dr. Jeffery Winston and I'm the director of the Oakwood Plantation Sanatorium. It's located about thirty miles southwest of Houston. We are only a fifty-bed sanatorium and we pride ourselves in assisting the mentally ill. Your condition is unusual, but we would be willing to keep you for a month or two and try to help you find out who you are. Perhaps, a family member might come forward during that time and hopefully, pay for the surgery your doctor has recommended. For now, though, you can stay with us. I will have someone pick you up later tomorrow morning. You will have to sign some papers. I'll be looking forward to helping you," Dr. Winston said, and left.

The next morning Alex was told to get dressed after breakfast. They led him to a small office and he was introduced to another man who was from the Oakwood Plantation Sanatorium. He introduced himself as Dr. Philip Seymour. He was a few years younger than Alex and he had been with the Sanatorium for about two years. He was going to assist in Alex's treatment. Alex found him to be personable and easy to talk to. Alex mostly listened as they rode to the sanatorium. He asked Alex a few questions, but when Alex was unable to give him any answers, he began talking about the sanatorium and what they did there.

They turned off the main road and pulled up to a massive, iron gate which was attached to a brick and wood fence that rose twelve feet from the ground on each side. After a few minutes a Negro man came running up and unlocked it. The private driveway was bordered by century-old pecan trees and its branches towered over the driveway creating a tunnel-like approach to the house. The structure was a stately, white, two-story mansion with huge columns in the front. There were no signs, except a small one to the right of the front door, that simply read, "Welcome to Oakwood."

Alex had no bags or luggage and he was wearing his suit and vest. He looked apprehensively at the magnificent foyer as they entered. Two nurses, both women, took Alex by the arm and walked him to the back of the house. He noticed that the main house looked like an estate home with a huge formal dining room on one side and a living room on the other. There was a massive staircase that arched up to the second story and there were large paintings on the walls. He noticed a huge library just past the dining room and the other doors were closed. He was led out the back door and passed under a huge gallery filled with rocking chairs, some with people sitting in them. Just to the right of the house was a long barn-like structure with no windows. One of the nurses used a key to gain entrance. It wasn't like the main house at all. There were no rugs on the floors and all the doors were closed. There were small openings in the doors that looked to be about ten inches square and bars in between. He jumped when someone's hand tried to reach through one of them and they screamed at him.

"Pay no attention to that one. She is not allowed out except a couple of hours a day," said one of the nurses.

They had walked past about ten doors, and came to another corridor that led away from that one. The nurse used another key to open it. Alex was beginning to get a bad feeling about this place. A large open room with tables and benches appeared out of nowhere and one of the nurses said that is where he would be eating his meals. After walking past a few more doors, they stopped and unlocked a door to a private room. It was small, with one bed and a thin mattress. There was a small sink and a chamber pot. There was nothing else.

Alex stopped dead in his tracks, and said, "I think there's been a mistake. I thought I was going to a hospital, not a prison."

There was a large man standing behind him now, blocking the door. The two nurses left and locked the door, leaving Alex and the large attendant alone. He was holding some pyjamas, and he told Alex that he needed to take his clothes off.

"I would prefer to leave," Alex said.

"I understand, sir; everyone says that when they first get here, but you will get used to it," he said.

Alex heard the door unlock and another male attendant came in with a large needle. The larger attendant grabbed Alex's coat and pulled it off. Alex held up his fist and before he could swing, the man grabbed his arm and pulled it behind him. He pushed Alex up against the wall and pressed his own body against Alex's back, while the other attendant pushed the needle through Alex's shirt and into his upper arm. Alex blacked out a few minutes later.

CHAPTER 7

Clarence had expected Alex back at work on Monday. When he didn't show up, Clarence figured that Alex was at the Indian reservation. At least that was what Alex told Clarence his plans were. Alex had told Clarence that after he got back from Galveston he was going to the Indian reservation to visit with Mary and her father, but that he for sure would be back at work on Monday. He wanted to keep his job. After he and Mary married, she would have the choice of moving to the Billings farm with him or she could stay on the reservation. Alex would be there with her on the weekends, if that was her choice. He had no intentions of leaving his job, he had assured him. Clarence decided to give it another day before he would start worrying. He had worked all day Monday in his office but he had to go to the rig at Spindletop on Tuesday morning. When he got to the stables, he noticed Pilgrim in one of the stalls.

"When did Alex get back?" he asked the blacksmith.

"I haven't seen Alex since Friday," he answered.

"You mean Pilgrim's been here the whole time?" Clarence asked.

"Yes sir and he's getting restless. You want me to walk him and leave him out in the corral for a while?" he asked.

Clarence told him yes and went back to his office. He searched his desk for the piece of paper that had Catherine's number written on it. It took him a minute, but he finally found it.

"I need to speak to Catherine Cooper," he said to the lady who answered the phone. Minnie Wyman told him she was no longer staying there and asked who wanted to know. Clarence told her who he was and why he was calling. He figured the old lady wouldn't cooperate unless he did.

"He was here Saturday morning and we visited for about an hour," Minnie said. "He told me he was going back to Beaumont on the noon train."

Minnie gave him the number for Catherine and he thanked her and hung up. Clarence was getting worried now. It wasn't like Alex to just leave and not call in; at least, not the old Alex. Catherine was on her way to the kitchen when the phone rang in the study. "Merit's residence," she answered.

Clarence recognized her voice and asked if she might know where Alex was. She told him that Alex had stopped by Saturday morning around 10:00 a.m., and only stayed for a few minutes. He had left to catch a train back to Beaumont. When Clarence told her he had not seen him and that Pilgrim was still at the livery stables, she was puzzled.

"I'll give him another day or two before I do anything. Maybe he decided to stay in Houston for a couple of days," Clarence told her.

Catherine made him promise to call her if he found out anything. She hung up the phone and began to worry. Brain injuries were nothing to ignore, but Alex seemed all right when he left. She remembered him kissing her and it encouraged her to kiss him back. He didn't seem to be acting any differently than he had right after his accident. He still could find his way around and he remembered some things. She was deep in thought when she heard John calling her from upstairs. She remembered she was getting him some orange juice so she told John she would be up in a minute.

She poured John some orange juice and met Martha carrying Daniel at the bottom of the stairs. Catherine bent over and kissed Daniel and he reached for her.

"I'll be right back," she told Daniel. "Your brother is waiting for me to get him."

Catherine took the juice in to John and told him she had to change Adam and nurse him. John kissed her on the cheek and told her to bring Adam in and sit by him while she nursed. She gave him a slight smile, but John knew her well enough to know something was bothering her.

Catherine joined John on his bed a short while later and began nursing Adam. She was quiet. John reached over and took her free hand. "You want to tell me what that phone call was about?" he asked.

Catherine looked away and took a deep breath. She told him about Clarence and who he was. "Alex never made it back to Beaumont on Saturday. No one has seen him. I guess I was the last one to talk to him," Catherine said.

John thought for a minute and then said, "Maybe he decided to just take off for a few days and sort through some things. He's been through a lot. Maybe he went directly to the reservation."

"I don't think so. His horse, Pilgrim, is still at the livery stables in Beaumont and he would not go on a trip without him. Pilgrim saved his life. Alex loves that horse," Catherine said.

"Look, Catherine, I know you love him, but he made a choice to leave you and marry someone else. He's not your problem. Let that Indian woman go look for him," John said.

Catherine wished it were that easy. Alex saved hers and Adam's lives. If he somehow lost all of his memory, he could be anywhere. The thought made Catherine shiver. There wasn't anything she could do right now, anyway. John's health had improved some, but she knew it was only temporary. He still needed her there and besides, she had two young boys to look after.

Since John was feeling better, Catherine started sleeping back in the boys' room. John wanted her to stay with him, but she knew she wouldn't be able to sleep now, and she wanted to be alone. Catherine spent the next three days dividing her time between John, the boys, and helping Martha and Amelia with the housework and cooking. They were paying a Negro lady to come in every day to do the laundry. Catherine had little time for herself, but the nights were hard and her nightmares were vivid and scary. She decided that if Clarence didn't call her by Friday noon she was going to call him.

The phone rang at 9:00 a.m. on Friday and Catherine ran to the study to answer it.

"I don't have any news, Catherine," Clarence said. "I sent one of my men to the Indian reservation yesterday and they haven't seen him since before he left for Galveston. I really don't know what to do," he said. "He could be anywhere."

Catherine hung up the phone and slumped into the chair. She put a call into Clay Segal. He answered the phone himself.

"I was wondering if you had gotten the judge's signature on the papers yet?" she asked.

"I sure did. I caught him on his break and he signed it last Monday. I already filed it with the clerk's office," Clay said proudly. "How's John doing?"

Catherine told him John was better and she thanked him for his help. She sat at John's desk mulling over her options. She wondered since she was no longer Alex's wife, whether she would have the authority to go to the police for help. She had to try, she thought.

Catherine lied and told John that she had to go to Clay Segal's office to sign something and she would be back in a couple of hours. She made sure the boys were dry and had been fed and she went to her room to make a quick change. After giving Martha instructions about Adam's next feeding, in case she didn't get back in time, Catherine put on her coat and walked to the trolley. Catherine had not been out of the house in over a week and she noticed that there were pumpkins and orange flowers popping up in front of some of the houses. It struck Catherine that Thanksgiving was approaching. She bit her lower lip and felt sick at her stomach when she realized that ever since she had come to America, something bad happened during the Thanksgiving holidays. Was Alex's disappearance just one more incident? She wondered.

When Catherine got to the police station she asked to speak to Sergeant Husky. She waited about fifteen minutes before she saw him coming through the door. He looked older than she remembered when she first met him. She was only fifteen when she and Minnie came to the station to find her mother. He introduced himself and asked how he could help her. When Catherine introduced herself his jaw dropped open. She was a woman now, and a beautiful one at that.

"I'm sorry I didn't recognize you," Husky said. "I heard of your plight in Beaumont and I'm glad to see you are well. How may I help you?"

Catherine took out a photograph and showed it to Husky. She told him that she and Alex had married, and Husky interrupted her before she finished. "That's the man I spoke to about a year ago. He came through here and told me he thought you were living in Beaumont and he was certain you were Catherine Merit. I sent a David Brooks wanted poster to the sheriff in Beaumont and someone killed him and claimed the reward."

Alex had never told her he had come to Galveston, but she tried to clear her head and get back to the matter at hand. "My husband, Alex Cooper, suffered a gunshot wound to his head. He recovered, but lost some of his memory. He left Galveston last Saturday morning to go back and finish his job in Beaumont, but he never made it there. He hasn't been seen by anyone since then. What would you suggest I do?"

Husky though for a few minutes and rubbed his chin between his thumb and fingers. "If I were you, I would cut his picture out of that photograph and take it to the newspaper. Ask them to print his picture in the newspaper and write a short article saying that he may have some memory loss due to a recent injury, and give them my name here at the police station as a contact. When it comes out in the newspaper, ask the paper to give you about fifty copies of that particular page and mail them to some of the surrounding towns and hospitals. He had to go through Houston to get to Beaumont on the train. I'd send it to the depot there as well as all the hospitals. Bring me a few copies and I'll send one to my brother-in-law in Houston, who's also a policeman, and to the sheriff in Beaumont. If that doesn't work, and he's not back home in a month, I know a good private detective, but he's expensive."

For the first time since Alex left, Catherine felt like there was hope. She thanked Sergeant Husky and left to go to the Galveston Gazette Newspaper office. When she got there she was introduced to a young reporter who listened to her story and took some notes. He took Catherine's photograph and cut out Alex's picture with some scissors. He assured her that it would run in the next day's paper.

Catherine made it home by noon and Adam was crying when she came in. What's wrong?" she said sweetly to Adam as she picked him up off the floor. Daniel was busy getting some things out of the toy box and Martha was nowhere in sight. She heard Amelia in the kitchen and went in.

"Where's Martha?" Catherine asked. She could see Amelia was stressed out.

"Martha got a call shortly after you left. Her older brother in Austin, Texas, died suddenly. She didn't want to leave, but I insisted. I knew you would be back soon. I'm sorry about Adam, he hasn't been fed yet," Amelia said almost crying.

"You go sit down and rest. I'll take care of Adam," Catherine said. "Can you keep an eye on Daniel while I go check on John?" she said.

Amelia answered, yes. Catherine was halfway up the stairs when the doorbell rang. Adam's crying was getting louder and louder. Catherine turned and went downstairs and answered the door. It was Carla.

"What on earth is going on? You can hear that kid screaming

all the way down the block. That has to be a hardship on John's nerves," Carla said as she went upstairs to see John. She stopped and turned before she got to the top of the stairs. "Would you be a dear and bring me a glass of water?"

Catherine didn't answer. She walked over to the sofa and unbuttoned her blouse. Adam is more important than getting your water, she thought to herself. Adam latched on to Catherine's right breast and stopped crying. Amelia was smiling at her when Catherine looked up.

"Good for you," she said.

Carla had only been upstairs for about thirty minutes when she came downstairs. Adam was asleep in Catherine's arms.

"I guess we need to talk about the funeral," Carla said.

Catherine and Amelia looked at each other, astonished at Carla's bluntness about John's impending death. Neither said a word and waited to see what else Carla might say.

"I think it just needs to be kept simple; only something at the graveside. My pastor, the one who married us, will say the eulogy, and Catherine, I would appreciate it if you and the boys did not attend. After all, he is my husband, not yours. After the funeral, I would like to meet with Clay Segal, as soon as possible, to go over the will, and discuss a more lucrative allowance for me?"

Daniel crawled over to Carla and tried to pull up on her leg. She pushed him aside and got up, causing Daniel to lose his balance and fall. He hit his head on the coffee table and started crying. Carla said nothing and walked out the front door. Catherine put Adam in Amelia's lap and picked up Daniel to check his head. She kissed him and asked if he wanted some juice.

"He's fine," she told Amelia, "but I don't look forward to sitting across from her in Clay Segal's office."

After Catherine gave Daniel his juice she came back in the living room where Amelia was cradling Adam in her arms. "Catherine, pay no attention to what she said. You have every right to attend

John's funeral," Amelia said.

Catherine didn't answer and excused herself to check on John. John had fallen asleep and Catherine sat in a chair beside his bed. He looked so peaceful. He hadn't had a haircut in while and she noticed how one of his curly locks had fallen into his face. He always kept his hair rather short and combed it straight. She wondered how long it would be to the end. John only got out of bed to go to the bathroom on his own, and he had stopped asking to see Daniel. She knew it wouldn't be too much longer. He ate very little and he slept a lot. He often wet the bed and apologized. As bad as it was, Catherine always approached John with a smile and a loving heart. He had told her on several occasions that if she were not there to take care of him, he would already be gone. She had a heart of compassion, and she made the end for him more tolerable. It had made it easier for John but Catherine's heart was aching. It was difficult watching someone you loved fade away in front of you.

The next morning, Catherine woke early and dressed. It was a dreary morning, with a mild mist in the air. She hoped the paper that had been delivered in the early morning hours was not wet. She smiled when she saw the paper boy had placed it under the awning of the front porch. She put the kettle on to make hot tea and she opened the newspaper as she placed it flat on the kitchen table. After scanning the first and second pages, her eyes focused on the picture on the third page. It was a bit blurred, but it looked like Alex and she quickly read the article underneath. "HAVE YOU SEEN ALEX COOPER?" was the headline. It gave a brief description of his age, height and weight and said that he was an oil scout for the Glacier Oil Company. They referenced his accident and said he had suffered memory loss and that his last sighting was at the Galveston train depot. Any information regarding his whereabouts was to go to the Galveston Police Department. Catherine read it again and hoped it would be enough to bring Alex home.

CHAPTER 8

Alex had slept for over sixteen hours and when he woke up, Phillip Seymour was standing over him with a stethoscope.

"Sorry we had to give you such a strong sedative, but you were a bit uncooperative last night," he said. "We need to give you a name and I was wondering if anything came to mind?"

Alex thought for a moment and said, "Adam seems to ring a bell."

"How about a last name?" he asked.

Alex thought harder and then said, "Cope, Coop, Cooper?"

"Sounds good to me," Dr. Seymour said and wrote it on his chart. "Tell you what; you've missed breakfast with the group, but I'll walk you down to the kitchen and see if they have a few biscuits and coffee left over."

Alex liked Dr. Seymour and felt more at ease with him than he did the night before with the two male attendants.

"We don't usually allow patients in the kitchen, because they might try and steal a knife, and hurt themselves. But after talking with you yesterday on our ride here, I've decided that while most of the people here have lost their minds, you've just lost your memory," Dr, Seymour said.

"So that's why they have all the locks and keys?" Alex asked.

"Yes, Dr. Winston didn't really think you belonged here, but after Dr. Peterson told him about your condition, he felt badly for you and agreed to take you on a short term basis. You're lucky," Dr. Seymour continued, "this place is very expensive."

"Maybe I could help out. I like horses and I see you have a corral and a barn. I could take care of the livestock and clean the barn," Alex suggested.

"Well, that's a step forward," Dr. Seymour said. "You just told me you like horses. I'll check with Dr. Winston and see what he thinks about you helping with some chores. You're not planning to run off, are you?" he asked.

Alex laughed and said, "I must admit I was ready to get out of here last night, but after thinking about it, I have nothing and no one. I need a safe place to stay, so I can work on getting my memory back and I guess this is as good a place as any."

The two men drank their coffee and Alex ate two biscuits with honey. When they finished, Dr. Seymour walked Alex back to a community room where there was a wall of books, several tables with puzzles and checkers on it, along with some other activities that the sanatorium used to try and engage the patients into doing something creative with their minds. Alex saw the two male nurses from the night before, standing by the door talking. There were also two female nurses and the room had about fifteen people in it. Some were in wheelchairs, staring into space. Others were either playing checkers or just sitting and reading. When he turned around, Dr. Seymour had disappeared.

Alex walked over to a book section and studied the books. One in particular caught his eye; *The Adventures of Tom Sawyer,* by Mark Twain. Alex lifted it out of the shelf and walked over to a chair and began reading. When he got to page ten, he noticed it was missing. He thumbed forward a few more pages and found page fifteen missing also. Further back in the book he noticed several chapters had been ripped out. Alex shook his head, and put the book back on the shelf. He took another book out and slowly turned the pages. This one had pages nine and thirteen ripped out, along with a couple of chapters in the back. He closed it and put it back on the shelf. He walked over to one of the nurses, who looked at him suspiciously.

"Excuse me," Alex said. "I couldn't help but notice that several of the books have pages missing."

"Most all the books are that way," she said and continued talking when Alex seemed to want to know why. "Some of the patients eat the pages. Others just tear them out because they have a bad feeling about that particular page number, or there is some reference on that page that reminds them of something."

"Are there any books to read that haven't had the pages torn out?" Alex asked. "I noticed a large library at the front of the house yesterday; maybe I could borrow a book from there."

"I'm sorry, but patients aren't allowed to read those books," she said as she turned and walked away.

Alex scratched his chin and thought for a minute. He walked over to the other nurse and asked if he might be able to talk to Dr. Seymour.

"He's in therapy," she said. "What do you want him for?"

Alex shook his head and walked away. There was a large window that overlooked the grounds, and there were bars on the outside of it interfering with a clear view. The window had not been washed recently and he made a mental note that that was also something he could do. He knew one thing for sure. Thirty days imprisoned in this place would surely drive him crazy. He felt like a caged animal. A buzzer rang and everyone stood up and began heading towards the large dining hall. There were no clocks, and Alex wondered why. He waited until the last person left and he followed.

They formed a line and each person picked up a tray. Food was slopped on a metal plate that had partitions in it, he guessed to keep the food from running together. At the end, a roll was placed on top and he was given a small wooden fork and napkin. Metal cups full of water were sitting on another table and you were supposed to pick one up and take it to a table. Alex asked if he could join some people who were already seated. No one said anything. He noticed one young woman who he determined to be in her middle twenties. Long, stringy hair and a nice enough looking face. She had bandages on her arms and he wondered if she might have tried to slash her wrists. Someone told him her name was Helen. Another woman at the table was older, maybe in her fifties, he thought. She had white, wiry hair and lots of wrinkles on her face. She had a scowl and Alex figured that she never smiled. The only man at the table besides him was a man in his thirties, and he had a uniform on that looked just like the one he was wearing. After they exchanged names, Alex looked at his food and wondered what it was. He poked at the meat and decided it must be some kind of sausage. There were beets, cabbage and two small potatoes, which he ate first. He finally decided to try the meat. It was tasty and he was hungry, so he ate everything including the roll.

Everyone stayed in their seats until another buzzer when off and they all stood up and walked to their assigned rooms. All of the doors were open and once they went into their rooms, the door was closed and locked. When Alex got to his room, he turned to ask the attendant a question but before he could, the man said, "No talking."

Alex walked into his room and heard the key in the lock turn. He stood there for a few minutes feeling hopeless, and like he didn't have a friend in the world. He sat on his bed for a few seconds and then lay down, staring up at the ceiling. He wondered what had happened to the picture he had in his vest pocket, but more importantly, he wondered who she was. A sister maybe, he thought, or a girlfriend?

Alex had fallen asleep and his dreams were sporadic and isolated. There was a fire and he was watching it burn. He saw a man with a noose around his neck and then he saw the man in a grave. The next images were of the woman in the picture he carried. She was holding a dead child and waving goodbye to him. His head was exploding and Alex sat up in his bed in a cold sweat. He was breathing hard and his head was pulsating. He put his head in his hands and he wanted more than anything to scream out loud, but he thought better of it. Crazy people did that, and he wasn't crazy. Alex lay back down and wondered if he could survive this mundane existence. He felt isolated and alone.

He heard the key in the lock and sat up when the door opened. "It's time for your therapy, Mr. Cooper," the nurse said. Alex jumped up and followed her. He was led into another wing of the building and through another door.

Dr. Seymour was sitting behind a desk. "Come in, Adam, and have a seat on the couch." Alex did as he was told.

"Normally, we would start off with some electrical shock therapy, but I understand you have a bullet fragment still in your head, and I'm afraid that might cause an adverse effect with the electrons. We don't want to fry your brain," he joked.

Alex found nothing funny about that.

"I would like to try hypnosis on you, but I will need your full cooperation. It's a means by which we take your mind back to a particular time and ask you questions about your life. Are you in agreement with that?" he asked. Alex agreed.

Dr. Seymour went through the motions, getting Alex to relax and count backward from ten as he followed a circular ring attached to a string that dangled back and forth in front of him. Once Alex seemed to have fallen under the spell, Dr. Seymour began a series of questions.

"Can you tell me your name?" he asked.

"Alex Cooper," he answered.

"How old are you, Alex?" came the second question.

"I'm eighteen," he answered.

"Where do you live?" was the next.

"At home," Alex said.

Dr. Seymour was amused by his answer and then said, "Where is home?"

"Denton, Texas," he answered.

"Who are you living with?" Dr. Seymour pursued further.

"My dad," answered Alex.

"Where is your mother?" Dr. Seymour asked.

"She died," Alex said sorrowfully.

Dr. Seymour felt that since this was his first hypnotic session with Alex, he would bring him out of his spell and they would talk about what Alex said. Before Alex woke up, Dr. Seymour told him he would remember everything they had talked about during the session.

Dr. Seymour was encouraged that Alex had been such a good patient. He asked Alex if he remembered who he was and he said yes and that his name was Alex Cooper. They talked about Alex's dad and if he knew what happened to his mother. Alex couldn't remember.

"Well, I think we've made progress today and we will try it again tomorrow," Dr. Seymour said.

"I need to ask you a couple of questions before I leave," Alex said. "I'm not good at sitting around with nothing to do. All the books in the patients' recreation area have pages missing and I have nothing in common with those people out there. I need to stay busy or I'm afraid I'll end up just like them," Alex said.

"I'll look into it," was all Dr. Seymour said.

CHAPTER 9

Martha was still not back from her trip yet, and John's days were numbered. Their food and supplies were getting low and Catherine waited until Alva, the help, came to do the laundry. Alva said she was happy to watch the boys and work on the laundry later. Catherine carefully peeked in on John and he was asleep, so she put on her coat and left. The next day was Thanksgiving and she and Amelia had already decided they would just have some homemade soup and that Catherine would pick up something more substantial for Daniel. Catherine had taken a large knapsack that she had quickly sewed up one day. It was one that she could carry across her chest to free up her hands so she was free to carry one of the children. Her first stop was the Galveston Gazette newspaper where she picked up fifty sheets of page three. Catherine dropped off ten copies of the newspaper at the police station and asked that they be put on St. Husky's desk.

The general store was packed with people getting last minute items for Thanksgiving and many of the shelves were empty. That fact had never crossed her mind. She had never been shopping for the Thanksgiving holidays and had no idea that she should have shopped earlier. She went up and down the aisles looking for items they could use. She grabbed the last loaf of bread, a soup bone, some vegetables, and then stopped at the meat counter. There was a long line, but she waited. The butcher suggested a small ham, which she took, and then she picked up a dozen eggs. Anything more and she wouldn't be able to carry it all. She walked in the front door two hours later. Amelia met her at the door.

"John needs you, hurry," she said.

Catherine put her things down by the stairs and ran up to John's room. He was crying and he grabbed on to her. She held him and told him she was sorry she wasn't there when he needed her. She quieted him and then he said, "I need to know that you have forgiven me, Catherine. I should never have given up hope that you would come back. I am sorry I didn't wait for you. Please, I need to know you forgive me."

"John, listen to me," she said tenderly. "Of course I forgive you. I didn't want you to wait. I had no idea what my fate was going to be. God spared me and I'm here now. That's what is important."

"I can't take the pain any longer, Catherine. Would you see if Father Jonathan could come over this afternoon and take my confession?"

Catherine said she would. She held John awhile longer and willed herself not to cry. She didn't want John or the children to see her falling apart. She helped him take a pill and he had difficulty swallowing it, but it finally went down. After fluffing his pillow and tucking the covers around him, she stood back and watched as he closed his eyes. His face was drawn and pale and she could see his bones protruding through his now withered skin and body. She left and went downstairs to use the phone in the study to call Father Jonathan.

Catherine and Amelia put the food away and waited for Father Jonathan to arrive. Amelia looked at her sadly.

"He's leaving us, isn't he," she said as she struggled to hold back her tears.

"I'm afraid so," Catherine whispered. When Father Jonathan arrived, Catherine took him upstairs and waited outside the door. She heard him give John his blessing and when John said, "Bless me Father for I have sinned," she left and went into her room and waited.

She watched, and when she saw Father come out of John's room, he motioned Catherine to follow him downstairs.

"John is at peace now. After his confession, he quietly went to sleep. He loved you very much, Catherine, and you, too, Amelia. He's no longer in pain."

The three adults sat in the living room, getting support from one another, and then Father Jonathan asked what arrangements they wanted to make for the funeral. Catherine told him that John's wife, Carla, wanted a graveside service and that her pastor was doing the eulogy. Carla did not want John to have a Catholic burial or mass.

"Then we'll have one without her. I know it will be early, but I will have my Friday 6:00 a.m. mass in his honor and then we will have the candle lighting. John and I have been friends ever since he was an altar boy and I was just a young priest. I am not going to allow that woman to deprive John of a proper goodbye.

Father Jonathan called the funeral home and asked that they pick up John's body as soon as possible. Next, he called Carla and told her that she needed to get with the funeral home to plan John's burial and to please let Amelia and Catherine know of the time.

"Do you want me to wait until the funeral home comes?" Father Jonathan asked. The girls agreed they were all right and there was no need for him to stay. They each hugged him when he left.

"I know it will be difficult for you to go upstairs and see John, but I'll help you go up the stairs," Catherine said.

Amelia shook her head, no, and left to go into her room. She closed the door behind her. Catherine stood at the bottom of the stairs looking up towards John's room. The boys were quietly playing on the floor with Alva and she turned and smiled at them. She wiped the tears from her eyes and walked slowly up the stairs. The sheet had been pulled over John's face and Catherine carefully pulled it back. She truly loved this man. She sat down beside him and took his hand. She smiled when she remembered the wonderful times they had had during their short marriage together, and she was comforted that he had chosen her to be with during his final days here on earth. She felt a peace in her heart that he was no longer suffering. It was a long, hard battle for him and he fought it bravely. Catherine bent down and kissed him sweetly on the lips. "I love you, John." She pulled the sheet back over his head and walked out, closing the door behind her.

After they picked up John's body, the funeral home attendant told Catherine and Amelia that the graveside service would be Friday at 10:00 a.m. Thursday was Thanksgiving and their employees would be off.

Catherine decided to make some calls before she checked on Amelia. She called Clay Segal first and he was still at the office. She told him of the arrangements. Before he hung up he told Catherine he would see her at the funeral.

"Carla has asked me not to come," Catherine said. "The boys and I will go there after the memorial and burial is over. There is a mass at 6:00 a.m. and then a candle lighting Friday morning, and I will be there for that," Catherine said. Clay said he would see her there. When she hung up, she called Minnie Wyman and gave her the news. Minnie gave her condolences and said she would see Catherine at mass on Friday.

Thanksgiving was difficult for Amelia. She hardly came out of her room. Catherine checked on her several times but knew she just needed rest. Catherine spent the day playing with the boys and she put on a pot of vegetable soup. She prepared lunch for the boys. Adam was almost five months old and he, too, had a hearty appetite. She was only nursing him twice a day now and she knew her milk was not enough to satisfy him. Her thoughts went from losing John to wondering where Alex might be. She was worried about moving into Amelia's house permanently. Losing John was hard enough for Amelia and Catherine knew how attached she was to the boys. Catherine decided to see if she could coax Amelia out of bed to come in the kitchen and eat some soup.

Catherine put the boys down for their naps and when she came back downstairs, Amelia was in the kitchen. Catherine prepared two bowls of soup and gave Amelia one.

"I know when you agreed to stay here; you had planned to only stay until John's passing. You are like a sister to me, Catherine. I was serious when I invited you and the boys to stay and make this your home," Amelia said.

Catherine thought for a moment and then said. "Nothing would please me more, but there are some things I need to take care of which might require me leaving town for a few days." Amelia listened as Catherine told her about Alex, his memory loss and his disappearance. He was there for me when I needed someone. I need to find him and make sure he is all right," Catherine told Amelia.

"You have been a wonderful friend to me, Catherine, and I admire you for the kind of person you are. John and Alex were fortunate to have married you. I want you to take care of things you need to do. Martha and I will be happy to look after the boys, if you need to leave town," Amelia said.

The two women hugged for a long time. Martha called after lunch to see how John was and when she heard of his passing she decided to cut her trip short and came back by train on Thanksgiving. She wanted to be there for the funeral.

Martha insisted on staying with the boys while Catherine and Amelia attended the mass. They decided the night before that Martha would attend the funeral with Amelia. Catherine had requested that the funeral home attendant pick her and Daniel up after the funeral and take them back to the cemetery for a private prayer. Before John died, he had made prearrangements with the funeral home and the cemetery. After he and Catherine had married he purchased three more vacant plots next to Anne's grave and it was his wishes to be buried next to her. Catherine knew Carla would be furious and it was probably best that she not attend.

St. Mary's Catholic Church was full and Catherine had no idea who a lot of the people were. Of course the mass was open to the general public, but the benches were overflowing with people. Amelia said a lot of the people knew John since he was a boy and some were friends of her parents and people he worked with. Clay Segal sat beside Catherine and Amelia at the mass. He offered to come back and pick Catherine up after the graveside service, but Catherine told him she had already made arrangements with the funeral home. She saw Sergeant Husky from the police department from a distance and she smiled at him and nodded. Tom Garret from the Grande Theatre was there along with his wife. The time went by quickly, and Catherine and Amelia approached the altar, made the sign of the cross, and then walked over for the candle lighting. It was daylight when they walked out of the church.

Martha had prepared some hot tea and scones for them when they got home. The boys were just waking up and Catherine changed them and brought them downstairs for breakfast. The carriage from the funeral home picked up Amelia and Martha and left. Catherine put the boys on the floor and watched as they began taking things out of the toy box. She had decided to leave Adam at home and only take Daniel. Daniel was fourteen months old now and walking. She hurried upstairs and grabbed Daniel's clothes and hardly left them out of her sight. Waiting was the hardest. She looked at Daniel and thought how much he had his father's mannerisms and then she looked at Adam. She tried hard not to think of David Brooks. But Adam was every bit his father. His facial expressions and his temperament were a direct reflection of David. He did not seem to have his father's volatile mood swings and she was thankful for that. Just then, she felt the baby move inside her and it almost surprised her. She thought of her unborn child and then she remembered her last kiss with Alex. She closed her eyes and relived the moment and then she stopped. This was a day to mourn the loss of John. She would have plenty of time to dream of Alex, she scolded herself.

Amelia and Martha got back home by 11:00 a.m. Carla was having a big gathering at her house, but only invited Amelia. She declined. Catherine put Daniel's coat on and then her own. It had rained earlier but had stopped. The carriage entered the cemetery grounds and Catherine saw the canopy and flower-covered grave. She got down and then picked up Daniel. They walked over and stood beside the grave. She took three white roses off the spray of flowers she had ordered for John's grave and put them on her mother's grave and then went back to John's. She said the Our Father and read the Twenty-third Psalm from the Bible. She had closed her eyes and was silently telling John goodbye when she heard Daniel say, "Da, Da," and pointed.

Catherine looked in the direction he was pointing and saw a man who looked just like John standing by a tree, waving at them with a big smile. He turned and took the hand of a woman who came out of the light. She smiled at Catherine and waved. It was her mother. The two turned and walked into the light. Catherine blinked and when she opened her eyes they were gone.

She picked up Daniel and said, "Did you see them?"

Daniel had a huge smile on his face and Catherine was smiling too. For the first time in a long time, Catherine felt at peace.

Amelia and Martha waited until Catherine returned and sat down at the kitchen table to have lunch. Daniel was in his highchair eating ham and green beans. Adam had been fussy so they had fed him earlier and he was already down for his nap.

"Carla certainly made a spectacle of herself at the service," Amelia said. "She cried out loud and made everyone uncomfortable."

Catherine looked at the newspaper that was sitting on the counter, open to the obituaries. Martha and Amelia looked at each other. Catherine got up and picked it up, reading it as she sat down. She revised the one John had given Carla to use. It barely mentioned Amelia as his sister and Daniel was not included in the list of family members. Catherine was furious.

"I hate it for John and for Daniel. I really didn't expect my name to be in there. John had given me the one he wrote before he gave it to Carla," Catherine said, "and it clearly mentioned Daniel."

Carla had revised it to read that he had two daughters and gave their names. It was already in print and there was nothing anyone could do about it.

Later in the afternoon the doorbell rang and Catherine opened the door. It was Clay Segal.

"I just came from Carla's little get together. She managed to stop crying at the funeral long enough to ask me to come for lunch. There must have been seventy-five people there," he said.

Catherine wondered why he came all the way over to see her. She had no interest in what Carla was doing.

"I just wanted to prepare you. She wants a meeting Monday morning to read the will and talk about her livelihood. I told her to come in at 10:00 a.m.," Clay said. "Will that work for you?"

"I suppose I can come in, if Martha will watch the children," Catherine said.

Clay did not get up to leave and Catherine asked if he would like some hot tea. He said yes, so she went into the kitchen to put the kettle on. She thought Clay had something on his mind other than the will and she wondered what it was. The tea pot finally whistled and she took the tray with cups and sugar into the living room. Amelia excused herself and went to her room, leaving Catherine alone with Clay. They each took a couple of sips and then Clay turned to her.

"I just wanted to tell you, Catherine, that I admire the way you waited on John hand and foot during these last few months. I knew you took your annulment pretty hard, and my heart goes out to you," he said. "I guess what I'm trying to say is that I understand your predicament, now that you are with child, and it won't be easy raising three children alone. I would be willing to marry you, and help you raise your three children. I'm not getting any younger and I'm a widower, myself. Will you marry me, Catherine? The sooner the better, since you are showing now."

Catherine's mouth dropped open and she found herself

speechless.

"Think about it a day or two. You can call me at home anytime," he said as he got up to leave.

Catherine walked him to the door and told him that she appreciated his offer, but that she was just fine raising three children by herself.

"Think about the children, Catherine, they need a father," he said and left.

Catherine sat down and finished her tea. Clay and John had grown up together. He was from an old Galveston family and he had a nice law practice. He was a bit podgy and he always looked a bit dishevelled, but that was not the reason Catherine told him no. She had no intention of marrying again, to Clay Segal, or any other man for that matter. She knew it would be difficult for the children, growing up without a father, but she would teach them to be strong. She also knew that she still loved Alex, and she had to find him, at any cost. Catherine's mind turned to John again and she knew that seeing him at the cemetery was just a mirage. Still, she smiled to herself. He had waited for them to come, before he left. He knew she was coming, she thought. She would always cherish that image; John, her mother, and then the light.

Catherine had not looked forward to Monday. Clay had made Catherine uncomfortable when he asked her to marry him. She said nothing to Amelia. There was no reason to and she felt it might upset Amelia in some way. Catherine took some extra time getting dressed for her meeting. She had washed her hair and the curly strands hung beautifully down her shoulders. She added a touch of rouge and lipstick and she was amazed at how much she looked like her mother. She put on her long coat and it barely covered her baby bump, When she walked downstairs Amelia commented on how beautiful she looked. Catherine smiled and told her she had a few errands to do and would be back after lunch.

Carla was already in Clay's office when Catherine got there.

Clay read the will and Carla interrupted him several times asking for clarity. When he finished, Carla turned to Catherine.

"Sweetie, I know you don't want to be bothered with all this legal stuff. Clay and I have been talking and he said you could withdraw as executrix anytime."

Catherine gave Clay an uncertain look. "Yes," said Clay, "you have that right."

"Since John is not able to speak for himself, I have to honor his request. The will remains as he intended it to be. I am not going to resign," Catherine said. "Now if there is nothing else, I have other appointments." Catherine got up and left.

Clay sat talking to Carla and Catherine wondered whose attorney he was. She would deal with him later, but she couldn't help but wonder if her rejection of his proposal had anything to do with him changing alliances.

Catherine stopped at the police station and waited a few minutes to see Sergeant Husky. "I wanted to thank you for coming to John's mass. He would have appreciated it," Catherine said. "I know it's still early, but have there been any calls regarding the article in the paper?" she asked.

"No, not yet; I've sent out some of the copies to Houston and Beaumont," Husky said.

Catherine thanked him and left. Her next stop was the general store to get some envelopes and then go to the Rosenberg Library. When she got to the library, she took out a pencil and paper. She looked at the large map of Texas and wrote down the names of cities surrounding the Houston area. She also added San Antonio and Austin. She looked up addresses of the police departments and also the names of the hospitals. Houston had several and she was afraid that once she made her list she wouldn't have enough copies. Before she left the library, she went to the second floor to the science section. She scanned the sections, looking for medical books about the cranium. She wanted to learn more about the human brain. She located one, and then selected another one on psychology. After stopping at the post office for stamps, she took a trolley to Minnie's boarding house. They sat at the kitchen table and Catherine told her how much she appreciated her friendship and that Amelia wanted her and the boys to stay with her. She said she would return another day to pick up the remainder of her things and settle up with rent. Minnie hugged her before she left and told her if anything changed, that she would always make a place for her there.

CHAPTER 10

Mary Windsong waited for Alex to return to the reservation and as the days slipped by, it was clear that he had no intentions of returning to the reservation to marry her, and be a father to her child. Three weeks had passed, when Dr. Windsong told her that there would be a wedding that night. She knew all the people in the reservation and wondered who it was. There was a knock on the door and Dr. Windsong opened it.

Grey Wolf was Mary's age. They had grown up together and played together when they were younger. They also liked to swim naked in the creek, until Dr. Windsong found out and forbade them from seeing each other for two weeks. Mary was fourteen at the time and Grey Wolf was like a brother to her. It was at that time that Dr. Windsong took out one of his medical books and explained to Mary about how babies were made. Having the illustrations made it easier for him to show her. After she realized that it was a natural thing for two people who were married and loved each other, she was embarrassed that Grey Wolf had seen her naked. She had started her period that summer, but she still liked teasing Grey Wolf, and by the end of summer he had kissed her. She called him Grey and his love for her grew over the years; he had already made up his mind that they would someday marry.

Mary felt differently. You don't marry your brother and she told him on several occasions that she did not love him the way a man and wife loved each other. He ignored it and decided to wait. He lost that hope the day Alex Cooper showed up, near dead, at the reservation. Mary looked at Grey Wolf as he walked in the door, still not knowing what was going on.

"Grey has asked me for your hand in marriage. Your baby is six moons away from delivery. The two of you will be married tonight," he said.

Mary started to open her mouth and refuse Grey's hand, but she stopped. She knew her father was right. Grey walked over and took Mary's hand.

"My father has told you about the baby and you still want to marry me?" she asked.

Grey said, "Yes."

"Then we will marry," she said, and went to her room and cried off and on most of the day. Dr. Windsong felt badly for her, but he knew that in time she would forget about the white man.

That afternoon, the Indian women came to the house and helped Mary get dressed. She looked beautiful in the doe skin wedding dress that had been passed around to other young brides on the reservation. The women placed elaborate feathers and brightly colored beads in Mary's hair.

There was a cool November breeze blowing from the south on the evening of the wedding. Mary and her father walked to the ceremonial garden that was used by the reservation for special events. Grey watched as she approached. He loved her more than anything, but it was not his intention to love the white man's child. He would deal with that in time. The drums, dancing and festival lasted until the half-moon appeared. Grey took Mary back to his small tent and waited outside while the women undressed her inside his tent. There was a small fire glowing beside the bearskin rug that lay beside it. Grey pulled the small covering aside and walked in when the ladies left. A glow from the fire reflected off Mary's smooth, delicate brown skin and Grey felt himself getting excited. He had waited for this time since he was a young boy. He was in full dress and he told Mary to remove his wedding garments. She complied. They stood, naked, and Mary gasped when she saw his large bulge. He turned her around, facing her away from him, and pushed her to her knees on the rug. He forced himself into her as she cried out in pain. Grey was a warrior and he performed as such. He was showing Mary how strong he was, and that she was expected to consent to his manhood whenever it pleased him. He collapsed beside her on the rug and fell asleep. Mary watched the embers in the fire as they slowly begin to fade. She had heard from many of the other Indian women what was expected on your wedding night. In all her imagination, this had to be the most horrible night she had ever experienced. She closed her eyes and remembered how beautiful and tender her nights had been with Alex. He was loving, gentle, and compassionate. That was not the way of the Indian men. They approached their women like they were instruments the men could play. They were harsh, uncaring, and as far as they were concerned, their wives' bodies belonged to the warriors, to do with as they pleased.

Grey woke up several times during the night and took Mary again, and he was content. Mary was his now, and no man would ever take her from him. If the white man came back for her, Grey would end the white man's life and he would make sure no one ever found his body. He would deal with the white man's child another time.

Alex had been at Oakwood Plantation Sanatorium for five weeks. They had not asked him to leave, as he was well-liked by everyone and he was earning his keep. At first it took him a couple of weeks to clean debris and junk out of the horse barn. Alex mended the fences to the corral and when he finished with that, he had begun working on the landscaping and gardens on the grounds. Oakwood sat on ten acres that had beautiful century-old pecan trees. Only the main house was surrounded by the towering wrought-iron fence. A barbed wire fence was erected on the outer perimeter of the land and it had been in disrepair for some time. Alex had permission to ride one of the horses and he made it a point to do it often. It enabled him to make his repairs on the fence much faster. It also made him feel human again. He had been moved to different living quarters at the back of the main house and it did not have a key or a lock. He was given regular clothes to wear and he was no longer considered a patient. Alex continued seeing Dr. Seymour twice a week, but he no longer did hypnosis. After two more hypnosis sessions, Alex was not able to recall anything that happened in the last five years.

He continued to have vivid dreams and they were often the subject of his therapy. Alex knew he didn't want to spend his life in the confines of the sanatorium, but it was safe and until he was ready to leave and find a job elsewhere, Dr. Seymour told him he could stay at Oakwood. Alex was allowed to take books from the main library and he spent his evenings in his small room reading and trying to remember. He was lonely and his only real friend was Dr. Seymour. Alex was longing for something more and he wished he knew what it was.

Dr. Winston called Dr. Seymour into his office one afternoon for a meeting. Dr. Winston picked up an article from an old newspaper and showed it to Dr. Seymour, who read it and then asked Dr. Winston if he wanted to make the call or should he. Dr. Seymour picked up the paper and went to his office and placed a call to the Galveston Police Department. The call was put through to Sergeant Husky. He listened intently.

"Are you sure?" he asked. "Well I'll be damned. Does he remember anything? Husky asked. "Awe, that's too bad," he said. "Let me get your name and number and have his wife call you," Husky said before he hung up the phone. He scratched his head. He had had a few calls from people who thought they had seen Alex on the train, but nothing could be traced. Now, someone had actually been able to give him information on Alex's whereabouts.

Catherine was on the floor playing with the boys when the phone rang. They had been actively engaged in playing possum and tickle. Catherine was breathing hard because they had been laughing and rolling on the floor. Amelia answered the phone in the study and walked into the living room.

"It's Sergeant Husky," she said.

Catherine jumped up and ran to the phone. After she answered, she listened intently. She wrote something on a pad, thanked him, and then hung up the phone. Her face was ashen and she stood looking at Amelia.

"They think they have found Alex," she told Amelia. "I need to make another phone call."

When Dr. Seymour answered the phone, Catherine introduced herself as Catherine Cooper. Her story was much too complicated to convey on the phone. "I understand that my husband, Alex Cooper, may be staying with you," she said. Dr. Seymour said he felt reasonable sure they were one and the same person.

He told her that Alex had been found at the train depot in Houston and he was taken to a hospital in Houston about three weeks before. His only memory was of the first twenty-five years of his life. They discussed the fact that Catherine should come to the facility and talk to Dr. Seymour first before they told Alex. She said she would leave on an early morning train the next day and Dr. Seymour said they would send a carriage from the sanatorium to meet her train. Catherine told Amelia what Dr. Seymour said and that Alex had total memory loss of the last five years of his life.

Adam was scooting around on the floor now and his new found freedom brought out more energy than Catherine could keep up with. Martha and Amelia both encouraged her to leave Adam and Daniel at home. She told them she might be gone several days and she wasn't sure if she would be bringing Alex back. If she did, she would have to find a place for them to move into.

"Don't make any hasty decisions," Amelia said. "If you are able to bring him back, he can stay in John's old room and you can move back into the boys' room. At least until you feel like you are ready to do something different. We can get Alva to spend a few extra hours each day and we'll get the rooms ready. You need to concentrate on Alex's health now."

Catherine hugged Amelia and thanked her for her generous offer. She knew part of the reason was that Amelia wanted to have the boys around and she understood that. They were all she had left.

Catherine took her large bag down from the closet to pack, expecting to stay three or four days. She hardly slept the night before she left. When she dressed the next morning, she realized that the clothes she had were getting very tight. She had not worn some of them for some time and she was panicked about what to wear. She came downstairs with open buttons and was almost in tears. Amelia was a good two sizes larger than Catherine and she took her into her room and opened the closet.

"I don't know what I would do without you," she told Amelia as she pulled a few things out of the closet. She tried on several things and selected two dresses and a skirt and blouse. She was over three months pregnant now, and she wondered what Alex would say about the baby. After she finished putting her things in her suitcase, Catherine made her way to the train station.

When Catherine got off the train in Houston there was a Negro man holding a sign that said "Cooper." She waved and walked up to him. He took her bag and helped her into the carriage. Thirty-five minutes later they were at the front gate of Oakwood. Catherine got down off the carriage and the Negro man took her inside and showed her into a small drawing room. Catherine sat for about fifteen minutes and then began pacing around the small room.

Catherine was looking out the window when she heard her name and turned around. There was a man who introduced himself as Dr. Philip Seymour and he smiled at her. He told her that he only had one hour to visit with her before he had to attend an important meeting. She followed him into his office and sat down in a chair in front of his desk.

Dr. Seymour told Catherine about Alex's condition since he came to the sanatorium. He told Catherine that part of the bullet went through his head and had left a fragment in his skull, and it was recommended he have surgery to remove it. Dr. Seymour felt strongly it had somehow moved and caused Alex to regress.

"How long have you been married to Alex?" he asked.

Catherine noticed he was looking at her baby bump.

"A little over three months," she replied. "He had left Galveston one morning to go to Beaumont. He worked there and came home on the weekends. When he didn't show up for work, they called to see when he might be coming in. That's when I realized something had happened," Catherine said.

"I'm really sorry I have to leave you, but one of our benefactors is stopping in for lunch and I have to meet with him for a couple of hours. You are welcome to walk the grounds or you can wait in our library. I'll see that you get something for lunch and you can leave your bag where it is. It will be safe," Dr. Seymour said.

"What if I run into Alex?" she asked.

"Just act normal. Watch his face and see if he recognizes you. He has your picture and he told me he looks at it often. We'll consider it as a test. If he doesn't make the connection, just tell him you are a visitor. I should be free around 3:00 p.m. By the way, we have a couple of rooms in the main house that we allow our guests to use. If you could stay overnight we could have more time to discuss your options," Dr. Seymour.

Catherine smiled and said, "That would be nice."

Catherine set out to explore the main house and studied the paintings that filled the hallways and vestibules. She wondered if they were of the original plantation owners. Catherine walked down a long corridor and she reached a large door. She tried to open it, but it was locked. She turned and went the other way and found two double doors with glass that opened to an outside veranda. She turned the knob on one and opened the door. The grounds were truly beautiful and she found herself outside under a covered porch with wooden rocking chairs and some tables. It was chilly with a slight breeze blowing from the south. She was glad she still had her coat on and she decided to sit in one of the rocking chairs. She was wondering what the history was on this plantation before it became a sanatorium.

"Ma'am," she heard someone say and when she turned and looked up, she couldn't believe her eyes. It was Alex. "Dr. Seymour asked me to take you into the employee dining room and have lunch with you. I don't normally do this kind of thing, but I guess no one else was available. Would you like to follow me, please?" he said.

Catherine got up, not sure what to say. She watched as Alex showed her the way and opened the door for her. He had lost at least fifteen pounds and his hair was a bit longer. He was dressed in khaki pants with suspenders, and a white, long-sleeved shirt. He looked more handsome than she had ever seen him. On the way, it struck her that he seemed to have no recollection of who she was. Maybe being pregnant had something to do with it, she thought. He showed her to a small table for two by a window and sat down with her. Catherine could see Dr. Seymour across the room with three other gentlemen and they all turned and looked at her. Dr. Seymour smiled and Catherine returned his smile. She felt awkward and vulnerable. Consider it a test, Dr. Seymour had told her earlier. She wondered who the test was for. It was obvious that Alex had no clue who she was.

A waiter walked over, wearing white gloves, and poured water into both of their glasses. He asked if they preferred meat or fish. Alex and Catherine said at the same time, "fish," and they smiled at each other. Alex was extremely polite and he asked her if she was visiting a family member. Catherine said she was considering the facility for a friend. Alex looked at her in a strange kind of way.

"Is something wrong?" she asked.

"Not at all," he said. "I don't get to eat lunch with a beautiful woman often, and it's really nice."

The waiter brought out two fruit salads and Alex waited for

Catherine to pick her fork up first. She asked him what his job was at the facility.

"Actually, I originally came here as a patient; apparently I had gotten shot and the bullet went through my head causing me to lose some of my memory. I now do odd jobs around the plantation and go to therapy twice a week," Alex told her. "If you are looking for a place for a relative, I recommend this place highly."

Catherine smiled and said it was really beautiful. While they ate their food, they mostly talked about general things. Catherine watched intently as Alex ate. She poked at her food but wasn't very hungry.

"You're not a very big eater," Alex said. "Your baby needs nourishment, too. Do you not like it?"

"Oh, yes, it's delicious and I know I need to eat more, but right now, I'm just not that hungry," she said.

Alex asked the waiter to bring coffee for him and hot tea for Catherine.

"I'm sorry," he said. "I should have asked you first. I don't know why I did that, except, you're British, aren't you."

Catherine smiled and said that she was from England and had only been in the United States about three years.

"I don't know a lot about England. I'm pretty sure I'm a native Texas. I found that out in one of my therapy sessions. I can only remember the first twenty-five years of my life. Dr. Seymour thinks I'm around thirty, so I'm hoping I'll remember the last five. They told me at the hospital in Houston that a fragment of a bullet was still lodged in my head and until it was removed, I may never remember," Alex said, staring past Catherine. A moment later, their eyes locked.

"Have your thought about the surgery?" Catherine asked.

"Of course, all the time, but like this place, it's very expensive and I have no money. They let me work here doing odd jobs to pay for my upkeep. They give me a room and food, and two therapy sessions a week," Alex said.

"So, you're saying that if you had the money, you would definitely have the surgery? I understand that it could be very dangerous," Catherine said.

Alex thought for a minute.

"I'm not sure I want to spend the rest of my life trying to figure out who I am. We're not made that way. I have a past and it's important to me to find out what kind of man I was."

He stopped and stared at Catherine and moved his hand over across the table and touched the top of Catherine's hand. She watched his hand and then looked up at him.

"You are the woman in my picture, aren't you?" Alex asked.

Catherine opened her purse and took out the picture she had brought. It was a picture of the three of them on their wedding day. She handed it to Alex. He took the picture and looked at it.

"The boy, is that my son?" he asked.

Catherine looked down and said, "No, this one is yours," and she patted her stomach.

Alex stood up and threw his napkin on the table.

"Excuse me," he said, and left.

Catherine was stunned and she looked at Dr. Seymour. Dr. Seymour could see that something had happened, so he got up and excused himself from his table and went to Catherine.

"I don't know why he left. I showed him a picture of us when we got married. He asked if the boy in the picture was his and I told him, no, but that the one I was carrying was. I'm so sorry if I upset him," she said, holding back her tears.

"Its fine, Mrs. Cooper. I have a session with him today at 2:00 p.m. You can wait in your room and I'll come for you."

Catherine got up and left the table. Everything seemed to be going so well. Maybe I just overwhelmed him, she thought. She walked back to where she had left her bag. It was 1:00 p.m. according to the large grandfather clock in the entry. She decided to find a telephone and call Amelia and tell her that she was going to stay overnight. She saw a cleaning lady and asked to use a phone. She was shown into a small waiting room and to a telephone on a small desk. Catherine picked up the phone and gave the operator the necessary information to reverse the charges. Martha answered and before Catherine could tell her she would be staying over, Martha began crying.

"I'm so sorry, Miss Catherine, Amelia went back to her room after you left this morning and now, I cannot wake her up. She was breathing, but unresponsive. I called an ambulance and they took her to the hospital. I'm so sorry, Miss Catherine, but you need to come home now."

"All right," Catherine said. "I'll be home late tonight and I'll call you when I get in. Are the boys all right?"

Martha assured her that they were fine. Catherine hung up the phone and felt completely overwhelmed. She saw some stationery on the desk and she picked up a piece of paper and wrote Dr. Seymour a message. "Family emergency; I have to go back to Galveston immediately, and will call you tomorrow." -- Catherine Cooper.

Dr. Seymour and Alex were in their therapy session when Catherine left in the carriage to return to Galveston.

"What made you angry?" Dr. Seymour asked Alex.

Alex thought for a moment. "Scared, I guess."

"What were you afraid of?" Dr. Seymour continued.

"I'm not sure. Sitting there with her made me feel a connection, but when she told me that the baby she was carrying was my child, I just got overwhelmed. I know it must have seemed rude to her, and I'm sorry. She is beautiful, but I reached over and touched her hand, and I didn't feel anything," Alex said sadly. "How can she expect me to just go back with her, to who knows where, and be a husband and a father?"

"I don't think she was expecting you to leave. I spoke with her for awhile this morning and she seemed to have your best interest at heart," Dr. Seymour told Alex.

There was a knock on the door and an attendant handed Dr.

Seymour a letter. He read it and folded it back up and looked at Alex. "It's from Catherine, and she says she has a family emergency and has to leave immediately. She will call me later." He handed the note to Alex and he read it.

"I guess I ran her off," Alex said sadly. "I didn't mean to offend her."

"At least we have confirmed who you are, and that's a starting place," Dr. Seymour said and continued, "What else did she say?"

She asked me if I would do the surgery if I had the money," Alex answered. "I told her yes. She said she came here four years ago from England, and I guess that's about it. I suppose I thought that if I met someone from my past, I'd remember, but I didn't."

CHAPTER 11

Catherine had just gotten to the train depot in Houston, Texas, to make the 4:00 p.m. train back to Galveston. She was anxious and worried not only about Amelia, but Alex. She hated just walking out like that and she worried he might think she abandoned him. Why, she thought, when I try to move forward with my life, there is always something dragging me back. She had stopped feeling sorry for herself a long time ago, while she was in captivity. It took too much energy, and now she needed to focus on the matters at hand. She decided to go to the club car. She needed something to steady her nerves.

She was going to be twenty-one years old in a couple of months and she had seen a lot of tragedy in her short life. She sat at a small table by the window and ordered a glass of wine. Two men came in from the other direction and sat at a table across from her. She could feel them staring at her and one of them said something she could not hear. They both laughed. She decided to ignore them and continued looking out the window. One of them walked up to the bar and ordered two beers. He put one in front of his friend and then sat across from Catherine at her table. He was probably forty, balding, and his clothes looked like he had been wearing them for several days.

"Where's your husband?" he asked her.

Catherine looked at him but didn't answer. She took a sip of her wine and continued to look out the window.

"I'm talking to you," he said in a loud voice.

"My husband is back in our private compartment and he is a policeman. Do you want me to get him for you?" she said, staring him the face. He grabbed his beer and went back to his friend's table. Catherine was upset, but she had learned a long time ago how to have a poker face. No man was ever going to intimidate her again, she thought. She finished her wine and got up and left.

Catherine decided to go home first and leave her bag when she got to Galveston. She wanted to check on the children and change into something more comfortable, just in case she needed to stay the night at the hospital. Daniel ran to the door when he saw his mother come in, and Adam began crying, holding his arms up in the air. Martha picked him up and took him to Catherine. The two boys were almost too big for Catherine to hold at the same time, but she managed. She took them to the sofa and hugged and kissed them both. Martha said she had checked on Amelia's condition by phone just before Catherine got home, and the prognosis was not good. Catherine made a quick change and put a few things in her knapsack just in case she stayed at the hospital.

Amelia had been placed in a private room and Catherine looked on the chart to see who the doctor was. His name was Dr. Samuel Allen. Catherine asked one of the nurses where he had come from.

"He came from Dallas, Texas, and he's a lung specialist," the nurse said.

Just then, Dr. Allen came in, and Catherine introduced herself as Amelia's sister-in-law.

"I'm afraid she has pneumonia. She is resting, but having difficulty breathing. I don't expect her to make it through the night. I have checked her medical history and apparently she has been suffering with lung disease for the past ten years. I'm very sorry," he said.

"Yes," Catherine said. "I'm aware of her illness. Her brother passed a couple of months ago and she has not been well since. He was her only living relative. I have been living with her and looking after her, but I had to leave town on some personal business and I feel terrible I wasn't here for her."

"Don't feel bad, Catherine, you're not being here would not have made any difference. Pneumonia is a powerful enemy to the lungs and the body and we haven't found a cure for it yet," Dr. Allen said. "You can go in and see her now. She might not recognize you, as she is sedated. It was nice meeting you," he said and smiled at her.

Catherine walked into Amelia's room. There was a tent over her bed and Catherine sat in a chair beside her. Amelia had been Catherine's biggest supporter and she never gave up on Catherine. She loved her like a sister. Catherine took her hand and she felt a slight squeeze. Catherine stood up and stared through the tent, but Amelia's eyes were closed. Amelia's hand went limp and Catherine saw that her chest was no longer moving up and down. She ran to the nurse's station and saw Dr. Allen. She followed him back into Amelia's room. He opened the tent and placed his stethoscope to her chest. He took a step back and shook his head and said, "I'm sorry."

Catherine sat back in the chair and put her head in her hands.

"Is there someone I can call for you?" Dr. Allen asked.

"I'll be all right. I just need a minute," she whispered. Catherine ran her fingers through her hair and shook her head. "I'll have the funeral home pick her body up in the morning," she said.

Catherine left and automatically walked toward the exit of the emergency room. She stopped before she got through the door when she saw how dark it was outside. She turned to go back in and ran directly into Dr. Allen.

"Oh, I'm so sorry," she said. "I didn't realize it was so dark outside."

"It's all right. May I see you home?" he asked.

"If you could just see me to the trolley, that would be wonderful," Catherine answered.

The weather was brisk and they walked quickly to the trolley.

Dr. Allen boarded the trolley with her. I take the same trolley," he said and smiled.

Catherine was quiet and did not feel like talking. She was thinking about having to plan another funeral. She pulled the lever when it approached her stop.

"Thank you," she said to Dr. Allen. He followed her and got off when she did. Catherine looked at him surprised.

"Well, I've come this far, I might as well see you home," he said.

Catherine turned and thanked him again when they got to her house.

"Are you sure you are going to be all right?" he asked.

"Yes, my children are with the nanny," Catherine said.

"You have other children?" he asked.

"Two boys. Amelia was their aunt. Amelia's brother, John Merit, was my husband and he passed a couple of months earlier from a blood disease. Thank you, again," Catherine opened the door and went into the house.

Dr. Samuel Allen stood outside the door, trying to take it all in. This beautiful, young, pregnant woman has two boys and she is a widow. How unfair, he thought. Samuel could feel compassion for Catherine because he was raised by his mother. His father had died when he was young and ever since he could remember; his mother had worked in a canning factory in a small town outside of Dallas. She saved everything she didn't have to spend and put it away for Samuel's education. It was never a question that Samuel wouldn't go to college, but his mother told him to do something useful with his life, and to pick something that made him happy. He knew by the time he had gotten to high school that he wanted to be a doctor. He took a special interest in the heart and lungs when his mother developed tuberculosis.

She had not been the only one from the factory to have this problem. The fumes from the gases they inhaled in the boiling room on a daily basis were lethal, only no one knew that. His mother had died a semester short of Samuel's graduation from medical school. He interned at Dallas General Hospital and when he read in the paper that Galveston, Texas, was short on doctors after the flood, he decided it was time for a change. He was twenty-six years old and loved what he did. He had a few distant cousins, but had lost contact with them years earlier.

Samuel liked working at a Catholic hospital and he and Father Jonathan became good friends. Samuel was protestant, but occasionally he would go to mass, just to humor Father Jonathan. He wasn't particularly religious, but he believed in a higher power and he saw miracles every day. It was his job to save lives. He felt bad that Amelia's disease had already done its damage by the time he began treating her.

Catherine Merit intrigued him. Actually, she reminded him of his mother. The two had a lot in common. She was attractive, caring and independent. He had seen Catherine talking to one of the nurses earlier that evening and they seemed to know her well. He asked, and was told that Catherine had been a medical student and interned at St. Mary's Hospital a couple of years earlier, but some unfortunate circumstances caused her to drop out. Samuel was even more intrigued, and decided his friend, Father Jonathan, might know some of the answers.

Martha was still up when Catherine came in and she and Catherine hugged, each trying to lift the other up. "I'm sorry that I forgot to ask how things went with Alex," Martha said.

"They did not go well. He did not remember me and unfortunately, I overwhelmed him. He appears to be in good health otherwise. There may be a possibility that an operation to remove a bullet fragment might help him regain his memory, but I didn't get that far with his doctor. I'm afraid it's been a very long day and I need to sleep. Catherine said as she got up. She kissed Martha on the cheek and thanked her for being so loyal.

Catherine tossed and turned all night. Her thoughts and dreams seemed to ramble and each time she woke up, which was often; ghosts of her past were speaking to her. She finally got up at 5:30 a.m. and drank some hot tea. She dressed early and looked at the clock. It was too early to make the phone calls she needed to make. Father Jonathan was the first one to call, simply because Catherine knew he woke up early, too. Father Jonathan had already been notified of Amelia's death. That was the first thing he did in the mornings; check the well-being of his parishioners. He visited with Catherine on the phone, and he could feel her pain. She had had so much of it, he thought. There was no reason to wait for notifications. Amelia had no other relatives and her only friends were Catherine and Martha. There would be a graveside service at 2:00 p.m. that afternoon. After Catherine and Martha fed the boys and gave them their baths, Catherine went into the study to make some more calls. She called Clay Segal and asked that he notify Carla. The next phone call was the one she was dreading.

"This is Dr. Seymour," the man said on the other end of the line.

After a thirty-minute conversation, Catherine asked what she should do next. She had told Dr. Seymour that there were ample funds to take care of any surgeries Alex needed, and that right now his welfare and health were most important. Dr. Seymour told Catherine that he had had a session the day before with Alex and that he thought it best that Catherine not return to the sanatorium until Alex asked for her to come.

"He's very confused right now and very overwhelmed. He needs time to sort out the information," Dr. Seymour suggested. She gave him her home phone number and address and he promised he would keep Catherine posted on Alex's condition.

Catherine made another call. "Clarence Henry, here," the voice on the other end of the phone said.

Their conversation was short. She just wanted Clarence to

know that Alex was safe and she gave him the name and address of the sanatorium. Clarence thanked her and hung up. She would have called Minnie, but Minnie had left a message earlier in the week that she was leaving the city for five days to visit her daughter in another town.

The funeral home carriage picked up Martha, Catherine, and the boys at 1:30 that afternoon. As they drove through neighborhoods, they saw Christmas decorations in front of the houses. Daniel and Adam got excited by all the colorful scenes, including a manger scene in front of one of the churches. Many of the houses had Christmas trees in their windows with brightly colored lights and tinsel. Catherine felt bad that she had not even thought about Christmas or a tree for the house.

When they got to the cemetery, a tent had been put up over the grave. It was threatening rain, but it was still dry. They were the first to arrive, and Martha held Daniel's hand while Catherine held Adam and walked over to John's and her mother's graves. A few minutes later, Clay Segal showed up and then Father Jonathan, accompanied by Dr. Samuel Allen. Carla did not come. The two funeral home attendants stood off to the side, and when they decided there would be no other participants, one of them nodded to Father Jonathan to begin.

The service was over in fifteen minutes. Catherine read the Twenty-third Psalm from the Bible and thanked everyone for coming. She walked over to Father Jonathan, handed him an envelope and kissed him on the cheek, and shook Dr. Allen's hand. She had been surprised that Dr. Samuel Allen had come, but perhaps he was at the hospital and Father Jonathan invited him, she thought. She walked over to Clay Segal and introduced him to Dr. Allen. Before she left, Clay said they needed to talk about Amelia's will and that Carla wanted a settlement. They agreed to meet the next morning at 10:00 a.m.

Father Jonathan and Samuel got back into their carriage and

made their way back into town. “Tell me about Catherine Merit,” Samuel asked Father Jonathan.

Father Jonathan thought for a moment.

“Her life has been one tragedy after another, since the day she set foot on American soil. She’s an incredible woman, the likes I’ve never met. If you are thinking of asking her out, I suggest you just try and be a friend. She will break your heart,” he said. Samuel and Father Jonathan rode the rest of the way in silence.

The next day Catherine went to Clay Segal’s office alone, leaving the boys at home with Martha. They discussed Amelia’s will, which John had had Amelia sign before their deaths. It left Amelia’s full interest in the house to Catherine along with the furnishings. She had a small $2,000 life insurance policy that would pay her burial fees and Clay’s legal fees first, and the remainder would go to Daniel for his education. Catherine would be paid the sum of $250.00 for being the executrix of John’s will, $5,000 would go to Daniel for his education and Carla would get the remainder after Clay’s legal fees were deducted. He gave Catherine a payment ledger and told her that the mortgage on the house was $65.00 a month and the payments had to be kept current each month. There was a balance due on the mortgage of $3,200.

“Have you thought about my proposal?” Clay asked. Catherine wondered at first what he was talking about and then remembered he had asked her to marry him.

“I’m not of the mind to consider marriage at this time. I appreciate your offer and consider it to be a very kind gesture. I must decline,” she said as she got up.

Clay’s small office was cluttered with papers and he only had a part time secretary, who was out that day. Clay got up and walked over to the door to open it. Catherine stopped because he was blocking her exit. She looked at him questioningly. Before she could say anything, Clay grabbed her and twisted her arm behind her back and kissed her. He caught her off balance and they fell to the floor with papers flying everywhere. Clay was on top of her, kissing her hard, and pinning her to the floor. She resisted as best she could, but his large body on top of hers prevented her from getting away.

"Please, please stop," she cried. "Please don't do this," she begged.

He had pulled her dress up and tried to enter her. She managed to free one of her hands, but he grabbed it and then she felt his fullness move inside her.

"Marry me, Catherine, marry me, marry me," he said over and over as he raped her.

"Please stop," she cried. "Please!" she kept saying

A few minutes later, he collapsed on the floor beside her.

She tried to get up but he pulled her back down to the floor and took her hair, pulling her face to his.

"You tell anyone about this and I'll say you encouraged me to have you. Do you understand?"

Catherine said nothing. Clay got up and buttoned his pants. He walked over to a mirror and took out a comb and ran it through his hair. Catherine sat up and Clay made no effort to help her. She felt violated and angry. She had considered Clay a good friend of the family and he had betrayed her. She managed to get up by herself, not looking at Clay. After she adjusted her clothing, she notice a cut on top of her wrist and it was bleeding. She took her handkerchief out of her knapsack and wrapped it around her wrist. When she looked up, Clay was gone. She saw broken glass on the floor and figured the glass that was on the table had fallen off and broken.

She gathered her things, walked out into the cold, and realized she had left her coat. She did not turn back. She was afraid he would attack her again, so Catherine began to walk fast down the Strand. She was close to tears and the horror of the moment was escalating in her mind. How could he? she thought; how could he? She was too upset to go home so she continued walking. Dazed and in shock, Catherine made her way down several streets.

CHAPTER 12

Fifteen minutes later she found herself in front of St. Mary's Catholic Church. She pulled on the handle of one of the massive carved wooden doors and it opened. She was shaking from the cold and she had hardly noticed that it had started raining the last six blocks of her walk. She disappeared into a rear pew and pulled down the kneeling bench. She knelt as she folded her hands in front of her face and softly cried into her hands. She thought she was alone in the church, but Father Jonathan had been up by the confessional when she walked in. He watched her for awhile, and then he decided to take a closer look. There was something white wrapped around her wrist and it was splotched with blood. He saw she was crying and he decided to give her a few more minutes. She had only been there about five minutes when she looked up and saw him watching her. She looked down and away, like she was ashamed about something.

"Come," he said softly as her helped her up. "Come into my office."

She got up and he put his arm around her while they walked together. He closed the door behind him and helped Catherine to a chair. She was wet and shivering. He took his overcoat off a hook from behind the door and put it around her. As he examined her more closely he realized she must have been attacked, as he saw bruises on her neck and other hand. He poured her a glass of water and told her to take a drink and she did.

"Who did this to you, Catherine?" he asked her softly.

Catherine shook her head and tightly closed her lips.

"Stay here and I'll be right back," he said.

Father Jonathan went into his private study off of his office and closed the door to use a private phone. "Yes," he said. "You'll need your black bag."

When he went back out Catherine was still in shock and staring at the floor. She was no longer crying, but shaking. A few minutes later, there was a soft knock at the door and Catherine looked up in panic.

"I have to go. I don't want anyone else to see me like this," she whimpered.

Father Jonathan walked over and put his arms around Catherine, and said, "Come in."

Dr. Samuel Allen walked through the door and Catherine looked at Father Jonathan like she had been betrayed.

"I'm going to give you something to make you more comfortable," Dr. Allen said as he took out a small bottle and a needle and administered the medicine. "Let me take a look at your wrist," he said as he took Catherine's hand. "It looks like there is a small piece of glass still inside the cut and I need to remove it. Will that be all right?" he asked Catherine. She shook her head, yes.

It was not the first time Dr. Allen had seen the aftermath of a rape. The receiving room in the emergency room of Dallas General brought many young girls through who had been violated by strangers, boyfriends, and even family members. It was that part of the job he least liked, but it came with his profession.

"Catherine, did he hurt the baby?" She looked away and shook her head, no. When she did, he saw a bite mark on her neck, and he instantly wanted to do harm to the man who had done this to her. "I'd like to take you to the hospital and do a complete examination on you," he said.

"No. Just let me go home," she said.

The two men looked at each other

"All right," Dr. Allen said, "but only if you let me see you home. I just finished my shift and I was headed that way anyway."

Catherine got up and said, "All right."

Dr. Allen waved for a public carriage to stop and he helped Catherine inside. He had put his coat around her when they left the church, and he sat beside her as they rode home. He told the driver to go on after he paid him, and he accompanied Catherine to the front door.

Martha was stunned when she saw Catherine and Dr. Allen. "She fell on the slippery street and she needs rest," he said.

Once inside, Catherine ran up the stairs and didn't say anything.

"She'll be fine after she gets some rest," he said. "I'll give you my phone number if she needs me," he said.

Martha thanked him and he left. When he got outside, the rain had let up, and he decided to walk to his small rooming house. He was off for twenty hours now, and he wondered what he could do to pass the time. He turned and looked at Catherine's house and remembered a conversation he had heard at the cemetery. Catherine was visiting with Clay Segal and he heard him make an appointment with Catherine at 10:00 a.m. that morning. It was 11:30 a.m. when he was called to the church. Dr. Allen turned and made his way to the Strand. He only walked a couple of blocks when he saw a small sign over a door that said Lawyer's Office, Clay Segal. When he walked in a buzzer rang and a few minutes later Clay Segal came out of an office.

Dr. Allen did not introduce himself again, because other than Father Jonathan, Samuel was the only other man at the funeral, other than the attendants and Catherine had introduced them.

"Already need a lawyer, Dr. Allen?" Clay said.

"I understand you had an appointment with Catherine Merit at 10:00 a.m. this morning?" he said more as a statement than a question.

"So what's it to you?" Clay asked him.

"She was molested sometime between 10:00 and 11:30 this morning," Samuel said.

"Don't know anything about that. Is she okay?" Clay asked.

"Tell me something. How did you get that blood on your shirt?" Samuel asked.

"Must have cut myself shaving this morning," Clay answered.

Samuel was tall and weighed about one hundred eighty-five pounds and Clay realized he was no match if Dr. Allen decided to put up a fight. Samuel took a few steps closer and asked Clary if he wanted to tell the truth to him or the police.

"Well, she wanted me to kiss her. She's been trying to get me in bed with her ever since her husband died. It may have gotten a little rough, but she seemed to like it at the time. I just gave her what she wanted," he said.

"You son-of-a-bitch," Samuel said. "If I hear you telling anyone that lie, you'll have to answer to me. Understood?"

Clay shook his head, yes.

Samuel left; afraid if he stayed any longer he might hit Segal. He couldn't afford to have something like that on his record. He walked back in the direction of Catherine's house.

"She'll break your heart," he remembered Father Jonathan say. He knew it was too late. He had already been drawn into her web and he was defenceless.

Samuel rang the doorbell and Martha answered the door, holding Adam in her arms. Daniel walked over and held his arms up.

"This is a nice welcoming party" he said, as he picked up Daniel.

He looked up and saw Catherine coming down the stairs. She had showered and her wet curls circled her cheeks and flowed over her breasts. She had on a simple dress and a cardigan sweater. He thought she was the most beautiful creature he had ever seen.

"I was in the neighborhood and thought I would come by and

check on you," he said smiling.

Catherine smiled and asked if he would like some hot tea. He said yes. He followed her into the kitchen with Daniel in his arms.

"He'll let you hold him all day," Catherine said. "He likes being on eye level with the grown-ups."

"Your boys are adorable," Samuel said.

Catherine walked over and took Daniel from Samuel and sat him on the floor. She gave him two cookies and said, "Go take one to your little brother." Daniel grabbed the cookie and ran into the living room.

Catherine and Samuel sat at the kitchen table drinking their hot tea.

"Thank you and I'm sorry I was so rude to you at the church. Being a doctor, I guess you figured out what happened to me. I would appreciate it if you didn't report it to anyone," Catherine said and looked at him.

He shook his head up and down, indicating that he understood, and then said. "I heard you at the cemetery yesterday making the appointment with your attorney at 10:00 a.m. this morning. You were at the church at 11:30. After I dropped you off, I went to his office. He tried to deny it, but eventually lied and said you had encouraged him to have you. I knew it wasn't true."

Catherine looked down and said, "He told me if I said anything that would be the story he would tell. He's a well-respected attorney from and old family. He's untouchable."

"He shouldn't get away with this Catherine," Samuel said.

"I appreciate your concern, but I can't drag myself or my children through some scandal that I know would only make the indignity of the rape worse," she said looking into his eyes.

He sighed and took her hand. "I can't begin to imagine how this must have been for you. Just promise me that if he tries to get close, you'll let me know," Samuel said. "I want to be your friend."

Catherine looked at his hand on hers and she slowly moved it and picked up her cup to take a sip. "I think it would be best if you stayed far away from me. People who get close to me sometimes get hurt. You seem like a very nice man and I'm going to be honest with you. My children are my life and there is no room for anyone else," Catherine said and looked away.

Samuel finished his tea and stood up. "I'm not asking to move in with you, Catherine, I just needed a friend, too." He turned and left.

Catherine felt the bite of his words and was sorry she had been so abrupt with him. It's for his best interest, she thought. He's handsome, smart and sweet. Some young nurse will latch on to him soon, and the nurse would make a better friend to him than she would. It really didn't matter anyway.

That night, her anger grew as she thought about Clay Segal and she hated him for making her feel dirty again. When he was raping her, she had a vivid picture of David Brooks on top of her; taking her body and her dignity. Clay Segal was no different than David Brooks. If John were alive he would kill him. She wished she could kill Clay Segal. What man would even want her? Even Alex had turned his back on her now. She was aching with loneliness and wanting more than anything for someone to love her.

A few days later Catherine had made an appointment for a check up with Dr. Copeland. She didn't think the baby had been harmed in any way, but she needed confirmation. She hadn't felt any movement and she wanted to be sure it was all right. She waited on the exam table and Dr. Copeland finally came in. He did a pelvic exam and then used his stethoscope to check for a heartbeat.

"Aw, there it is," he said. "The baby is doing fine. Are you feeling all right?" he asked. Catherine assured him she was fine and thanked him.

When Catherine wasn't playing or taking care of the children she stayed in her room. Martha knew something had happened, but she knew Catherine was not ready to tell her. Finally, she couldn't stand it anymore.

"It's only three days before Christmas and you've done nothing for your children. I know something happened when you had your accident, but your children can sense your unhappiness. Why don't you get out of the house and go Christmas shopping?" Martha suggested. "Take your time. The children will be fine with me."

Catherine walked into the study and looked at the phone. Maybe she did need a friend. She called the hospital and asked for Dr. Samuel Allen. When he came to the phone, Catherine said, "I thought about what you said about being a friend, and I was wondering if you're not busy at the hospital on Christmas, we would like you to join us for dinner."

"That sounds great. I'm on a twenty-four hour shift from Christmas Eve until noon on Christmas day. Give me a couple hours sleep and I'll be there. Is four o'clock too early?" he asked.

"That would be fine." Catherine said. She walked out of the study and told Martha she was going shopping and that they were having company on Christmas for supper. Martha smiled. It's time something nice happened to her, Martha thought.

Catherine spent the next two days shopping for Christmas presents and getting the house decorated for Christmas. She found a real fir tree for sale on a vacant lot. She bought it and they delivered it that afternoon. She had already rummaged through the attic for decorations, but she bought a few more just in case. Martha, Catherine, and the boys decorated it. Most of the decorations were on the lower limbs because that was as far as Daniel could reach. Adam seemed more interested in tearing the paper up, but they had a lot of fun. She made the grocery store last on her list: fresh vegetables, lamb, mashed potatoes and a cream pie. Martha had made the grocery list and promised to show Catherine how to cook everything. They had prepared the cake the day before and Catherine set the dining room table with some antique dishes that she bought at the thrift store. She felt sad when she realized that she and John had never sat at this table nor eaten off these dishes. It didn't seem fair, she thought.

On Christmas morning, the boys tore into their presents. Catherine had hidden some of them from the boys, so there would be some things under the tree when Samuel got there. While the boys took their afternoon nap, Catherine picked up their mess and helped Martha in the kitchen.

The phone rang at 1:25 p.m. It was Samuel. He wanted to call and let her know that there had been an automobile collision with a train. Six people had died and there were at least fifteen more waiting for treatment. He didn't think he would be able to get there in time for dinner. If he could see his way clear, he would call her, but not to wait on him. Catherine, Martha, and the boys sat quietly at the dining room table and had dinner. Martha could see the disappointment in Catherine's face and she wondered why things were always falling apart around Catherine.

"Thank you, Martha, for making me get up and look after my children. This has been the most wonderful Christmas I can remember. The boys have certainly eaten well and I can see they are exhausted from playing all afternoon with their toys," Catherine said as she smiled at her. "You've done enough. If you will put the boys to bed, I'll clean everything up."

Martha picked up Adam and she took Daniel's hand and they slowly walked up the stairs. Catherine watched as Daniel carefully lifted one foot up on each step. When he got to the top, he turned and smiled at his mother. She blew him a kiss.

Catherine turned the water on under the kettle and put water in the sink to soak the dishes. There was enough food left over to feed them for a week, she thought. She washed and dried the dishes for what seemed like hours. She left the pots and pans on the drain board to dry and she poured herself a cup of tea. She looked at the clock in the hallway and it said 9:35 p.m. She wasn't angry at Samuel, just disappointed. She had been through traumas at the hospital lots of times and you never had time to look at a clock. Saving a life was what a doctor did and she knew Samuel had done the right thing. Perhaps it was best. She couldn't deny she found him attractive. His boyish grin was very appealing. She was about to turn the light out when she heard a light knock on the door.

"Who is it?" she asked through the door.

"Samuel," he answered.

Catherine opened the door.

"Forgive me?" he asked and he held out some flowers. "I saw the light on in the living room and I was hoping you were still up."

"Have you eaten?" Catherine asked.

"No, and I'm starving," he answered.

Samuel not only had flowers, but his arms were filled with gifts. She took some of them and put them under the tree. He took off his coat and handed it to her and after she hung it up he followed her into the kitchen.

"Have a seat and I'll heat some food for you."

"You wouldn't have a beer in the icebox, would you?" he asked sheepishly.

"No, but I have some wine," she said, and she poured them both a glass.

"Merry Christmas," they said in unison as they toasted and laughed.

Samuel told Catherine about the accident as he ate his meal. They were shorthanded with the holiday and all and it was stressful for everyone. He was surprised that when he used a medical term, Catherine knew instinctively what he was talking about. He asked her where she had learned it and she told him about going to medical school and working at the hospital.

"I really miss it," she said.

"Maybe someday you'll be able to finish and get your degree," he said.

"That's a wonderful dream, but I need to save my money for my children's education. As soon as the baby comes and I'm able, I'll come back to work at the hospital as a nurse. I spend my spare time reading the medical books and keeping up with the new things the doctors are trying."

"You know, my mother felt the same way you do. She never bought anything for herself because she put all her money away for me to go to school. She died a semester too soon. I regret that she wasn't there to watch me get my medical degree. She deserved it as much as I did."

Samuel praised Catherine on the food and she shared a few stories about Daniel and Adam opening their presents. They sat at the table talking and sipping the wine. Catherine finally got up and put the dishes in the sink. When she turned around, Samuel was standing beside her and they were looking at each other. She looked down, but he lifted her chin up. Their lips were almost touching. Samuel pulled her closer and they kissed. They were both apprehensive at first, and he felt Catherine pulling away. She looked up at him and there was a feeling of need and want inside both of them. They embraced each other and kissed again. She finally pushed him away.

"I'm, I'm sorry for leading you on, please forgive me."

"We both wanted the same thing, Catherine. You don't have to apologize for being attracted to me. God knows, I'm attracted to you," Samuel said.

"I think it's time for you to go," she said.

"May I call you?" he asked. "Friend, to a friend?"

Catherine didn't answer. She handed Samuel his coat and told him she had a nice time. He tried to grab her hand, but she took a step back. She smiled sweetly and said goodbye.

Samuel started walking and turned and looked back at the house as the light in the living room went out. I'm infatuated with a woman who's pregnant and has two kids. I must be out of my mind, he thought.

As Catherine started to go up the stairs, she stopped and walked over to the tree to turn out the Christmas lights. There was a small silver package with a white bow on it and her name was written on the card attached to it. She picked it up and carried it upstairs. She undressed and put her gown on and crawled into bed. She had laid the gift on her pillow and she stared at it.

She shook it first and something inside moved. She opened the card. "To Catherine, May your days be embellished in happiness. Your friend, Samuel." She smiled and held the card to her heart. She carefully opened the package, not wanting to tear the paper. When she opened the box she pulled out something wrapped in a piece of rice paper. It was a beautiful ivory hair barrette with tiny sparkly rhinestones decorating it. She clipped it in her hair and put the paper back in the box. Just tonight, she thought, just tonight I'll pretend to be a happily married woman…but then, again, she wasn't and it was a dream she knew would never come true. Her thoughts drifted to Alex and she wondered what they did at the sanatorium at Christmas time. She missed him terribly and she was sure that Samuel was just a stand-in for him. It wasn't Samuel she was kissing, it was Alex. Or was it? She fell asleep wanting someone to hold her and tell her everything would be all right.

CHAPTER 13

Catherine had hoped that she would hear from Dr. Seymour regarding Alex's care so she put a call in to his office the day after Christmas. She was told that he had been on a two-week sabbatical and would return after New Year's. Next she asked to speak to someone who could give her an update on her husband, Alex Cooper. She was told someone would have to call her back.

It was afternoon when someone from the sanatorium called her. He introduced himself as Wyatt Anderson, one of the head nurses. He told her Alex's condition had not changed and that he was in good spirits. Catherine asked that Dr. Seymour call her upon his return and hung up, uneasy, and feeling helpless.

A few days before New Year's Eve, Samuel called and said he was all alone on New Year's Eve and if he promised to be good, could he come over for just an hour or so. "I don't want to be alone, Catherine, I need a friend," he said.

Catherine finally agreed when he said, "I'm on my knees begging, Catherine," he laughed.

She finally gave in. She had to admit, it did give her something to look forward to. Martha had left for a couple of days to go see her family in Austin and she was all alone with the boys. She called the grocery store and asked them to deliver some groceries. The weather was too unpredictable and shopping with the boys was difficult. She decided to cook something that she knew how to prepare. She decided on meatloaf, mashed potatoes, and green beans. She had it ready early so that all she had to do was heat it up when Samuel got there.

The boys had been bathed and were playing in the living room with their toys when Samuel rang the doorbell. He was carrying a large bag filled with wine, French bread, and cheese. He was wearing some casual pants and a flannel long-sleeved shirt and he reached down and kissed her on the cheek. After he put the groceries in the kitchen, he sat on the floor with the boys and they crawled all over him. They handed him some of their toys and he played liked a child. Catherine smiled as she watched them interact. He lifted Adam up in the air and he giggled loudly. Daniel waited for his turn and he couldn't have been happier. She knew he missed his daddy. Catherine put the food in the oven to warm and went in and sat on the floor and they played for almost an hour.

"They have a lot of energy," Catherine said.

"They're supposed to have a lot of energy," Samuel replied.

Catherine brought Samuel a glass of wine. He got up and sat on the sofa beside her and they watched as the boys played. Catherine excused herself to put dinner on the table and when it was ready, she picked up Adam and told Daniel to go in the kitchen and find his place at the table. He had a booster chair in a kitchen chair and he waited with his arms in the air to be picked up. Samuel picked him up and sat him in the chair. She wiped the boys' hands with a clean rag and pointed to a chair for Samuel, while she finished getting some butter from the icebox. Samuel didn't sit down yet. He waited until Catherine was ready and he pulled her chair out for her and then he sat down. Catherine motioned to the boys and they put their hands together and bowed their heads while Catherine said grace.

"That's amazing," Samuel said. "The boys are so well behaved."

"I threatened them," she whispered and laughed.

The boys were quiet after they ate their dessert and Daniel was yawning.

"I think it might be bedtime," she said. "We usually don't eat this late."

She got up and wiped the food from their faces and put Daniel on the floor first.

Samuel got up and said, "Let me help," and he picked up Adam. They went upstairs together and Samuel helped Catherine put the boys' pyjamas on and put them in the crib.

"They sleep together in the crib?" he asked.

"I tried putting Daniel in his bed, but he keeps crawling back in the crib with Adam," Catherine said.

Catherine and Samuel walked back downstairs and into the kitchen. "I'll do the dishes later," she said.

"No, I'll help. It won't take that long if we do them together," Samuel insisted.

When they finished, Samuel filled their wine glasses and they went into the living room.

"Tell me about yourself, Catherine. I recognize you have a British accent. Where were you born?"

Catherine thought for a few seconds and bit her lower lip. "I've been trying to think about how to give you bits and pieces of my life, but that wouldn't be fair to you. I'm sure after you hear my story you'll understand why I will probably never marry again. You may not want to be my friend when you hear the whole story. I want to warn you, it's not pretty and I'm certain when you hear it, you'll not want to be with me." Samuel listened intently.

Samuel felt her pain, as she walked him through the past four years of her life in America. The more he listened, the more he was astounded that any woman could bear this much pain, and still be sane.

"So, Daniel and Adam are half brothers and the baby you are carrying is Alex's child?" Samuel asked.

Catherine shook her head, yes. "And you are no longer married to Alex, right?

"That's right," she said.

"I still want to be your friend," Samuel said and he kissed her on the forehead. "I'm sorry, Catherine," Samuel continued. "I must admit, I'm overwhelmed."

She shook her head yes and got up and walked over to the closet, taking Samuel's coat off the hanger. He took it from her and put it on.

"I just need a few days to digest all of this," he said.

Catherine didn't look at him when she opened the door. He kissed her on the cheek and thanked her for dinner.

"Just one more question," he said before he walked out the door. "Are you still in love with Alex?"

"Yes, yes, I am," Catherine answered.

She knew when Samuel left she wouldn't be hearing from him any time soon. Until she had actually told the whole story at one time, she didn't realize how horrible it sounded. No man would want her now, and Samuel not only knew about her past, he knew about her recent rape. Men like Samuel did not marry women like Catherine. She sat on the sofa and poured herself another glass of wine. It seemed to dull the hurt. She knew that Samuel assumed that all of her children had the same father and that he had recently died. Adam was a child out of wedlock and her unborn child was also a child out of wedlock, because she had the marriage annulled. Inwardly, she knew her past would always create problems for the present and the future. She just had to pray that the children would never find out.

CHAPTER 14

It was January 8, 1903, when Dr. Seymour finally returned Catherine's call.

"I've made an appointment for Alex to see a specialist at Houston Memorial Hospital on January 21st, and I think it would be a good idea if you could come here for a couple of days. He's beginning to accept the fact that he's married and going to have a child and he wants to do the right thing. I'm afraid he still does not remember very much," he said.

"Of course, I'll come, just let me know where and when," Catherine said.

Catherine needed to go to the bank, but she kept putting it off because it was across the street from Clay Segal's office. It was getting close to her trip to Houston and she needed to confirm the balance in their joint checking account so she decided she needed to just do it, and stop being afraid.

She was surprised when she saw their balance was over $75,000. The deposits had been coming from Alex's employer and he must have had everything transferred before his accident. She was relieved that it would be more than enough to cover his surgery and the sanatorium if it were necessary for him to return there. She worried that since they were no longer married, she should probably put her money from the farm in a separate account. She took the $45,000 which was her money from the farm and opened up an account in her name. She withdrew fifty dollars in cash to take on her trip. She also stopped and bought two new dresses and a new coat for her trip.

Dr. Segal wanted to meet with her and Alex together in his office the day before Alex's appointment. Catherine left on the twentieth, leaving Adam and Daniel in Martha's care. She was nervous as she waited in the grand hall of the Oakwood Plantation. A young woman took her to Dr. Segal's office and when she entered, both Dr. Segal and Alex stood up. Alex was wearing the suit he had worn when they got married. She smiled and shook Dr. Segal's hand. She waited to see if Alex was going to shake her hand, but instead he reached down and kissed her cheek. Catherine smiled back.

Dr. Segal spoke first. "I've made an appointment with a new doctor who has joined Houston Memorial and is a specialist in head injuries. They have a new version of the x-ray machine and he will compare it to the x-ray that Alex previously had two months ago. It's important to see if there has been any movement. Once he decides whether surgery could help Alex's memory, they are prepared to begin immediately, scheduling surgery the next morning. Alex, you can decline the surgery at any time before it begins," Dr. Seymour said.

Catherine looked at Alex and said, "How do you feel about this, Alex? I don't want you to feel pressured to do it."

Alex looked down at his hands, folded in front of him, and said, "No one can tell you how it feels to live in a vacuum. It seems like when I make a little progress and I think I remember something, it goes away. If I do nothing, I will probably spend the rest of my life here. I want to be the man I was, even though I have no idea who that is. I need to made sense of things."

Alex and Catherine sat and talked in a small conference room after their meeting with Dr. Seymour. Catherine only told him general things about her past. She never mentioned David Brooks and her life in Beaumont. She mostly answered Alex's simple questions. They had a quiet dinner together and then Alex walked her upstairs to her room. Before he left, Catherine took Alex's hand and looked at him.

"Alex, all I ask is that you let me be your friend. Neither of us have very many, perhaps you more than I. I want you to do this for yourself. Whatever the outcome, I'll always be your friend. Whether you remember me or not; we started out as friends."

Alex smiled at her, still holding her hand. He took a step forward and drew her close to him. It was a soft, gentle kiss at first and then he kissed her again. He smiled at her and said goodnight.

The next day Catherine could tell that Alex was anxious on their ride into town. She took his hand and held it, smiling at him.

When they arrived at the hospital, Catherine waited while Alex was taken to another area of the hospital for the x-rays. They waited for almost an hour before Dr. Marcus Stein met them in his office.

"The brain is made up of many specialized areas that work together. The cortex is the outermost layer of brain cells. Thinking and voluntary movements begin in the cortex. When Alex was shot, it fractured the skull and a small fragment of the bullet was left touching the outer layer of the cortex. The skull helps protect the brain from injury, but in Alex's case, the fracture compromised this, which is causing Alex to remember some things and not others. There are millions of nerve endings that move this information around. What I am trying to say is that it is a very risky and dangerous surgery and there could be many consequences."

"Like death," Alex said.

"Well, I wasn't going to be that blunt, but yes, death," Dr. Stein answered and continued, "The area is still in the process of healing and you could leave it alone and live to be an old man. I doubt that you'll forget what you have learned in the last month because it seems to have stabilized and won't be moving again, unless you have another head injury."

"So, will Alex remember from the time he was admitted to the sanatorium and everything forward?" Catherine asked.

"Yes, I believe he will. Dr. Seymour says he still has a lot of the skills he learned at his job. He remembers things like putting a saddle on a horse, shaving, simple things. Alex, I understand you have been reading a lot since you were there. Do you remember the things you read?" Dr. Stein asked.

Alex answered, yes, and that he had remembered Catherine's last visit. "I remember just about everything since I've been at Oakwood."

"It's your decision to make, but if it was me and I had a chance to start over with my life again, I don't think I would risk the surgery. Death, loss of eyesight, hearing and even more memory loss could be the result of removing the fragment. You can go back to the sanatorium and think about it. I'm not going anywhere. Just have Dr. Seymour give me a call with your decision," Dr. Stein said.

Alex and Catherine got up slowly, trying to understand what their options were. Catherine didn't think of it as an option. It was a death sentence if he had the surgery, she thought, but didn't say anything to Alex.

"There's no urgency, Alex. You can go back to the sanatorium and stay until you feel you are ready to leave. We can visit with Dr. Seymour and perhaps you can have the therapy on a more regular basis. You have money," Catherine said.

"I just don't want to be unfair to you," he said.

"I didn't say anything about this to anyone, because I was afraid if the truth were out, that it would be difficult for you to get the proper help without a wife. Before you had your relapse, you wanted to go back to Beaumont where you were working and you asked me for an annulment. You didn't think it was fair to me to be married to a stranger. You had been in Galveston signing the papers and our marriage was annulled that morning when you went to Houston and had your relapse. I did not tell you at the time that I was pregnant, because you didn't seem to want to be married to me anymore," Catherine said quietly.

"I need you to come back with me and tell Dr. Seymour what you just told me. Are there any other lies you need to tell me about?" Alex asked.

Catherine didn't answer. They rode back to the sanatorium in silence.

When they arrived at Oakwood, Alex helped her off the carriage and showed her to a small waiting room. He told her to wait. Catherine had never meant for it to be a lie, but the more she thought about it, the more she could see why it seemed to be to Alex. Dr. Seymour joined her in the waiting room and closed the door.

Catherine explained to Dr. Seymour that the reason why she said she was still married to Alex was because someone at his work had called to report that he was missing. An annulment meant that they were not married and she wanted to report him missing to the police. Only a relative could do that. She was the one who had put the notice in the paper and had hoped that Alex would remember her. She apologized and said she had his best interest at heart.

"Alex said that you said he had money."

"Oh no, he thinks I did this for his money?" she asked.

"That's what it sounds like," Dr. Seymour said.

Catherine took their joint check book out of her purse and handed it to Dr. Seymour. "If I wanted to keep the money, I wouldn't have tried to find him. I love him. Tell him he is free, and that I won't bother him anymore. Just, please take care of him," she said.

The Oakwood carriage was not available and Catherine had to wait for over an hour for a public carriage to come from Houston. She kept looking at the door, hoping that Alex would come into the waiting room, but he didn't.

Catherine had missed the train going to Galveston and she sat on the bench staring at the empty tracks and wondered how her life had come to this. It was after midnight when Catherine finally got into Galveston. She knew the trolleys had stopped running and she sat on a bench outside the train station in the dark. A slight mist had begun to come down and it was a twenty-block walk to her house. Many of the street lights along the way were still in disrepair since the storm and Catherine was afraid to make the walk alone. She waited awhile and the carriages had also apparently stopped coming. Catherine took Samuel's card out of her purse and looked at it. There was a home number on it.

"Dr. Samuel Allen," he answered on the second ring. "Hello is anyone there?" he asked.

"This is Catherine," she said in a meek voice.

"Where are you, are you all right?" he asked.

"I'm at the train station. I just got back from Houston and I don't have a ride home and I'm too afraid to go by myself and I was wondering…."

"I'll be right there. Just wait," Samuel said.

Fifteen minutes later, she saw a man with a large umbrella walking towards her. "You should have called me from Houston. I would have been happy to meet your train," he said.

"I didn't know I would get in so late and that there would be no carriages. I'm really sorry to put you out," she said.

"Catherine, you didn't put me out. It's just not safe for you to be out this late at night. Things can happen. I had just gotten off my shift at the hospital an hour ago and you're lucky I was home," he said.

Samuel picked up her bag and pulled her close to him under the umbrella. He saw a small café that was open and said, "I haven't eaten all day, do you mind?"

Catherine was glad to get somewhere warm and she hadn't eaten all day either. After they ordered, Samuel asked, "Did you go to Houston to see Alex?"

"Yes, I did," she answered.

"Is everything all right?" he asked.

Catherine told Samuel what had happened. "Why is it, that when you try to do the right thing, it often backfires on you?"

Samuel took her hand and said, "Alex is not a well man, Catherine. You should not blame yourself. At least he'll be able to get proper help now, and you won't have to feel obligated anymore. You need to concentrate on you and your children's lives now. You've fulfilled your commitment to him. You need to move on."

Catherine shook her head in agreement. After they had eaten, Catherine said, "I know you are right, and I want to thank you for being my friend."

CHAPTER 15

It had been two months since her trip to Houston and she had heard nothing from Alex or Dr. Seymour. She figured that since she was no longer married to Alex, Dr. Seymour had no obligation to tell her of his progress. Still, she was concerned and decided to pick up the phone and make the call. He was in therapy and asked if he could return her call. It was 5:30 p.m. when the phone finally rang. She had just finished feeding the boys and they were playing on the floor with Martha. Catherine answered the phone in John's study.

"Hello, Dr. Seymour, I just wondered if you might tell me how Alex is," she asked.

"Alex couldn't be better, Catherine. So far, he has managed to remember just about everything since he first came here. We do therapy every day, now, except Sundays, mostly memorization and memory recall therapy, and he's looking forward to making a new life outside the sanatorium," Dr. Seymour said.

"What do you mean by a new life outside the sanatorium?" she asked.

Dr. Seymour hesitated for a few seconds and said, "He's getting married next month to a socialite from Houston. Her brother is on the board of directors here and they met when she volunteered over the Christmas holidays. I'm sorry, Catherine, I know that's not what you wanted to hear."

Catherine hung up the phone without saying anything. She felt numb. A few minutes later, she told herself Alex was happy now and that was what she wanted for him. It was for the best and she hoped more than anything, they would be happy and have lots of children. She was five months pregnant now and she felt her baby moving and she touched the spot on her abdomen. She hated that her baby would never know its father, but then neither would the boys.

Catherine opened up the ledger she kept on top of the desk and looked at it. She did some calculations and realized that unless she started working, she would go through the money she had in about six years and that would leave nothing for Adam and her baby for college. She decided to call the hospital the next morning.

Catherine knew the director fairly well and he told her that they had an opening for a nurse on the 9:00 p.m. to 6:00 a.m. shift six nights a week. She told him she would have to take off for about a month around June 20th to have her baby, but she really needed the job. He remembered Catherine and knew she had great skills, so he told her she could start that next night. She needed to come in sometime before 9:00 p.m. to fill out some papers. She said she would be there.

Catherine sat on the sofa and told Martha her plans. She would work nights and be home during the day for the boys. For the first time she felt excited about something. She would sleep when the boys took their naps. She only needed five or six hours sleep, she told herself. She decided to stay up late and then told Martha to wake her at 9:00 a.m., so she could begin adjusting her sleep habits. The boys had started sleeping later, and often didn't get up until 9:00 a.m.

Catherine stayed up until after 1:30p.m. studying her medical books, and was exhausted. She had no trouble going to sleep. Martha woke her up at 9:00a.m.and together they fed and bathed the boys. Catherine played with them for a couple of hours and then read them some stories. Adam didn't always sit still during story time, but Catherine used puppets and toys to make it more interesting for him. She finally took a break and decided to make some hot tea and read the paper. She almost spit her tea out when she turned to the second page and read that socialite Carla Merit had wed attorney Clay Segal. Catherine froze. They were her enemies and they were two of the few people who knew her secrets. She knew both of them hated her and she knew she would have to be careful.

Catherine left after the boys were fed and had their pyjamas on and she stopped at the Mercantile to buy a couple of lab coats. She had kept a couple of Amelia's dresses that were loose around the waist and they were both light colored. They would have to do. After she completed the paperwork, she was assigned to the emergency room for the night. She had not heard from Samuel Allen since the night he met her at the depot and she supposed that was best. He didn't seem to be happy when she called him. If he was working, she would just be professional and not mention it.

When her shift began, she found herself in the middle of chaos the moment she got there. The waiting room was filled with about eight patients and all of the exam rooms had people waiting. She was told to check the patient in exam room two. Catherine went in and found a man who was having chest pains. She took his history and then began checking his vital signs. Her back was to the opening when Dr. Allen walked in.

"What do we have here?" he asked.

Catherine turned and gave him the information. Samuel didn't say anything to her. He introduced himself to the patient and began questioning the man. He listened to his chest with his stethoscope, and told Catherine to give him an aspirin and monitor him every fifteen minutes.

Catherine said, "Yes Dr. Allen."

He told the patient he would be back in an hour to check his progress.

The remainder of the night was pretty much the same. Things had begun to quiet down about 1:30 a.m. and Catherine went into the doctor's lounge to take a short break.

"How's the first night going for you?" Samuel asked Catherine.

"It's really nice to be back," she said.

"Martha watching the boys?" he asked.

"Yes, I don't think I could do this without her," Catherine said.

Samuel poured himself some coffee and joined a young nurse at a sitting area in the corner. Catherine looked out of the corner of her eye. She had never seen her before. She figured she was about her age and she was petite with short black hair. She had a pleasant face and a pretty smile. Catherine smiled to herself. Good for him, she thought. A buzzer rang and Catherine took the last gulp of her tea. She ran to the emergency room and met a man and a woman who was in labor. She took the woman into one of the exam rooms and began getting her history. The woman told her she had been in labor about twelve hours and that the midwife who was supposed to deliver her baby was already engaged with another patient and she told her to come here. After the woman undressed, Catherine checked to see if the baby was crowning. She walked out and told one of the nurses to get Dr. Allen immediately. The woman was in a lot of pain and Catherine was trying to calm her. Catherine closed the curtain and met Dr. Allen as he came in.

"The woman in exam 4 is in labor. I think the baby is breech," she said.

Dr. Allen walked over to the bed and checked the patient. We need to get her into surgery immediately." He walked out and talked to the woman's husband and then went back in and said, "I want you to assist me in the operating room, Catherine."

They both washed their hands and went into surgery and Samuel asked Catherine if she had ever delivered a breech.

"Yes, several," she said.

"Okay, then this one is yours. Tell me what you are going to do first," he said.

"I'm going to attempt to turn the baby first. Once I confirm where the umbilical cord is, I'll complete the turn and hopefully he or she will slide right out," she said.

"Let's see you do it," he said.

Catherine walked up to the lady and told her what she was going to do and that after she turned the baby she would let her know when to push. Catherine worked her small hands up to locate the cord and folded the baby's feet and legs up as the baby began to turn. She took her time checking the cord each time and once the baby was in place and its head began to crown, she told the woman to push. She had successfully delivered a healthy baby boy weighing in at 5 pounds, six ounces.

After they had finished and cleaned up, Samuel said, "Good job, Dr. Catherine," and he smiled at her.

When Catherine's shift ended, she waited at the back entrance for daybreak. The trolley didn't begin running until 6:00 a.m. so she sat and watched. A few minutes later she heard laughter coming down the hall, and turned to see Samuel and the young nurse leave together. He nodded to her, but kept walking. She watched as Samuel took the nurse's hand and disappeared into the dark. She remembered when John used to meet her at the hospital and they would walk hand in hand together to the trolley. It was nice to have those memories, she thought. Samuel was sweet like John and she was happy that he had found someone. She knew he hated being alone all the time.

Friday was Catherine's day off and after tending to the boys, she forced herself to go into the study and pay some bills. She hadn't looked at the mail in a couple of days and she picked up the small stack that had accumulated. She shuffled through the first few bills and stopped when she came to a letter from Oakwood Plantation Sanatorium. It was Alex's handwriting and addressed to Catherine Merit. She stared at it a few moments before she picked up the letter opener.

Dear Catherine,

Dr. Seymour suggested that I should write you and thank you for all you did to find me. I am feeling much better now and hope you are well. I have decided to move on with my life and I hope you will do the same. I will be married next month to a lovely young woman who has helped me with my therapy and progress. She understands my situation and I couldn't have asked for a more caring and loving woman. I love her, too, Catherine. It would probably be best, when the baby arrives, that you give it the last name of Merit, since the marriage was annulled. My new, soon-to-be wife does not know about the baby, and it is my hope that she not find out. If you find in the future, you need money for the child, it would be best if you just contacted Dr. Seymour.

My best to you,
Alex

Catherine found it difficult to swallow and she sat back in her chair, staring out the window. She wanted to be happy for Alex, but she really had not had closure until now. Martha was playing on the floor with the boys and Catherine got up and went upstairs. She opened the door to the closet and went in and closed the door. She didn't want the boys to hear her cry. She sat on the floor in the dark, small closet, underneath some of John's old suits, and reminded herself she was going to take them to the thrift store. She pulled one of John's coats off the hanger and held it up to her face. She sobbed into it, willing the past and the hurt to leave her. She stayed there for about fifteen minutes, dried her eyes and took a deep breath. She could do this, she thought; she had to move forward.

It took a few days for Catherine to adjust to the long hours and intermittent sleep. She tried to get six hours sleep, but most of the time she had to settle for five or less. The baby would be coming soon and she was looking forward to taking a month off. Dr. Allen and Catherine were working the same shift one night when he told Catherine to take the history of a young, fifteen-year-old girl who had cramping in the abdomen. The girl told Catherine her name was Alice Beranger and she had started her period and the cramps were really bad. Catherine took her temperature and was asking her questions, when the girl's mother walked in.

"What do you think you are doing?" she yelled at Catherine. "Get out," and she pointed to Catherine. "No whore is going to treat my baby," Carla Segal said.

Dr. Allen came in and tried to calm Carla down. "I'll calm down when you get that whore and her bastard baby out of here."

Catherine left and Dr. Allen turned to Carla and said, "Ma'am, if you don't quiet down, I'm going to have to ask you to leave." He left and went to find Catherine.

Catherine was standing outside the emergency room door when he saw her and he went to her. "You want to tell me what just happened in there, Catherine?"

"That was John's second wife. She's married to Clay Segal, now. They both know about my past. I'm sorry," Catherine said.

"Go take your break, we'll talk later," Samuel told her.

Catherine was in the doctor's lounge when Samuel came in and sat down with her. "There's nothing seriously wrong with the girl; just normal menstrual cramps. I gave her some syrup and sent them home. I'm sorry she treated you that way. You didn't deserve it. Are you all right?" he asked.

"I guess so. Carla never thought Daniel was John's child. She and Clay are the only ones who know the truth, and that all three of my children will have Merit as their last name. It was the way John wanted it. He did it for me and the children. I'm afraid she and Clay won't let it rest. They hate me," Catherine said.

"This will all blow over, Catherine. There's nothing they can do about it," Samuel said.

"I hope you are right," Catherine said.

It nagged at her that she would constantly be defending herself and her children. Galveston was a small town and she remembered John telling her that Carla's favorite pastime was gossiping with her friends. He said that if you ever got into bad favor with Carla, you were doomed.

Several weeks later, Catherine was working at the hospital when she felt a sharp pain in her abdomen. It was a couple of weeks earlier than she had calculated and wondered if the baby was coming early. Ten minutes later, she felt her water break. She was on the floor mopping it up when Samuel came over to her.

"What happened?" he asked.

"My water broke," she said.

Samuel reached down and pulled her up and looked at her, shaking his head in unbelief. "Leave it and go to an empty exam room, now. Put on a gown and I'll be there shortly."

Catherine had taken her clothes off and had just tied the gown around her neck when Samuel came in. He helped her onto an exam table and when she turned her back he noticed the healed lacerations on her back and legs. She turned and looked at him, but didn't say anything. "How far apart are your pains?" he asked.

"I'm not sure; I've only had one small pain. Labor for the two boys was only about an hour for each one," Catherine said.

Samuel had left for a few minutes and when he came back, the young nurse he was dating followed him into the exam room. It made Catherine feel awkward.

"This is Ellen. Ellen, this is Catherine. I need to give you a pelvic, Catherine, and check to see where the baby is. Will that be all right?"

Catherine said, "Yes." She tensed when she felt another contraction, but she did not cry out in pain. She breathed out slowly and then took a deep breath.

"The baby isn't quite ready yet. I expect it will be another hour or so and I'll come back and check on you," Samuel said. "Are you all right with me delivering the baby, or do you want me to get Dr. Copeland out of bed?" he asked.

Catherine had another contraction and she held in her scream and sucked in her breath, letting it out slowly. Samuel watched her. "You can scream when you have a contraction. I know it must be painful."

Her face grimaced and he could tell there was another contraction and they were getting closer. Samuel checked on the baby and he said, "No time to call Dr. Copeland, the baby's coming. Push," he told Catherine.

Catherine heard a small cry and Samuel held the baby up for Catherine to see. "It's a girl," he said smiling at her.

She grinned and then closed her eyes. Ellen and Samuel were busy taking vital signs of the baby and when Samuel went back to check on Catherine, she was unresponsive. He had remembered that Catherine had told him about how she had almost died when she delivered Adam. He checked her and saw she was bleeding profusely. He hollered at Ellen to finish with the baby and help him. Twenty minutes later Samuel had stopped the bleeding, but Catherine had lost at least a pint of blood. Once she was stabilized, Samuel left the exam room and went outside and sat on a bench. It was a warm June day, but the fresh air seemed to clear his head. He had never been so scared. He was afraid he might have lost her. Ellen came out and asked if he were all right. He had never told Ellen that he and Catherine were anything more than doctor and nurse working together.

"I just got hot and light-headed in there. Just needed some fresh air," he said.

Once Catherine was settled in a patient room, Samuel went in to her. He stood watching her and thought about the permanent marks on her back and legs. He checked her vital signs and was worried about the amount of blood she had lost. Come on, Catherine, he thought to himself, you can do this. He had to go back and work in the emergency room, but told the nurse on that floor to call him if there was any change. He wanted someone checking her vital signs every twenty minutes and keeping a log of it. As he was walking back to the emergency room, he silently prayed that she would recover. Her three children needed a mother. They were too young to be orphans, he thought. He was back in her room at his first opportunity. She was still alive and her breathing seemed to improve. His shift was over at 5:00 p.m. and when he got off he went to Catherine's room and stayed with her. Ellen had been watching him the whole time and after her shift ended, she found Samuel in Catherine's room. He was sitting in a chair, just watching her.

"I've never seen you so concerned about a patient," Ellen said.

"She doesn't have any family," Samuel said.

"What about the father?" she asked.

"He didn't stick around," Samuel said.

"And you know that, how?" she asked.

"Look, I've known Catherine since I came to work here. We're friends and that's all," he told her.

Ellen turned and left. Samuel didn't go after her. They had been dating for almost six months and Samuel tried to love her. He knew she was crazy about him, but he just didn't feel the same way about her that he did Catherine. Ellen had tried on several occasions to get him to spend the night with her. She had told Samuel that she already lost her virginity to a college sweetheart and that she was all right having sex before marriage. For some reason after she told him that, he slowly lost interest in her and refused to sleep with her. He worried that she might try and get pregnant and then he would have to marry her. It was time he broke it off, he thought.

At 8:00 a.m., he sent word to Father Jonathan and then called Martha and told her that Catherine had a little girl during the night and was resting now. He told her Catherine had lost quite a bit of blood and was resting. He assured her she would be fine. He wished he really felt that way but there was no reason to worry her, too.

Fifteen minutes later Father Jonathan tapped on the door and Samuel walked out in the hall with him. He told Father Jonathan what had happened and that he needed to pray for her. He thought she had a fifty-fifty chance of making it. Father Jonathan walked back into Catherine's room and Samuel watch as he kissed his rosary and made the sign of the cross. He closed his eyes, too, and bowed his head, praying that she would pull through. After Father Jonathan left, Samuel walked back over to the chair and took Catherine's hand. He sat close to her, still holding her hand. He looked up when he thought she moved, but she didn't open her eyes. He sat back in his chair and closed his eyes and slowly drifted off to sleep. Ellen had walked in an hour later and saw Samuel asleep, holding Catherine's hand. She turned and left the room.

Samuel was exhausted and had not slept for over twenty-four hours. The nurses came in and out, checking Catherine's vital signs, but he slept through their visits. At 1:15 p.m., he woke up and grabbed Catherine's chart. Her pulse had grown stronger, she had no fever. She was out of the danger zone and he breathed a sigh of relief. He wanted to check on the baby so he decided to take a break and stop at the nursery.

He watched from behind the glass as a nurse picked up Catherine's baby and began feeding her. She had a full head of curly hair and he smiled when he thought she was going to inherit her mother's beauty. He knew Catherine would be pleased that she had a girl. He went into the nursery and asked the nurse to bring the baby to Catherine's room when she finished. He was hoping that Catherine would wake up soon, especially if she felt the baby next to her. Samuel was standing over Catherine's bed when she woke up.

"You really scared me and I'm glad you made it," he said smiling. "They're bringing your little girl in shortly so you can see her. Are you feeling better?" he asked and poured her a glass of water.

She drank some through a straw and licked her lips.

"How long was I out?" she asked.

"You were out just a little over nine hours. You lost almost a pint of blood before I could stop the bleeding. You'll need to stay in bed and rest and if you feel like it you can go home in a couple of days," Samuel said. "I called and told Martha and she said the boys were fine."

Just then a nurse came in with her baby and Samuel helped Catherine sit up.

"She's beautiful," Catherine said smiling at her. Thank you," she said to Samuel. "I'm going to name her Emma after my grandmother."

Samuel told her it was a beautiful name. He kissed Catherine on the forehead and told her he would check on her later.

CHAPTER 16

Three weeks later, and 115 miles northeast of Galveston, Texas, on a quiet Indian reservation outside of Kountze, Texas, Mary Windsong had been in labor for almost twenty hours. Her father was the medicine man and he had stayed by his daughter's side without leaving. Her husband, Grey Wolf, paced outside the small frame house where Mary grew up, and he damned the white man who had gotten her pregnant. Mary's heart stopped beating and her father had no choice but to open her womb and take the baby, before it died, too. Her father cried when he heard the young girl cry. Grey Wolf heard the baby cry, too, and he went back into the house. Mary's bleeding womb was still open and Dr. Windsong had not had time to cover it. Grey Wolf yelled a wild cry and put his hand to his head.

"No, no, my Mary, no," and he ran out the door.

Dr. Windsong put a blanket over Mary's body and sat down and cried. His only daughter was dead and her young daughter would now have to grow up without a mother. He knew the gods were angry that Mary had gotten pregnant by a white man. Why you didn't take the baby instead, he mumbled to the gods. My Mary is gone. Several women from the reservation had come when they heard Grey Wolf yelling. Dr. Windsong handed the baby to one of the women.

"Go find Flying Bird, who birthed her child a month ago. She will have to nurse Isabella, my granddaughter, and we must plan for Mary's burial."

Grey Wolf came back after the women took the baby.

"The baby must die, too," he said. "She is a half-breed and I will not raise her."

"She is my daughter's baby and I will raise the girl as my own. You will not touch her," Dr. Windsong said.

That night, Mary's body was lying on a large rock near the burial grounds of the reservation. A huge bonfire lit up the Texas sky while the braves danced in rhythm to the beating drums. Dr. Windsong was in full medicine man dress and he held his spear up chanting to the gods in front of the fire. The ceremony lasted until the partial moon faded over the Texas sky, and then Mary was wrapped in doe skin and taken to the burial grounds. Her husband, Grey Wolf, used his hands to cover Mary's body with the black dirt. She had gone with the spirits to the gods and he swore revenge. He would see to it that the little girl would not live past her second birthday.

Samuel had taken Catherine home from the hospital two days after Emma was born. Daniel and Adam were fascinated by the tiny baby and every time she made a sound, Daniel would say, "Baby, baby."

Catherine was still weak and Samuel had told her to stay quiet and not to lift the boys. "You need to rest," he said. "I'll check on you later."

Samuel had begun his nightly shift that evening and Ellen approached him. "I just wanted to tell you that I think I'm going back to San Antonio. My old friend from college called me and he wants to get married," she said as she watched Samuel's reaction.

"Congratulations," Samuel said. "I hope you'll be happy."

"Is that all you have to say?" she said tearfully. "Tell me you want me to stay. Tell me you want to marry me and I won't go."

"Ellen, I know that we've dated for awhile, but I never said I loved you," Samuel said. Ellen stormed out and Samuel shook his head. He liked Ellen and she was fun to be with, but she was spoiled and demanding. He was actually relieved that she walked out on him.

Samuel called Catherine several times over the next couple of weeks and he had hoped she might invite him over when she felt better, but she seemed quiet and distant. He knew it was not unusual for a woman to be depressed after she gave birth and it had to be worse for Catherine, since Alex was not there. After a week, he couldn't stand it anymore. When his shift ended he would be off for twenty-four hours and he was going crazy not seeing her. He decided to call Catherine and ask if he could come over. Martha answered the phone and told him Catherine was resting. He asked Martha what they needed from the store and Martha told him she was about to call the store and have some groceries delivered. Samuel wrote down her list and told her he would be there after lunch.

Samuel went up and down almost every aisle and picked up the things from Martha's list. He did add a few things. He picked up hot dogs and buns, fresh fruit, cheese, scones and a bottle of wine. He had two bags of groceries and he hailed a carriage, afraid the trolley would be too risky.

Martha told Catherine that Dr. Allen had insisted on coming over and offered to pick up groceries for them. She still felt weak, but she put on a dress and sweater before she went downstairs. There was a knock on the door and Catherine answered it. Samuel's arms were filled with bags and she took one from him and thanked him for being their delivery service. They laughed. Emma was in a basinet by the sofa and after they put the groceries in the kitchen, Catherine walked over and picked Emma up. Samuel took her and was amazed at how alert Emma was.

"Will you stay for dinner?" Catherine asked. He smiled and said, "I was hoping you might ask me."

Catherine made the hot dogs Samuel had brought and the boys loved them.

"I think I just found their new favorite food," Catherine said. She and Samuel did the dishes and Martha took the boys upstairs and put them to bed.

After pouring two glasses of wine they went into the living room. “Ellen and I aren’t seeing each other anymore,” Samuel said.

“Is that a good thing, or a bad thing?” Catherine asked.

“She was a nice girl, but I felt she was trying to push me a little too hard about getting married,” Samuel said.

“Alex is getting married,” Catherine said solemnly.

“I’m sorry, Catherine,” Samuel said.

“I’m fine with it now. I must admit, it hurt at first, but I had to remind myself that he wasn’t the man I married. I can’t imagine what it would be like to lose your memory and not know who you are. I want him to be happy, whatever choice he makes,” Catherine said.

They talked awhile about relationships and Catherine apologized that she was getting sleepy.

“I still don’t have the energy I had before Emma was born, and I’m sorry about that.”

“Catherine, you lost a lot of blood and I must confess I thought you weren’t going to make it. You don’t have to apologize. I’m just glad you are getting better,” Samuel said as he got up to leave. He told her to call him if she needed him and she said she would. He leaned over and kissed her on the cheek. “Friends?” he said.

“Always,” Catherine answered

CHAPTER 17

The Board of Directors at St. Mary's Hospital met the first Monday morning of every month. Father Jonathan was not on the board but they would often invite him, if it concerned matters of the church. After the general discussion of the budget and other hospital related problems, the Director, Arthur Massing, said there was an unusual matter that they needed to discuss regarding an employee. It had been brought to their attention that a young nurse by the name of Catherine Merit had an inappropriate reputation and she was currently on medical leave and would not be rehired.

Mr. Massing looked at Father Jonathan and said, "We are aware that you have known the Merit family for a number of years. We have been told that Catherine Merit now has three children and that they each have a different father and that she has taken it upon herself to give the two children born out of wedlock her former husband's name."

"That is correct," answered Father Jonathan. "However, it was John Merit's wishes and his intention to allow Catherine to use his family name for all three of her children so that they would all grow up as brothers and sisters. Yes, she has had some unfortunate circumstances in her life, but I don't feel she should be expelled from society because of conditions beyond her control."

"That may be so," Massing said. "But we are a Catholic hospital and we have to protect our reputation and our public image. The board has concluded that it is not in the best interest of the hospital to rehire her. If there is no further business, our meeting here is adjourned. Father Jonathan, could you stay for just a few minutes after everyone leaves?"

Father Jonathan waited until everyone left the room and Massing approached him. "I know you are partial to Catherine Merit and I don't expect you to agree with our decision. Would you like to be the one to tell her or should I call her and tell her on the phone?" asked Massing.

Father Jonathan was taken aback by Catherine's abrupt dismissal and felt the least he could do was visit her at her home and tell her the board's decision. It was not something he would be looking forward to. After calling Catherine on the phone he told her he wanted to drop by for a visit later that afternoon and Catherine said she would be looking forward to seeing him.

Father Jonathan was on time for his 3:00 p.m. visit with Catherine. She had prepared hot tea and some scones and the children had just gotten up from their nap. Daniel screamed and ran to Father Jonathan when he walked into the living room where the boys were playing. Father Jonathan scooped him up into his arms and kissed him. Adam tried to crawl over to them, but he had not yet discovered how to move his arms and legs in a forward position so he just rocked back and forth. Catherine picked up Adam and they all sat down on the sofa. The boys went back to their playing and Catherine poured some tea.

"You are looking very well, Catherine," Father Jonathan said. "Where is Emma?"

"She is upstairs with Martha taking a nap. She will be up soon," Catherine said. "How are things going at the hospital?"

"Actually, Catherine that is one of the reasons for my visit. I don't want to beat around the bush, so I'm going to tell you something that displeases me greatly."

Catherine listened intently. She could tell Father Jonathan was upset.

Father Jonathan told Catherine about the board meeting and their decision not to hire her again. He said he had no idea who lodged the complaint and he tried to speak in her behalf, but the decision had already been made before he had gotten to the meeting.

Catherine sat silent for a few seconds and then said. "I know who made the complaint and I don't blame you. I appreciate your speaking on my behalf, but I am afraid I will always be defending my past and protecting my children. You are a very good friend and I appreciate your honesty."

"You said you knew who made the complaint?" Father Jonathan asked.

"I'm not sure whether you heard or not, but Clay Segal married Carla Beranger Merit a few months ago. Before I had Emma, Dr. Allen and I were working in the emergency room when Carla brought one of her daughters in because of cramps. When she saw me, she started screaming and calling me a whore. I had to leave the exam room," Catherine said.

"I do remember that now. Dr. Allen told me," he said. "I had not heard of their marriage. Clay and John were best friends and he was also your attorney. Why would he turn on you?"

"I know you will not repeat this, but do you remember the day you found me in the church and you called Dr. Allen to treat my wound and give me something to calm my nerves?" she asked.

"Yes," he answered.

I had a meeting with Clay that morning. He had asked me on several occasions to marry him and I refused. After our meeting he attacked and raped me. He said if I reported it, he would just say that I was the one who wanted to have sex with him and that I had changed my mind after I cut myself," she said. "I know it sounds unbelievable, but I did not want a scandal, and I knew with his background and family name that no one would believe me. I told Dr. Allen because he had heard me make an appointment with Clay that morning and he put two and two together. Now that they are married, they both hate me.

Father Jonathan shook his head and took Catherine's hand. "You must not let them get the better of you Catherine."

"It's too late, now. I'll be fine. Perhaps now is the time for me to go back to medical school. I may be able to intern at John Sealy Hospital at the school. Thank you for coming and being such a good friend," Catherine said and kissed his hand.

Father Jonathan left and knew Catherine was right. She was from a foreign country and she was a woman alone with three small children. The fight would be too great for her and she would not win. It was not fair, he thought. He said a rosary for her when he got back to the church.

Samuel called her that evening after he had heard the news from Father Jonathan. He was angry and wanted her to come forward and talk to the board.

"You have let it go, Samuel," Catherine said. "If I make Carla and Clay any angrier, there is no telling what they might do. You could lose your job if you stand up for me and I couldn't bear that. Please, I'll be fine. I've decided to go back to medical school in the fall."

Samuel was having to work two shifts and would not be off until noon the next day and asked if he could come over then. "Samuel, I think it would be best if we didn't see each other for a while. I'll call you," Catherine said, and hung up.

The next Thursday was June 25, 1903, and Adam was going to be one year old. Catherine decided to take the boys to the beach, except she felt Emma was too little.

"Go ahead," Martha encouraged her. "I can take care of Emma."

Catherine thought it might do her some good to get out of the house, so she packed a lunch and put the boys in their swimsuits. Adam was almost walking now and Daniel could walk very well on his own. She finished putting the last things in her knapsack and they walked to the trolley. They had to make one transfer, but she managed with the help of a nice lady on the trolley and they made their way to Murdock's beach house. She rented a large umbrella and had it up on a flat area of the beach that was not heavily occupied. The boys were fascinated with the water and Catherine walked to the edge and sat down in the water with Adam on her lap. Daniel picked up sea shells and brought them back to his mother and the boys played in the water for awhile.

"Mind if I join you?" Samuel asked. Catherine looked up in surprise. "I called the house and Martha told me you were here and told me where you were going to be sitting. I hope you don't mind if I crash the birthday party. It was my day off and this is the first time I've ever been here."

"It's a big beach," Catherine said teasing him.

Samuel grinned at her. "May I take Daniel into the waves? I'll make sure we don't go out too far."

Catherine smiled and said, "Sure."

She had never seen Samuel without a lab coat or long sleeves. He had a nice body, she thought. She watched as Daniel and Samuel jumped the waves, laughing each time. She really liked Samuel, but she was still afraid of getting too close. She had had her heart broken so many times and she didn't feel she was worthy of him. He deserved someone without a past; someone with a good upbringing and someone with a place in society. She would only bring him heartbreak.

Samuel shared their lunch and he brought snow cones for all of them. Catherine had the boys lay on a towel under the umbrella so they could take a nap. Catherine and Samuel lay down beside the boys and talked. Samuel wanted so badly to lean over and kiss her, but he knew it wasn't a good idea. He decided that when she was ready, she would have to kiss him first. He would just wait however long it took. When the boys woke up they let them play in the water for a while longer and then Catherine decided they had had enough sun. Samuel helped her and the boys get home and she invited him in. Catherine nursed Emma while Samuel sat and watched. When she finished, she put Emma in the basinet and went back to the sofa. Martha had taken the boys upstairs to take a bath.

"Thank you for coming. It was a wonderful day, Samuel," Catherine said as she leaned over to kiss Samuel on the cheek. Samuel turned and they were looking into each other's eyes. He gently pulled her to his lips and they kissed. Sweetly and tenderly at first, but it grew into a more passionate kiss. They were both breathing heavily and they both wanted more. Daniel came running down the stairs and crawled up into Samuel's lap. They both laughed.

Samuel stayed for dinner, but the opportunity for another kiss did not happen and he knew it would be awhile before he had another chance. Having three children underfoot was not the perfect environment for having a relationship. They were rarely alone, not that he wanted to take her to bed, but he knew what she meant when she said she was not right for him. He wished he could get her out of his mind. The more he was away from her; the more he wanted to be with her. There was just something about her that kept drawing him to her. He decided he would try harder to stay away.

Catherine was sad when Samuel left. It had been a memorable day for her, too, but when Samuel left he didn't ask her to call him, and he didn't say he was going to call her. Their interrupted kiss was not timely and she could see the disappointment in his face, although he tried to hide it. It was probably for the best that Daniel interrupted them. There was no hope that she could have a relationship with any man. Her children and her future were all she could think about now. Having a boyfriend would just complicate things, she thought. When Catherine got into bed that night, her thoughts went back to the day Adam was born and she couldn't help but cry when she thought about Alex delivering Adam. A whole year had come and gone and she was alone again except for her three children. She still loved Alex, and she knew in her heart, she would always love him.

Six weeks later it was Daniel's birthday, August 15, and medical school was going to start the next week. Catherine knew the boys had such a good time on Adam's birthday, so she decided to repeat it, only this time she decided to call Samuel and ask him to join them. She had not spoken to him since Adam's birthday and she wondered if he might be off. She called his home number first but there was no answer. Samuel was with a patient, so she asked the nurse to have him call her and she left her number. It was four hours later when he called and he seemed rushed.

"I hadn't spoken to you in a while, and Daniel's birthday is Saturday and I wondered if you might want to join us at the beach to celebrate his second birthday."

"I'm afraid I can't, Catherine, but thanks for thinking of me. I hope you and the boys are doing well," he said.

"Oh, we're fine, and you?" she asked.

"Couldn't be better," he answered. "Everything is good. I'm sorry, but I have to go." And he hung up.

Catherine looked at the phone, surprised by the fact that Samuel hardly acknowledged her. She repeated the conversation over in her head. Maybe he has found another girl friend. She was sure that was what it was. Still, she missed him terribly.

When Samuel put the phone down he started feeling bad. He had started dating again, but with no one special. Actually he was dating a couple of girls. He was not serious about either of them and he was off Saturday and really had nothing to do. He had thought about asking one of the girls to go to the beach, but decided against it. Maybe he would surprise Catherine and just show up like last time. He still had time to think about it, so he went back to work.

The paper on Friday threatened a storm, so Catherine decided they would just stay home on Saturday and have cupcakes. It was really too hard to try and keep up with both children by herself on the beach anyway. When the boys took their naps, she told Martha she was going shopping for a few presents for Daniel.

On Saturday, the sun was up and shining brightly through the white clouds in the sky. Catherine looked up when she went out to get the newspaper and thought again about going to the beach, but decided against it. She had already planned their day. She would have birthday cake after lunch and then Daniel and Adam could open presents. Since the boys' birthdays were so close together, she always got them both something on their birthdays so the other would not feel left out. She knew they liked hot dogs so that would be an easy lunch to prepare.

Samuel was standing on the pier at Murdock beach at 11:00 A.M. looking up and down the beach. He waited thirty minutes and then went in to phone. "Hi Catherine," he said, "My plans changed and I was wondering if you were going to the beach today?"

"I was afraid the boys would be too much for me to handle and the paper said it was supposed to rain, so we are celebrating here. We are having hot dogs for lunch and you are welcome to come over," she said.

"That would be great. Be there in an hour," Samuel said. He had just enough time to go home and change. He thought he might look foolish showing up in a bathing suit. He had brought both boys a present so he tucked the bag back under his arm and ran to catch the trolley he saw coming in the distance.

It was straight up noon when Samuel knocked on the door. Martha answered the door with Daniel at her feet and Emma in her arms. Adam was already in his highchair eating some peas and Catherine was getting the lunch ready. She had some ribbon dangling down from the light fixture and a special hat she and the boys made for each of them to wear. Daniel was excited when he sat in his booster chair. Catherine said grace and the boys bowed their heads. Before Samuel sat down, Catherine kissed him on the cheek and he pulled Catherine's chair out for her. Martha joined them and they all had a fun lunch. Afterwards, they sang happy birthday to Daniel and Catherine put a candle on his cupcake for him to blow out. Having finished their cake, they all went into the living room and Daniel opened presents while everyone watched. Catherine handed Adam a present to open and he handed it to Daniel. The children were finally put down for a nap and Catherine and Samuel were alone.

"I'm glad I decided to come. I haven't had this much fun since my birthday when I was six years old," he said, and laughed.

They kissed for a while and their desire for each other began to escalate.

"Come to my place with me, Catherine." Samuel said breathing heavily and looking at her. Without saying a word, Catherine got up and told Martha they were going on an errand and she would be back later. They left, holding hands and practically running to catch the trolley.

They could have walked, but Samuel was afraid Catherine might change her mind. He still couldn't believe she actually took him up on his offer. Ten minutes later, they were at his door.

His room was small, but neat. He had two fans that criss-crossed the room and the windows were up. It was a hot, steamy day, but as soon as they got through the door they were in each other's arms. Samuel pulled Catherine closer and held her face in his hands. He kissed her on the mouth, moving around to her neck, and feeling the heat turn on in their bodies. Catherine was kissing him back and she was sultry, sexy and she wanted him, too. They began taking each other's clothes off, exploring the naked parts of each other's body as they shed a layer of clothing. They were anxious as Samuel picked up Catherine and carried her to his bed.

"Do I need to put on protection?" he whispered to Catherine.

"No, it's all right, my period is soon."

After he laid Catherine on his bed, he took a step back and looked at her beautiful body. She held her arms out, inviting him to take her and he did. He had never felt this way about any woman and he felt as though they were one. Catherine cried out softly in quiet gratification as she climaxed first and Samuel followed. Their bodies were covered in each other's sweat and they lay motionless with their arms still around each other. Neither spoke. Samuel was perplexed by Catherine. She had rejected his advances for months and now, here she was lying in his arms after their intimacy, and it seemed perfectly normal. He didn't think he would ever figure her out, but for now, it was the most satisfying experience he had ever encountered. A short while later Catherine got up and went into the bathroom. When she came out she started getting dressed and Samuel got up and dressed, too. He watched as Catherine tried to straighten her messy hair. She walked over to him and put her arms around him and hugged him. She looked so innocent when she looked up at him and he gently kissed her.

They stood looking at each other, wanting the other to speak first. The moment was awkward and Catherine finally said, "Walk me home?"

Samuel smiled at her. "I guess that means you can't spend the night."

"Sure, but it might be crowded with the three children here," she teased.

Samuel shook his head and took her hand, pulling her through the door. He knew what she meant by her remark. She was reminding him that she had obligations, commitments, and he had none.

When Samuel got back home, he lay in bed staring at the ceiling, thinking of Catherine and he could still smell her sweet perspiration on his pillow and he took a deep breath, wanting her to be there with him. He knew if he asked her to marry him, she would say no. Maybe Father Jonathan was right. She was going to break his heart. He just needed to be patient. Maybe she would come around in time. It was too late, now. He was already in love with her.

Catherine found it difficult to sleep that night. She had taken a lover and she felt guilty that it was Samuel. He meant a lot to her and she was hungry for him. It had been over a year since she had been with Alex and she didn't think she would ever want to have sex with another man. She smiled when she thought of Samuel's love-making. He was sweet and tender and she hoped he had enjoyed it as much as she did. She knew it could not happen again. Today the timing was right but the next time it might not be and she could not risk getting pregnant. She also knew that with school starting next week there would be no time for Samuel, or any other man for that matter. Finishing medical school was going to be her priority, second only to her children.

CHAPTER 18

Catherine had to take a series of tests to determine where she would begin her studies at medical school. She had missed so much schooling. She was surprised when she tested out as a senior, surprising her professors as well. It would be a challenge, taking a full load of classes and then working at John Sealy Hospital as an intern. She would have little time for herself and she was determined on spending as much time with the children as she could. She had stopped nursing Emma, and Emma loved Martha. Catherine gave Martha a nice raise and allowed her to have one day off each week. Alva came on the day Martha was off. It was a rigorous schedule but Catherine was determined that she could do it for the next nine months.

Samuel called frequently at first, but Catherine's busy schedule allowed little time for them to be together. Catherine really missed him and she was hoping that perhaps during her Christmas break they might see each other. She called the hospital a few days before her break and left word for him to call her, but he didn't. She wondered if he got the message, but did not call him back. She tried his home a couple of times, letting the phone ring only two or three times. Perhaps its best, she thought; she was afraid she would not have the will power to resist his advances. He was not only a skillful doctor, but he was a skillful lover and he had awakened a need inside her that only he could fulfill. She thought about him often in between her dreams of her former husbands who had also fulfilled that hunger inside her.

She wondered if Alex had been able to remember anything of his previous life with her. She had no trouble recalling her days and nights with him. Occasionally she would still wake up with a nightmare where Alex was trying to rescue her from David Brooks and each time in her dream he fell short of rescuing her. She wondered what that might mean. She wished that she had been the one to have memory loss. She knew in her lifetime that David's skeletons in her mind would continue to haunt her. She would be twenty-one years old in a few months and she felt much older.

It was the first day of her Christmas break when she got a call from a woman who identified herself as the daughter of Minnie Wyman. She told Catherine that Minnie had passed during the night unexpectedly and that she was calling to give Catherine the news. Minnie had been taken to the hospital the day before because of chest pains and she died peacefully at the hospital. The funeral would be at 2:00 p.m. that afternoon.

Catherine arranged for a carriage to take her and Daniel to the funeral. Adam was walking and getting into everything and she knew he would be a distraction so he stayed home with Martha and Emma. After the funeral Agnes Pennington, Minnie's daughter, asked Catherine to stop by the house to talk about Minnie's estate.

"My mother loved you like a second daughter and she talked about you often. It is her wish that she bequeath the boarding house to you. It is paid for and I am having the lawyers draw up the deed in your name. Unfortunately, she only has one boarder, Professor Gordon. She is leaving all of the furniture, as I have no need for it," Agnes said.

Catherine was surprised. She had regularly visited Minnie over the past year and she and Minnie were very close, but she never expected Minnie would leave her the boarding house.

"I really don't know what to say," Catherine said.

"I am happy for you. I told my mother, I had no interest in the boarding house and she told me that she had changed her will, leaving me all her money and you the boarding house. I know it probably needs repairs, but at least I won't have to worry about selling it." Agnes went on to say, "The attorney's name is Clay Segal. She had told me that he was a friend of your first husband."

Catherine didn't say anything, but thanked her and told her that Minnie was a wonderful, thoughtful woman and she loved her dearly.

When Catherine got home, she wondered how she could ever face Clay Segal again. She was terrified of him now and decided to pick up the phone and call William Monroe, the attorney she had hired to help her when she tried to regain custody of her son, Daniel. She waited a few moments before he came to the phone.

"Hello Mr. Monroe, this is Catherine Merit and I need to retain your services again on another matter," she said. She told him about inheriting the property and that Clay Segal was the attorney for the estate.

"Why pay me when the estate is already paying Clay Segal?" he asked.

"Mr. Segal married John Merit's second wife, and his alliances are with her. They both have ill feelings towards me and I do not care to sit across a table with him. I am happy to pay your fee to do that for me." Mr. Monroe said he would contact Clay Segal regarding the property.

Five days later, Catherine was in Mr. Monroe's office signing some papers. The property would be signed over to her after the judge had approved the probate papers, in about thirty days. After Catherine left, she decided to stop by St. Mary's Catholic Church and take Father Jonathan a small Christmas gift. She knocked on his door and he was happy to see her. Father Jonathan had said a rosary for Minnie Wyman and had done the graveside service, but they had not had a chance to talk at that time. They visited about her going back to medical school and her children, and she told him that she missed St. Mary's Hospital. John Sealy Hospital was a much smaller hospital with fewer beds and it lacked the excitement of working in a larger hospital. Before she left, she asked him how Dr. Samuel Allen was.

"He is wonderful. He's been dating a really nice girl whose father is on the board. I would be surprised if they didn't announce their wedding plans soon."

"That's wonderful," Catherine said. "I hope they will be happy."

"And what about you, Catherine?" he asked.

"Between my children, going to school and working, I have little time to think about anything else. I plan to graduate next May and then I suppose I will try and find employment at a larger hospital, perhaps Houston," she said.

After they talked, Catherine left and walked over to St. Mary's Hospital. She had planned to do some shopping on her way home, but wasn't in the mood. The weather was nice so she decided to walk over to a park bench outside of the emergency room. Her mind went back to the day David Brooks had abducted her not too far from where she was sitting. It was a horrible memory and she wondered if she might ever get past it. She got up to leave when she saw Samuel and an attractive young woman walking towards a small restaurant and go in. They were holding hands and were deep in conversation. They did not see her. She was saddened by the fact that she was not the one holding his hand, but knew it was for the best. She knew Samuel would have made a good father to her children and a wonderful husband, but she did not want the curse that surrounded her to follow him.

Catherine went out of her way to make Christmas special for her children, even though her heart was not in it. Everyone she had ever loved, excluding her children, was gone, and she hid her feelings of loneliness well. It was the dark nights that made her feel so incomplete. She knew that once she was out of medical school, she would be able to plan her future. Just get through these next few months, she kept telling herself.

The children were all napping, having spent the morning tearing through presents and playing with their new toys. Martha was away visiting her family, so Catherine put on a kettle of water and was preparing some hot tea. She thought she heard someone at the door and listened. It was a strange sound, like something hitting the door. She opened it slowly just as the last egg hit the door. She saw two boys run away. She carefully stepped out the door and was shocked to see dozens of egg shells and egg yolks all over her porch. When she turned, the word "whore" was painted on her front door. Tears began trickling down her cheeks. It was one of the most disgusting things she had ever seen. How could people be so cruel? She went back in and closed the door quickly. The phone was ringing and she picked it up, not saying anything.

"Catherine, Merry Christmas," Samuel said in a cheerful voice.

She sniffed and took a deep breath and said, "Merry Christmas."

"You don't sound very well. Is everything all right?" he asked.

"Uh, yes, we're fine," she said.

"Catherine, I know you better than you think I do, and I can sense things aren't fine. I'd like to come over and see you and the children," he said.

She sniffed again and said, "Today really isn't a good day, maybe later in the week. Thanks for calling," she said and hung up.

Catherine went to the back porch and picked up a large bucket and a brush. She filled it with soapy water and carried it to the front porch. She looked at the mess and was overwhelmed and wasn't sure where to start, so she sat in the wooden rocker and stared at the word, "whore." She knew it was her Christmas present from Clay and Carla. Awhile later, she saw a man walking down the street and she quickly took the brush and dipped it in the water, trying to wash off the indignant word. She was crying while she scrubbed. Someone took the brush out of her hand and she looked up. It was Samuel. He helped her over to the rocking chair and told her nicely to sit. He took the brush and cleaned the door and washed the egg off the walls.

"I need to get some more water and a broom. Could you help me get that?" he asked. They carefully cleaned their feet and went into the house. He told Catherine to wait inside and he would finish cleaning it up.

Catherine had poured two glasses of wine and was sitting on the sofa when he came in. She watched as he walked into the kitchen and washed up.

"Do you have any idea who might have done this?" he asked as he walked over and sat beside her.

"My gut tells me that Carla and Clay had something to do with it." She told him about Minnie's will and that she had her own attorney work with Clay so she wouldn't have to see him, and she figured that might have made him mad.

"I'm really sorry, Catherine," he said as he put his arm around her. She cuddled with him and they sipped their wine. "I've missed seeing you," he whispered.

"I've missed you, too," she said.

"I know you have been busy with school. Father Jonathan told me you were a senior this year and that you were working at John Sealy Hospital," he said.

"Yes, I spoke with him a few days ago. He told me you might be getting married soon and I'm happy for you," she said.

"Are you really?" he asked. "Because that's why I wanted to come over, Catherine. I've tried to care about her and I keep comparing her to you. I know you have intentionally shut me out, because for some reason you don't think you are good enough for me, or that there is some kind of curse hanging over you. That day we were together in my room, I know you felt the same way about me that I did you. I want the whole package, Catherine, you, the kids, Martha, all of it. I want to marry you."

Catherine looked at him like she couldn't believe what he was saying. "I know it does sound crazy, but I've lost two husbands, my mother, my sister-in-law and a good friend, I have three children, each fathered by a different man. Why would you want me when there are so many other women without the kind of baggage I carry?"

Samuel looked at her and said, "I've tried very hard not to love you, Catherine, because you have consistently told me how you will never marry again. But you aren't anything like those other women. You're strong, compassionate and caring. That's the Catherine I love. Just give me a few months. We can work through all of these things," Samuel pleaded.

"You've only been around the children a few times and you have no idea what a madhouse it can be around here. The children are always on their best behavior when you are here and I need you to see them as they really are. They can be temperamental and moody and the boys sometimes fight. The next semester will be crazy with me working and trying to finish school," Catherine tried to explain.

"Catherine, just give it six months. If we can make it through that without any major problems, then after graduation, we'll get married," Samuel protested.

Catherine looked down and said, "Six months?"

"Six months," Samuel repeated.

"All right, I'll give it a try," she said. "But only on the condition that you'll be honest with me and if you feel that it's too much, you'll tell me and we will part as friends." Samuel agreed.

They held each other and kissed. Samuel knew he had thrown a lot at her and she needed some time to embrace the idea. "I think we should not tell anyone about our plans. That way if you change your mind, people won't associate you with me," Catherine said.

"I don't care what people think, Catherine, but I do need to break up with Allison, the girl I'm dating now. I'll tell her that I'm not in love with her, since that is the truth. I won't tell her I'm in love with someone else. Just so you know, you might start planning the wedding because I'm not going anywhere," he said, as he smiled at her.

"I had promised to join Allison and her family this afternoon at an open house that her family is having. I'm sorry I have to leave now but after today, I'm yours and I love you, Catherine," he said as he kissed her goodbye.

Catherine kissed him goodbye, but didn't answer him back. Samuel knew he loved Catherine much more than she loved him, and he felt that she was holding back, afraid of being hurt again. He had six months to prove to her that they were meant for each other. He dreaded going to Allison's house to tell her that they were not going to see each other again and he hated that it had to be on Christmas day. He touched the small box in his pocket with the engagement ring. Had Catherine told him no, he was planning to ask Allison to marry him. He was going to be twenty-eight years old on his next birthday and he wanted children of his own. Catherine was his first choice, but Allison was a nice girl and he felt that if Catherine was not in the picture, Allison would have made a suitable wife for a doctor.

CHAPTER 19

Samuel had a busy work schedule during the Christmas holidays and he was with Catherine and the children during his days off. He had tried to get New Year's off, but most of the doctors were married and had families and he understood that. They were rarely alone and he knew that once Catherine went back to school that they would only be able to see each other once or twice a week for a few hours. It was more difficult than he thought it would be.

Catherine knew that it had to be frustrating for Samuel, but she tried to warn him. She decided that she would plan something for just the two of them. After carefully checking her calendar and finding out what Samuel's schedule was, she made arrangement with Martha so she could be away for a night. She told Martha that she had taken a shift at the hospital and would return the next day.

Samuel had just gotten home from his nightly shift when he heard the knock on his door. He had already taken his shirt and undershirt off and just had his trousers on when he opened the door slightly to see who it was. He grinned when he saw it was Catherine and he grabbed her and pulled her inside. He took her small train case and put it by the chest of drawers and then took her in his arms.

"I have been dreaming about this. You have no idea what this means to me," he said holding her.

Catherine pushed him back and slowly took off her gloves in a seductive way. He was watching her as she opened the front of her dress, exposing her beautiful bosoms.

"Do you need some help?" he asked.

Catherine gave him an alluring smile and took his hands and looked at them. She brought one of his hands up and put it on her breast and then took the other one up to her mouth, kissing his palm first and then putting two of his fingers up to her mouth while she kissed them sweetly. Samuel closed his eyes, feeling the rush of excitement as it exploded through his body. He removed Catherine's clothes and she helped him take off his pants and underwear. Samuel picked her up and pulled the covers back on his bed. He felt like he was being drawn into a magical cavern. The pleasure of her body overwhelmed him and he had to fight to hold back the blood flowing into his organ. He didn't want it to end and he knew Catherine wasn't ready yet. He turned her over on her stomach and began caressing her body and kissing her back. He had forgotten about the scars she had endured during her capture and he vowed she would always be safe with him. She turned back around and he could see she was ready as she mounted him and they exploded in utter relief and pleasure. They lay together touching and kissing, enjoying the moment after, their bodies fulfilled and nourished. It was these small moments in time that would get them through the next few months. They slept and Catherine woke first. She knew Samuel had not slept in twenty-four hours so she left him a note telling him she was going shopping for their dinner and she would return shortly.

Catherine quietly left and walked the six blocks to the general store. She smiled to herself and couldn't believe that a man like Samuel Allen was in love with her and wanted to marry her. Life was good again and she prayed that God would keep Samuel safe. She was picking out some fruit and she heard a young girl say, "Look, mother, that's the woman from the hospital."

Catherine looked up and saw Carla and her two daughters staring at her. She quickly selected some fruit and turned to leave. Her basket caught the corner of a small display with candy on it, knocking several of the candy bars off. She stooped down to pick them up and when she got up Carla and her two girls were staring at her. Catherine went to the checkout and Carla followed.

When Catherine opened her knapsack to get her change purse, there was something foreign inside. She took it out, and it was a larger coin purse that did not belong to her.

"Oh my word!" Carla screamed. "You stole my purse. Give that back to me," she said as she grabbed it.

Everyone in the store looked at Catherine. "I have no idea how that got in my knapsack," she cried out. The store manager came over and asked Carla if she wanted him to call the police.

"No, but if I were you, I'd make sure she never set foot back in your store," Carla said.

"But I didn't take that," Catherine said.

"I think you need to leave before Mrs. Segal changes her mind and asks me to call the police," the manager said.

Catherine left, willing herself not to cry. She walked slowly back to Samuel's apartment. The door was unlocked and she quietly went in. Samuel was still asleep and she sat and watched him for a while. She picked up her note and put it in her knapsack. It's always going to be like this, she thought. While she was writing another note, Samuel woke up and watched her.

She was about to put the note on the table, when Samuel said, "You're leaving, just like that," and she stopped. He sensed something wasn't right. She didn't turn around. Samuel walked over to her and turned her to him. When he saw her face she looked away. "Did I do something wrong?" he asked. She bit her lip and he could see tears in her eyes. "I'm not letting you leave here until you tell me what is wrong." He pulled Catherine over to the bed and made her sit beside him. He pulled the covers over his naked body.

Catherine told him about leaving to pick up some food for them and she told him about her encounter with Carla and her daughters, and how embarrassed she was. She was still holding the note in her hand and Samuel took it from her. He read it and looked up at her, reading the note out loud. "Find someone else. I'm not good enough for you." He sighed as he read it and pulled her into his arms.

"Catherine, you aren't alone anymore. You can't let these people control your life. I know it's difficult to have people treat you like this, but they are the ones who are the bad people, not you," Samuel said softly.

"I'll never be able to show my face again at that store. They think I'm a thief," she said.

Samuel didn't have an answer and thought for a moment. "When you graduate, we can move anywhere you want. We'll both be doctors and we can open up our own practice. I've been saving all my money and if we are frugal, we can start over with a new life someplace where people will appreciate you. I need you, Catherine. We need each other and I want you to stop running away from me when something bad happens to you."

"I wish I could make you understand," she said.

Samuel kissed her. "Catherine I understand more than you know. There are bad people in this world and they have chosen you as their victim. The next time it happens, I'm going to do something about it. For now, can we put it behind us? How long can you stay?" he asked.

"I told Martha I would be back tomorrow morning. She thinks I'm working," she answered.

Samuel fell back in the bed. "Oh God, I love you," he said, pulling her to him. "I'm going to get dressed and we'll go somewhere nice to eat."

Samuel worked hard trying to get Catherine's mind back on him and not on the meeting she had with Carla at the grocery store. Catherine began opening up over their lunch and she asked him what he thought she should do with Minnie's boarding house once she became the owner.

"I suppose we could sell it and use the money to open up a

clinic," she said smiling at Samuel.

"That's your decision, Catherine," he said. "But after school is out, will you be selling your house, too?"

"Of course," she said. "I have other means, also," she said. He looked at her, not sure what she meant by that. "Didn't you know I was a wealthy woman?" she asked teasingly.

"I guess I never thought about it," he said. "I just thought you were comfortable since you had the house and a nanny," he said.

"I still have about $42,000 that I received from the farm in Beaumont," she said.

He looked at her and said, "Now that I found out you are a wealthy woman, you couldn't possibly get rid of me." They both laughed. The tension had finally eased and Catherine was back to her usual sexy, sultry self. He picked up her hand and kissed her fingers. "What would you like to do the rest of the day?" he asked.

Catherine leaned over and whispered something in his ear and Samuel gave a wide grin, and said, "Check, please."

They walked, hand and hand, back to his apartment. Catherine called Martha to check on things, and then Samuel took her in his arms again and kissed her. The rest of the day they made love, talked, slept, and made love again. Before they knew it, it was morning again and time for Samuel to go back to work. The next day was New Year's Eve and Samuel apologized that he had to work. They knew it would be awhile before they saw each other again.

The weeks went by quickly and Samuel arranged to be off on Catherine's twenty-first birthday. Samuel had received a couple of letters from Houston General Hospital asking if he would be interested in working with a world famous pulmonary doctor. He had no idea where they had gotten his name, and was flattered that they wanted him to come for an interview. He called Catherine and asked if she could manage to get away that Friday and Saturday so she could go with him. She hated cutting classes, but agreed to, not wanting to disappoint Samuel. Catherine arranged for Alva to come during the day and help Martha with the children. Martha was perfectly capable of taking care of the children on her own, but Catherine felt better knowing that she had some back-up. The boys were both toddlers and Emma was six months old, and she knew they could be a handful.

Catherine had shopped for a few new things to wear before her trip and she was excited when Samuel picked her up in the carriage early that Friday morning. They took an 8:00 a.m. train to Houston and Samuel had booked a large suite in the Pullman car. He had arranged for breakfast to be brought to their cabin at 8:45 AM and they dined like royalty. Samuel's appointment was at 11:00 a.m. and after dropping off their luggage at the front desk of the famous Roosevelt Hotel, which was close to Houston General, Samuel left for his appointment and Catherine went shopping. They were to meet back at the hotel at 4:00 p.m. Catherine had not been back to Houston since she and John had been there several years earlier and it seemed to have grown a great deal in the last few of years. More beautiful boutiques lined the main street and there were more automobiles than she had ever seen. It was bustling with activity and after having a light lunch and shopping for a couple of hours, she went back to the hotel.

The room was ready when she got there and she picked up a key to their room. She stopped when an elevator door opened. She had never before been on an elevator and she asked where the stairs were. When they told her that her room was on the eighth floor, a bellman asked if he could escort her up. It was a strange feeling standing inside a square box as it lifted her up. It had stopped on two other floors before it came to a stop on the eighth floor. When they got off, the bellman showed her to her room. Their luggage was waiting in the room and she tipped the bellman and thanked him. The room was large and beautifully decorated. She walked over to a door that opened out to a small wrought-iron terrace and opened it. The cool breeze chilled her as she watched in amazement all the automobiles and street cars from eight stories up. She smiled and thanked God for bringing her Samuel. She was looking forward to beginning a new life in a new city and knew that once she left Galveston, all her history and past life would be left behind.

She went back in and looked at the clock. It was 3:30 p.m. and she decided to take a bath and change clothes. Samuel would be there soon. She piled her hair up, leaving the curls to fall randomly where they pleased, and put on one of her new dresses. She felt pretty and she knew Samuel would approve. Her dress was cut lower than she usually wore, exposing the fullness of her breasts. It was 5:30 p.m. when she looked at the clock again. She walked out onto the terrace, but the evening air was beginning to cool down what was otherwise a beautiful day. She walked back in and closed the door. The phone rang and she rushed over to get it.

"Catherine, I'm so sorry. I've been in meetings all day and now they want to take me to dinner. I'm not sure when I'll get through. I know we were going to celebrate your birthday tonight, but I hate to tell them no," he said sadly.

"You go. I'll be fine. I'll just order room service and I'll be here when you get in," she said.

Catherine looked around the beautifully decorated room and knew that Samuel was genuinely sorry he had to leave her alone. She wasn't ready to eat dinner yet and remembered that she had seen a bar just off the lobby at the hotel. She knew it wasn't really proper for a lady to go to a bar alone, but maybe she would just walk around and if it were not too crowded, she would order a drink. Catherine felt awkward going into the bar alone so she sat in a chair in the lobby facing the elevator. A bellman asked if he could get her something and she asked if he could get her a scotch from the bar. A short while later he brought it to her.

It was interesting, she thought, watching all the people come in and out of the hotel. As she sipped her drink she wondered where they were from. She noticed an attractive man and woman come in the lobby door from outside and walk over to the elevator. She watched and it suddenly came to her that the man looked just like

Alex. When he turned around in the elevator and faced her, he saw her, too. They stared at each other until the door closed. Catherine was surprised that they happened to be at the same hotel at the same time. Was it fate, she wondered. The woman he was with was very pretty and she wondered if she were Alex's wife. The thought of him no longer wanting to be married to her made her sad, and even though Samuel was going to be her husband, she couldn't help but admit that part of her was still in love with Alex.

She was holding her drink and looking at the ice in the glass when she heard someone said, "Catherine?"

She looked up and Alex was standing in front of her. She felt her heart skip a beat. There was an empty chair next to her and he asked if he could join her. "It's nice to see you again. Are you here alone?" he asked.

"No, no, I am here with my fiancé," she answered. "Was that your wife you were with?"

"Yes, her name is Meredith," Alex told her.

"I'm surprised you remembered me," she said.

"I still have your picture," he said. "You were expecting when we last saw each other."

"Yes, I had a little girl. Her name is Emma," she said.

"So where is your fiancé?" Alex asked.

"He is a doctor and is here for an interview at Houston General. They wanted him to have dinner with them and he'll be back soon."

"I'm glad you've moved on, Catherine, and I want to thank you for going to the trouble of finding me. I'm doing much better, but I still have no recollection of my past. I did send for Pilgrim. We are living outside of Houston on Meredith's family ranch. I still go to therapy at the sanatorium three times a week," Alex said.

"I've gone back to medical school and will graduate in the summer," Catherine told him.

"That's great. Will you be moving to Houston?"

"Maybe, it depends on whether Samuel gets the job at Houston General," she answered.

"Well, I need to get back upstairs. It was good seeing you, Catherine," Alex said, and left.

Catherine watched as he walked over and waited for the elevator. When he got on it, he turned and looked at her and smiled. Catherine couldn't help but wonder that if he had not met Meredith, would she be the one on his arm. It made her begin to wonder if she loved Samuel because he was conveniently there. She needed to be sure before she married Samuel and then regretted it. Catherine picked up a Houston newspaper and took it upstairs to their room. At least it would help her pass the time.

For some reason, she turned to the want ads in the back of the paper. They were mostly just ordinary jobs for ordinary people. There was one in a bold square that caught her eye. It was an ad for the city of Rosenberg, Texas, seeking a medical doctor to open a practice there. It went on to say that the town was rapidly growing, had railroad connections, and was located on the outskirts of Houston. She tore the ad out and put it in her purse, thinking it might be something to look into, if Samuel did not get the job. She ordered a bowl of soup and some fruit from room service. She really wasn't hungry, but knew she needed to eat something. It was 9:00 p.m. when she finally took off her clothes and went to bed. It was nearly midnight when she heard Samuel come in. She had left a small light on in the corner so he would be able to see. It only took him a couple of minutes to go in the bathroom and undress. He crawled under the covers and wrapped his arms around her. His hands were cold and she shivered when he touched her.

"I was hoping you might be awake," Samuel said.

When she turned towards him she could smell liquor on his breath and he smelled of smoke. She knew he wanted her and she was half-asleep, but she succumbed to his advances. "We need protection," she said.

Samuel stopped and walked over to his bag, fumbling through it. A few minutes later he came back and had sex with her. It was over in a few minutes, and he turned over and went to sleep.

Catherine lay awake staring into the dark. She knew that sex wasn't always going to be an exciting encounter, but they weren't even married yet. She had just hoped for more. Maybe it was because she saw Alex earlier, but she knew that was only a part of it. Samuel was only interested in his own personal gratification and not hers, and that struck a nerve with her.

She got up before Samuel the next morning and ordered room service. She was sipping her hot tea when he woke up and got out of bed.

"How was the meeting last night?" she asked.

"They want me in a couple of weeks," he said.

"You mean they hired you?" she asked.

"Yes, they did, and at twice the money I'm making now," he said.

"Oh, Samuel, that's wonderful," Catherine said cheerfully.

"There's one more thing, though," he said, and waited a minute before he told her the rest. "I'm afraid we'll need to put off getting married for at least a year. The reason why they sought me out was because they wanted someone who was unencumbered and didn't have a family. I'll be practically living at the hospital, learning, doing surgery, and looking after patients. I hope that's not a problem. I really do want this job. They asked me if I had a woman in my life and I lied and told them, no."

Catherine didn't answer him. "I haven't told them yet, Catherine. If you don't want me to take it, we can just stay in Galveston." He assured her.

"It's an opportunity of a lifetime," she answered. "You have to take it. You do want it, don't you?"

"Of course, more than anything, but I made a promise to you, too," he said.

"I won't hold you to it. Remember, I told you that if you wanted to change your mind at any time, just be honest with me," she said.

He hugged her and thanked her. "If it's all right with you, can we catch the next train to Galveston? I have a lot of things I need to do," he answered.

Catherine walked over and began putting her things in her bag. Samuel was so excited about his new job, he had forgotten about Catherine's birthday. It's not that important, she told herself. She was actually surprised that she wasn't mad or upset. She thought of Alex again and decided that seeing him was the best present she could have gotten.

CHAPTER 20

Samuel slept on the train most of the way. They were in a small compartment and Samuel had put his feet up on the side of the seat she was sitting on. She stared out the window and reminded herself that life was always full of surprises; some good and some not so good. Samuel saw her home and left, promising to call her soon. Once school began she knew she would be busy and they wouldn't be able to see each other very much. She was excited to see the children, but Samuel didn't ask to come in. When he left, she had a feeling she might not see him again anytime soon. How could he be so madly in love with her one day and out the next? She couldn't help but feel betrayed. She would miss him a lot, she knew, but she was happy for him.

Now she had to decide what she was going to do after she graduated. Staying in Galveston was not an option. After she put the children to bed, she took the small piece of paper she had torn out of the newspaper, went into the study, and wrote a letter inquiring about the job they had advertised for a doctor in Rosenberg, Texas. She told them she would be graduating in May and that she was a widow. She would mail it the next day.

A week had almost gone by when Samuel finally called her. He was leaving a week earlier so that he could take his time finding a place to live. He said that he wanted her to come to Houston in a couple of weeks to see him and he would let her know when he was off.

He told her to be strong and that they should stay in touch. Catherine felt empty when she hung up the phone. It bothered her that he didn't think her important enough to come see her before he left.

The remainder of the school year flew by, and Catherine was graduating at the top of her class. Samuel had called her a couple of times when she wasn't home, but he didn't leave a number. She had gotten a reply from her inquiry about Rosenberg, Texas, needing a doctor. They thanked her for inquiring, but they really were looking for a male doctor with more experience. Her house had been egged two more times and each time she was able to clean it off before the children or Martha got up. Catherine had sent out other inquiries to surrounding hospitals even as far as San Antonio and Austin, Texas. Most did not answer her inquiry. Catherine was looking forward to graduating. Martha and the children were coming to the ceremony, and she bought new outfits for all of them.

There were forty-five in her graduating class and that year she was the only woman. When they called her name and she went up on stage to get her degree, the boys pointed and said mommy. She blew them a kiss and they clapped.

Catherine had a lot of time to think about what she was going to do. She had sold Minnie Wyman's boarding house and contents two months earlier and she cleared $1,800.00. She had told the real estate agent that she was interested in some real estate in Rosenberg, Texas, and he gave her the name of another real estate man who lived there. She had been speaking to him about a home that would be large enough for her family to live in and have a couple of extra rooms for a medical practice. He had called her a couple of times, but she felt the properties just were not large enough.

It was a week after graduation when the real estate agent called her from Rosenberg and told her about a large, two-story home at the edge of town that was older and needed some work, but it was large and had a carriage house. There were four bedrooms and two baths upstairs and a large living room, separate dining room, a parlor, two kitchens and a bathroom downstairs plus a large suite for the owner. She asked him what train came through from Galveston and he told her she would have to switch in Bay Town, Texas, and then come to Rosenberg. She made an appointment to meet him in Rosenberg on Friday and he would meet her at the depot. She decided to take Emma with her. Martha could handle the boys just fine, but they demanded a lot of attention and she didn't want Martha to get stressed out by having to look after Emma, too.

Catherine had been to the library several times looking at maps of Texas and trying to get her bearings. Rosenberg, Texas, was just eighty miles from Galveston and 38 miles from Houston. Being in between the two cities would give them several options for small weekend trips and they could be at the beach in Galveston by train in a couple of hours. For some reason this just seemed to feel right. If no one wanted to hire her, she would just open up her own practice. When she spoke to the real estate agent in Rosenberg, he told her they still did not have a doctor and she was excited about the possibility.

Catherine had packed a bag for her and Emma and told Martha she would be back in about two or three days. She had shared her plans with Martha, and Martha agreed to move there temporarily until Catherine could find adequate help. Martha had wanted to move back to Austin, where her family lived, and Catherine couldn't blame her. Before Catherine left she called her own real estate agent, Mark Graham, and asked him to come over and look at her house. She needed to know how much she could get for it and how long it might take to sell it. Mark Graham was very optimistic and told her she could expect to get around $4,500 for it because it was not very old. He felt it would sell quickly and that he had several buyers he could show it to. Catherine thanked him and said she would call him when she returned.

Catherine was excited when she and Emma got in the carriage to leave for the depot. She felt for the first time she was taking charge of her life. Emma was a sweet child and had a precious disposition.

She had just turned one year old and she reminded Catherine of her own sister who had died so young. It was Emma's first train ride and she would point and say, "See?"

They were in Baytown in forty minutes and they only had to wait thirty minutes for the other train to come and take them to Rosenberg.

Michael Atwood had grown up in Rosenberg. His family owned a large ranch and much of the property in the Rosenberg area south of the railroad tracks. They made a lot more money when the railroads came through, and they owned interests in two paper mills, a bank, and a real estate development company. Michael Atwood graduated from Harvard with a degree in banking and returned to Rosenberg to manage the family's business when his father died. Michael was twenty-six at the time and that was five years ago. He was tall, was nice looking, and he had a receding hairline. He was not handsome, but he was pleasant to look at. His sister, Meredith Atwood, had married a man by the name of Alex Cooper and they lived in a smaller house on their ranch. It was her second marriage. Meredith was tall, with long brown hair and she was pretty. Her first husband had died in a terrible accident at the ranch. Michael had two small children, a boy five years old, and a little girl who was three. Michael's wife had suffered most of her life with depression and was currently residing at Oakwood Sanatorium, five miles east of Rosenberg. She had tried to commit suicide twice and the last time their little girl, Heather, had found her.

Michael Atwood had a young apprentice he had hired to help him with the real estate business, and he had asked Michael to show a property for him the next day as he had to be out of town.

Michael was familiar with the property because his family owned it. The house was older, but in a good location. He was told to meet a Dr. Merit on the 11:30 a.m. train. Michael was anxious to meet this doctor. They had been advertising in the Houston paper for over six months in hopes of finding a doctor who would be willing to set up his practice in Rosenberg.

He was standing in front of the tracks outside the depot when the train pulled in. The train was on its way to San Antonio, and few people got off. After the train left, a woman holding a young child was trying to pick up her bag. Michael walked over to her and asked if he could help her, and he picked up her bag.

"I'm supposed to meet a Mr. Reynolds," she said.

"Are you Dr. Merit?" he asked, surprised.

"Yes, I'm Dr. Catherine Merit," she said.

"My apologies," he said, "Mr. Reynolds had to go out of town and I'm Michael Atwood. He asked me to show the property. I must admit, I was expecting a man."

"Well, I'm sorry if I disappointed you," she said. "Oh, and this is Emma."

Michael was taken aback by Catherine's strong personality. She was mature, confident, and didn't look over nineteen years old. "So you're a doctor," he said.

"Yes, women can go to medical school and become doctors, too," she said. "Is the property close by?" she asked.

"Not too far, my automobile is just in front," he said.

Michael put Catherine's bag in the back seat and helped her and Emma get in.

Catherine had never been in an automobile before, but she wasn't about to let Michael know. If she was going to be the town's new doctor, she had to act like she had been around. They rode through the main street of Rosenberg and the little town had an atmosphere of enchantment. It was clean and all the buildings looked like they were well taken care of. It had a small hotel, several shops, a bank, telegraph office, and stables, among other businesses. The courthouse was in the center of town and she saw a general store and two cafés. When they arrived at the property she was surprised that it actually was an older Victorian style house on a beautiful, treed lot. The landscaping was a bit overgrown with vines hugging the exterior of the columns. It was surrounded by a white picket fence and there were a number of stately old towering oak trees in the front and back yards. There was a wide porch with a large gallery across the second floor. It was impressive. There was a no trespassing sign up, and the downstairs windows were boarded up.

Michael helped Catherine get down with Emma. He took her arm as they walked up the four front steps and then he took out a large set of keys and unlocked the front door. Catherine walked slowly through each room.

"Mr. Reynolds had told me that this property had not been on the market very long," she said. "It seems to have been vacant for some time."

"Yes, actually the family just recently decided to sell it," Michael said.

"I'm curious about one thing," Michael said perplexed. Why would you leave Galveston to come to Rosenberg and set up a clinic?"

"Because you don't have one. Mr. Reynolds said they were asking $1,200.00. Would that include the furniture?" she asked.

"Yes. The family has no need for the furnishings. Much of it probably just needs to be thrown out," Michael stated.

Catherine just looked at him and walked over to the staircase. "May I see the upstairs?" she asked.

"Of course. Would you like me to hold Emma while you go up the stairs? I have a three-year-old daughter myself," he said.

"We live in a two-story home now, and I often carry two of my children upstairs, one in each arm. I think I can handle this," she said.

Michael was beginning to feel a bit intimidated and very few people ever intimidated Michael. He had to admit, she certainly could handle herself and she seemed fearless. She must have had a strong father, he thought. After Catherine looked through the upstairs, she said. "I would like to see the rest of the property now."

They went back downstairs and Michael showed her the rest of the downstairs and then took her to the carriage house in the back. There were two more rooms and a water closet on the second floor of the carriage house that used to be slave quarters. Michael walked around to the side of the carriage house and showed Catherine a large door that, when opened, showed a set of stairs leading to a storm cellar.

"I'll have my men take off the boards we hammered over it to keep the children and vagrants out. We don't have too many tornadoes, but they did have one in Sugar Land a couple of years ago when the storm hit Galveston," Michael stated.

"I'm very interested and would like to buy it," she said. "How soon do you think we can close?"

"Mrs. Merit, I mean Dr. Merit, I want to warn you that none of the men in this town are going to want to be treated by a woman," Michael said.

"Tell me, Mr. Atwood, do you also have women and children living in your fine town?" she asked.

"Well, yes," he answered. "At least half the town."

"Fine then, the men can just go to Houston when they get sick and I'll take care of the women and children. I'm curious, if you had a choice to take your three-year-old daughter to a local doctor rather than drive an hour into Houston, where would you take her?" Catherine asked.

"Right now, I have to take both of my children to Houston," he said. "It would be nice to have a doctor here."

"If you could just forget my gender for the moment, I would like to take care of the business at hand," she said.

"Fine, we'll just need to go back to my office up the street," he replied.

Catherine noticed as she got back in his automobile that they were about six blocks from the edge of town. She could also see the small depot and the water tower from the front yard of the property.

She looked at the front of the house again and pictured a sign that would say Catherine Merit, MD, and she smiled to herself. As they approached the small town, she saw a new building under construction and she asked what it was.

"That is going to be the new school. It's to open in the fall. You said you had another child?" Michael asked.

"Yes, I have two sons, three and two years old, and Emma is one," she answered proudly.

Michael was surprised and figured Catherine was much older than she looked. He wondered what happened to her husband, but was afraid to ask.

When they got to Michael's office the sign on the door read, Conveyor of Land and Property. Impressive, she thought. She had to admit his office was beautifully decorated. It had an imported oriental rug, a huge carved wooden desk and several old oil paintings on the wall. He took out some papers and asked her some questions, writing her answers down as she gave them to him.

"Are you going to need to obtain a loan?" he asked.

"No, I prefer to pay cash," she said and took out her check book. She wrote the check for the full amount and handed it to him. I would like to make some improvements to the property and I was wondering if you might have some names of workers you could give me."

"I could take care of that for you. I have a construction business, also. How long will you be in town?" he asked.

"I plan to stay a couple of days so I can get everything lined up before I go back to Galveston and sell my house," she said. Emma had fallen asleep in her lap and she asked Michael if he could carry her bag to the hotel for her.

"It would be my pleasure," Michael said. "Would you like to meet me back here tomorrow morning? We can go back over to the house and you can tell me what you need my men to do in the way of repairs and improvements."

"That would be nice," she said. "I'll make a list this evening. I'm an early riser so is 8:30 a.m. too early?" she asked.

"I'll be looking forward to it," he said.

Michael took Catherine's check and told her that he would get his lawyers to draw up the necessary papers for signing and have them ready the next day.

He walked her over to the hotel and waited while she checked in. He offered to buy her dinner, but she declined and it didn't surprise him. She seemed to be a woman of determination and she wasn't going to take nonsense from anybody. He smiled when he thought about what the men on the city council might say when they found out Rosenberg now had a new female doctor; especially one as beautiful as Catherine Merit. It was time the city of Rosenberg had a little spice sprinkled on it, he thought to himself.

Catherine and Emma took a bath and changed clothes. She wasn't sure what time the sleepy little town closed for the night, and she wanted to get supper before it did. They made their way down to a small café and went in. The waitress handed them a menu and told them they could sit wherever they wanted. It was not crowded, so they took a small table by the window where they could look out. It wasn't long before other people began coming in to the café and stared at her.

By the time their food came, the café was packed. Two women stopped and introduced themselves, and Catherine introduced herself and Emma. "Are you the new lady doctor everyone is talking about?" one of them asked.

Catherine smiled and told them she was. She thought it funny that she was the new attraction in town and everyone wanted to see her. Catherine and Emma bowed their heads while Catherine said grace. Emma said "Amen" and everyone in the café said "amen," also. Emma laughed.

"Hello, I'm Pastor Homer Watkins, and I would like to invite you and your family to church when you move here," he said. "We're so glad to have you."

Catherine thanked him and tried to resume eating. She had never had this kind of attention in her life and it reinforced the fact that she had made the right decision.

The next morning Catherine and Emma walked to Michael Atwood's office. They were a few minutes early so they took their time, looking in store windows.

"Good morning, Dr. Merit," Michael said as he greeted her on the street. "You are an early riser," he commented.

Catherine smiled and told him good morning and asked if he might show her through the house one more time before she signed everything. They drove the short distance to the house and Catherine took a small notebook and pencil out of her knapsack. She made notes as she walked through the house and Emma tagged along, holding her skirt. When she got to the main kitchen, she picked up Emma and sat her on the center island counter and continued to make notes. When she finished they continued their inspection in every room. They were there for over an hour. Michael had noticed a drawing of the downstairs floor plan on one of her sheets of paper and a drawing of the upstairs on another. He commented that he was surprised the drawings were so accurate.

"I'm fortunate to have a photographic memory," Catherine said. "It came in handy during medical school and math happened to be one of my stronger subjects."

Michael was impressed by Catherine's extraordinary mind; brains and beauty, he thought to himself. He was going to enjoy getting to know her. Michael could have given Catherine over to Eric Reynolds, since he had returned to work that morning, but Michael decided he wanted to personally handle this sale. After all, the property did belong in the family trust, and besides, nothing as exciting as Catherine Merit had come to Rosenberg in a long time.

Michael and Catherine spent most of the morning going over repairs and improvements to the house and Catherine gave him her home phone number in Galveston so that he could call her with an estimate. Michael gave Catherine a preliminary estimate of $875.00 and said he would confirm it with her by the middle of next week. It was time for lunch and Michael had set up an appointment with his lawyer at 1:00 p.m. to sign the closing papers. He insisted on taking Catherine and Emma to lunch and Catherine accepted.

Michael wanted to know more about Catherine so he decided to tell her a little about his past in hopes of her opening up about hers. Catherine had noticed that Michael was wearing a wedding ring and thought nothing of it, except he mentioned his two children earlier and nothing about a wife. It did make her curious.

"My family was part of the earlier settlers here in Rosenberg. I spent my teen years at a military school in Virginia and then went on to Harvard Business School. I met my wife during the summer of my junior year and we got married. She was from a well-respected family in Houston. We didn't know each other very well and found out that our parents had planned our meeting in hopes that we might someday get married. Anyway, she had some emotional problems and after our second child she had a nervous breakdown. She's currently in a sanatorium not far from here.

"Oakwood Plantation Sanatorium?" Catherine asked.

"Yes, it's not that big. How did you hear of it?" he asked.

"From the medical school," she lied.

"What about you, Catherine? You're from England?" he asked.

"Yes, my mother and I moved to Galveston when I was fifteen. Tell me about the history of the house," Catherine said, trying to change the subject.

"The property belonged to my great-uncle and his wife. They never had children, so they willed it to the family trust," he said and continued. "So is your mother going to stay in Galveston?" he asked.

"My mother died shortly after we got to Texas," she answered. "You said you had a sister?" Catherine changed the subject again.

"Yes," he said. "She got married a few months ago to someone she met when she was visiting my wife at the sanatorium. Actually, she volunteered there so she could keep an eye on her progress. Her husband, Alex, was there because he had suffered memory loss, but they had an instant attraction to each other and married."

Catherine felt a stab in her stomach when she made the connection. "Are you all right?" he asked. "Is something wrong with your food?"

"No," she said. "I just remembered something I forgot to do before I left home," she hated lying, but if she had any reservations about moving to Rosenberg before, there was certainly cause to be concerned now. "I'm sorry," she said as she got up. "I need to make an important phone call, if you'll excuse me. I'll meet you back at your office at 1:00 p.m."

Emma was through eating and was playing with her food. Catherine wiped her mouth and hands and picked her up and left.

Michael stood up when Catherine left and wondered what could be so important that she would leave without finishing her meal. She's a woman, he had to remind himself, and they were unpredictable. Catherine certainly tried to fit into a male role, but she was still a woman.

Catherine went to her room and put Emma down for a nap. She took her watch out of her purse and looked at it. 12:10 p.m. She started pacing the floor. She had already given Michael the check and she loved the house. How could this be happening? Never in her wildest dream did she imagine that she would move this close to Alex. She knew he would recognize her. What would she say to him? What about Emma? Her mind was racing and she took several deep breaths. If she stayed in Galveston, she would be constantly looking over her shoulder and besides, she couldn't find a job there. She had made at least fifteen inquiries and no one wrote her back. Catherine was stressed. Something was telling her moving to Rosenberg was the right decision. If she did encounter Alex, she would have to pretend she didn't know him and he would just have to do the same thing. Besides, what were her chances of meeting him?

Catherine woke Emma from her nap and they made their way to Michael's office.

"Is everything all right?" he asked. "Yes," she answered. "Everything's fine."

When they went into Michael's office, he introduced her to his attorney, Steven Findley, who went over all the paperwork with Catherine. She signed everything and Michael gave her a key to the property. He asked if he could keep one so they could begin the work on the house when she gave him permission.

"Will you be leaving today?" Michael asked

"Yes," I need to go to Houston and order my medical supplies and equipment so that they will be here when I come back to Rosenberg. I guess I need to go to the post office and see if they could hold my supplies until I come back," she said.

"Why don't you use my address here?" Michael said. The post office is small and may not have room. I have an empty office and I will be happy to store it there for you. It will be safe," he assured her.

"That would be most kind of you," Catherine said.

Michael gave Catherine his calling card with his phone number and address on it and told her to call him if she needed anything. He asked her when she wanted to move in and she said that as soon as he let her know the work was done, she would move in within a week. He told her it could be finished in thirty days and she told him that was perfect.

Catherine checked out of the hotel and walked with Emma to the depot. She still had knots in her stomach. She prayed that she had made the right decision and decided that if the shoe was on the other foot, Alex would probably do the same thing. Just because he lived near here was no reason why they couldn't live in the same town, she thought.

The next morning Catherine and Emma boarded the train to

Houston. She hadn't slept much the night before. Her dreams of a new future in Rosenberg and all the changes she was making kept her awake much of the night. I know this is the right thing to do, she kept reminding herself. When she woke up the next morning, her thoughts were now on Samuel. Her last dream had been of the two of them getting back together. She smiled and decided she would give him a call when she got there.

Samuel had left the hospital phone number and his address with Martha the last time he called, which had been several months ago. When Catherine got to the Houston depot, she called the number at the hospital and was told Samuel was off until the next day. She felt a rush of excitement when she hailed a carriage ride and gave the man Samuel's address. It was in a really nice part of town and all of the buildings looked like beautiful brownstone cottages.

"We're here," the carriage driver said, and helped Catherine and Emma down. He rode off before Catherine could ask him to wait. She stood outside Samuel's door for a few seconds before she knocked. She smiled when she thought about seeing him. It had been five months. She pulled the knocker and hit it four times, waiting for the door to open. She almost gave up when no one answered, but then the door slowly opened and a woman with messy hair and a robe on answered the door.

"I'm sorry, I must have the wrong address," she said.

"Who is it?" she heard Samuel call from the back.

"It's a woman and a little girl. She thinks she has the wrong address," the woman replied to Samuel.

The door opened further and Samuel, also in a robe, was standing by the woman looking at Catherine.

"I'm, sorry," she said. I do have the wrong apartment. Catherine turned and walked away.

She had walked halfway up the street and then sat down on a bench trying not to cry. Emma was sucking her thumb and clung to her mother's skirt. Catherine was embarrassed and scolded herself for acting so foolishly. She knew she had no right to expect that Samuel wasn't dating someone. They had hardly spoken since he left, and she was surprised that she felt deceived and rejected.

Samuel hurriedly dressed and left to find her. He saw her sitting on a bench and walked over and sat beside her. "I'm sorry, Catherine, I guess I should have told you that I was dating again. We just kept missing each other on the phone. You could have called first," he said.

"I did call the hospital, but you only gave me your home address. I didn't have another number. It's all right. I didn't expect you to wait for me," Catherine said softly.

"Hi, Emma," Samuel said cheerfully. "She has really grown. Look, I would like to see you. Could you maybe come back in an hour?" he asked.

"Sure," Catherine said.

Samuel kissed her on the cheek and said he would be looking forward to it. "I've missed seeing you, Catherine."

Catherine smiled at him and walked to a nearby trolley. She had no idea where the trolley was going but she just wanted to get away fast. She needed to close the chapter on this part of her life. She had reservations about marrying Samuel from the beginning and she always relied on her instincts. It was time she moved on.

Samuel knew when Catherine left, she wouldn't be back. He still had feelings for her, but she carried such a heavy load of responsibility and he just wasn't ready to carry that load. He liked being the new doctor and he had six floors of nurses in training and at least a third of them were not married. He was working hard and on his one day off each week he usually entertained one of them at his home. There was also a young woman living next door to him who went to night school. She usually didn't get home until late and she would often wait until his shift ended at midnight. She frequently spent the night with him, too. Life couldn't be better, he thought. He was sorry Catherine had to find out the way she did. He did feel a bit of remorse after she left. He had bedded numerous women since he had been in Houston, but none of them measured up to Catherine. She was special and he hoped he wouldn't regret letting her go.

CHAPTER 21

The June heat did not fare well for the Indian reservation in Kountze, Texas. There was a drought and food was scarce. Grey Wolf had made up his mind that when the timing was right, Isabella would simply disappear. He had planned that she would drown in the creek, but the drought had dried up the water and Dr. Windsong never let Isabella out of his sight unless she was being watched by one of the other women. Grey Wolf was still holding a grudge against Alex Cooper because Mary Windsong had died in childbirth. He had married Mary, but did not want anything to do with her child. Dr. Windsong had been taking care of Isabella since she was born and had loved her as his own daughter.

One morning Isabella was standing behind the screen door crying. Her diaper needed changing and she had been standing there for some time. Grey Wolf rode up on his horse and one of the women said they had not seen Dr. Windsong and would he go in and check on him. It was almost noon, and he asked how long the little girl had been at the door. "She had been coming to the door off and on since the sun rose," one of the children said.

Grey got off his horse and went over to the door. He pushed Isabella back and she fell on the floor crying. Grey walked through the house and back to Dr. Windsong's office. Dr. Windsong was slumped in his chair. He had apparently died during the night. Grey walked out and told one of the women to change and feed Isabella and that he was taking her to her father, since Dr. Windsong had died.

Thirty minutes later Grey mounted his horse and one of the women handed Isabella to him. He rode off quickly. He headed toward Beaumont, but after he got to a grove of trees several miles from the reservation, he stopped and slid off his horse, still holding Isabella. He took her over to a tree and told her to wait there. He carried his bow and arrow on a sling around his body and he pulled out an arrow from its quiver. Isabella was the reason Mary had died, and it was time for Isabella to leave with the spirits and join her mother, he thought. He put his arrow in his bow and began pulling it back, aiming at Isabella's heart. A butterfly flew and landed on Isabella's shoulder; she was fascinated with it. Grey took aim and closed his left eye. He released the arrow and it flew just over Isabella's left shoulder. Grey was surprised. He never missed his target. Isabella was still standing and the butterfly was perched on the tip of the arrow that had struck the tree behind Isabella. Grey took another arrow and placed it in his bow again and the butterfly flew and landed on Isabella's shoulder again. He could not release the arrow.

He saw Mary's face. At first it was just a blur and he closed his eyes and opened them again. He saw Mary standing in front of Isabella this time, frowning at him and he fell to his knees and beat the ground with his fists. When he looked up Isabella was handing him a flower she had picked. Grey picked up Isabella and put her on his horse and pulled himself up behind her.

It was unusual to see an Indian riding bareback, with a small child, coming down Main Street in Beaumont. Grey could not read and he asked someone where Glacier was, and they pointed. Grey took Isabella off the horse and carried her inside as he opened the door. Clarence was about to leave and almost ran into them.

"This is the white man's child. Her grandfather, Dr. Windsong, and her mother, Mary, are both dead. She belongs to the white man now," Grey said and left. "She is Isabella," he called over his shoulder. Clarence watched as Grey jumped on his horse and rode off towards the reservation.

Before Catherine checked into the hotel, she decided to call Martha so she could check on everything before she stayed another night. “I’m so glad you called,” Martha said. You need to call Clarence Henry as soon as possible. He says it’s urgent.”

Catherine wrote the number down and then placed the call. “Thank God you called,” Clarence said, “I didn’t really don’t know what to do.”

Clarence told Catherine about Grey Wolf bringing Isabella to the office and that he had no idea what to do with her. He had not spoken to Alex since Alex had picked up Pilgrim, and that was over six months ago; Clarence had no idea how to reach him. Catherine told Clarence that she was in Houston and would take the next train to Beaumont. She asked him to please get her a room at the hotel. She thought she could be there in two hours.

When Catherine hung up the phone, she picked up Emma and hailed a carriage. She was at the train station and the train to Beaumont was just about to leave. She was panting when she got on the train and found a seat by a window. Emma needed a change and Catherine thought she might be getting hungry. After she changed her, she made her way to the dining car and found a table. She ordered a glass of milk and a cheese sandwich. Emma ate all of it and finished off the milk. Catherine was just having hot tea and had planned to eat Emma’s leftovers, but there were none. She really wasn’t that hungry anyway, she thought.

Emma fell asleep after they returned to their seats. Catherine stared out the window and wondered why things were always changing. She was not sure why, at this time, Isabella would come into her life. But she was Emma’s sister and the thought of her going to an orphanage made her shudder. She thought of Samuel and had to remind herself that he wasn’t the right man for her and she was glad they had not gotten married. Young, attractive, and well educated doctors did not marry women like Catherine. She was damaged property and she had to stop thinking that her life might be anything like normal. She had to be brave for her children. She looked at Emma sleeping and wondered what Isabella would be like. She was excited. Two boys and two girls close to the same age meant that they would have each other and she was pleased about that. Catherine had been close to her own sister even though there was several years' difference between their ages. Emma and Isabella were probably less than a month apart.

They were in Beaumont an hour later. Clarence was waiting at the train station with Isabella. "I'm glad you were close by. I don't know what I would have done with her if I had to keep her overnight," Clarence said.

Emma and Isabella were both standing and looking at each other. Isabella was wearing a prairie dress that was a bit too large for her and she had on a pair of moccasins. Emma was carrying one of her favorite dolls and she handed it to Isabella. The girls took an instant liking to each other. Clarence picked up Isabella and Catherine picked up Emma, and they made their way to the hotel.

"Is Emma Isabella's half-sister?" Clarence asked.

"Yes, and thank you for calling me. I'm not sure Alex will acknowledge her, and if he doesn't, then she can live with us," Catherine said.

"You are an amazing woman," Clarence said. "Do you have any idea where Alex is?" he asked.

"I have a good idea," Catherine answered.

"Keep in touch with me," Clarence said and Catherine promised she would.

After they checked into the room, Catherine went into the bathroom and turned on the bath water. Isabella's hair was matted and dirty and looked like she had not had a bath in several days. When the tub was half full she undressed both girls and put them in the bath tub. Isabella was quiet, but seemed pleasant enough. At least she wasn't crying. She wondered what happened to Mary. Clarence said that both Mary and Dr. Windsong were dead and she had no idea what could have happened to them. When Catherine pulled Isabella's hair out of her face she was amazed at how much the girls looked like each other. Isabella's skin was a few shades darker and her hair was jet black. Emma was fair with light brown hair. Both girls had a strong resemblance to Alex, and Catherine smiled.

She ordered food to be sent in to the room that night, and all three ate well. Catherine wanted to catch the 8:00 train out in the morning so they all went to bed early. The next morning Catherine dressed Isabella in one of Emma's dresses and Isabella put her arms around Catherine's neck and hugged her. Catherine was overwhelmed, and hugged her back. She looked at Emma and then Isabella and said, "Sisters," and she smiled. Both girls smiled.

While they were on the train, the girls communicated in their own language and held hands most of the trip. Catherine busied herself making a list of the items she needed to buy when she got to Houston. Catherine checked in at the Roosevelt hotel for one night. Being Sunday, all the suppliers were closed and she planned to go first thing Monday morning to make her purchases for her medical business. She asked one of the bellmen if any of the shops were open on Sunday and he gave her a list of shops that opened for a few hours after lunch, and the addresses.

They ate an early lunch at a café across from a park and after they finished she walked to the park, where the girls played on swings and a seesaw. Catherine spent the next few hours shopping for clothes for the children. She also bought Emma and Isabella a doll. She let them pick out the one they wanted and Catherine was not surprised when Isabella picked up an Indian doll. She was about to pay for them when Emma pulled on her skirt and pointed to an Indian doll.

"Do you want one like Isabella's?" Catherine asked, and Emma shook her head yes and handed the other doll back to her. "I guess we will take two of this one," Catherine said to the clerk.

Catherine also felt an instant bond with Isabella. The girls had the same temperament. Both were easygoing and mild mannered. She was relieved. At first she worried that since Isabella had been taken from her home that she would be difficult and upset, but figured that having Emma with her made Isabella feel like she was wanted. She smiled to herself at how easy it was going to be to love Isabella. She had no idea what she would say to Alex. It was a complicated situation and she silently prayed that God would give her strength and wisdom to do what was right for Isabella.

Alex Cooper and Meredith had married five months earlier, and Alex continued to visit with Dr. Philip Seymour at Oakwood once a week. They had gone back to the hospital two months ago for another x-ray and visit with the surgeon, when he ran into Catherine at the Roosevelt Hotel.

Alex adored Meredith. She was compassionate and caring and most of all, patient, and she was easy to talk to. He was not surprised he had fallen in love with her. He liked her family and Michael and Alex became very good friends. Michael lived in the family's ranch house with his two children and a nanny and Alex and Meredith lived in a smaller house on the back two acres on the ranch. Alex made himself useful on the ranch, taking care of the horses and cattle and doing just about anything Michael asked him to do. Pilgrim had joined him and Alex liked the open air and space the ranch provided.

In his sessions with Dr. Seymour, he continued to remember bits and pieces of things in his past but it was like a jigsaw puzzle that had been thrown about on the table and it was difficult to put the pieces together. Dr. Seymour had suggested that since Alex seemed to be pleased with his new life, there was no reason to muddy the water with his past.

"The future is what is important right now," Dr. Seymour told him.

Alex understood that, but he was still haunted by dreams of Catherine and he knew they would not go away. He told Dr. Seymour he had recognized Catherine when he last saw her and he felt happy to see her, but Dr. Seymour didn't think it important. Still, Alex felt a nagging urge to be with Catherine. It was like she had a magic spell over him. He never mentioned it to Meredith because the last thing he wanted to do was hurt her. She was his life now, and she was three months pregnant.

Alex and Meredith frequently ate dinner at Michael's house. He had a full-time housekeeper and cook, and Michael liked the company of adults. He did love being with his children, but he and Meredith were close and he really liked Alex.

"I sold Uncle Phillip's house to a new doctor," Michael said at one of their dinners. Alex and Meredith listened as Michael told them about Dr. Catherine Merit. Alex tried not to act too interested, but asked if she had a husband that was coming with her. "I got the impression that she was a widow," Michael said. "I must say she is very smart, and has an incredible memory. I would say she has to be at least twenty-one, maybe twenty-two years old."

"Why do you think she picked Rosenberg?" Meredith asked and Alex wanted to know also.

"She saw the ad for a doctor in the Houston paper. I told her the town was looking for a male doctor because I didn't think the men would be willing to have a woman examine them. She said she didn't mind just looking after the women and children; if that was a problem for the men, they could go to Houston." They laughed.

"Seems to me, she might be well suited for the job," Meredith said.

Catherine couldn't help but be concerned about Martha on their way back to Galveston. It would have been too difficult to explain Isabella to her on the phone and she hoped Martha wouldn't want to quit since there was another child in the picture. She knew how difficult three children were under the age of three and now there were four. Both of the girls had fallen asleep. Emma was in the middle and Isabella was sitting on the other side of her and they were holding hands. She smiled at the fact that Emma had a sister now. The boys had each other to play with and now the girls would have each other. Catherine thought back to when she last saw Alex and when he neglected to ask her about her baby she decided Alex did not remember her telling him that the baby she was carrying was his. Catherine was also tired after spending their last day in Houston shopping and ordering medical supplies. The girls had been patient but were tired from the exhausting day, also. They were all asleep on the train when the conductor announced the Galveston stop.

Martha sat stone faced when Catherine got home and told her about Isabella. She wasn't surprised after Catherine told her the story that she agreed to take her in. Isabella and Emma were sisters and it would have been devastating for the girls not to grow up together. Martha had a sister and she knew the bond she had with her sister was irreplaceable. After a few days, Martha couldn't help but fall in love with Isabella, too. Both girls were a joy, but the boys were another story. Adam was selfish and was always creating confrontations with Daniel and sometimes, the girls. Daniel was easygoing and always gave in to Adam. He loved his little brother. Four was a handful, but Catherine patiently managed to keep peace most of the time.

The real estate agent brought several prospective buyers through Catherine's house after she placed it on the market and the third family made Catherine a reasonable offer which she accepted. They also agreed to buy some of Catherine's furniture that she felt she didn't need since the other house was furnished. She had spoken with Michael Atwood several times and it seemed the repairs and improvements were coming along nicely. Catherine had scheduled a mover to load up the things she was sending to Rosenberg and if everything went according to schedule, they would be in their new home by Adam's second birthday on July second.

Several days before their move, Catherine stopped to visit with Father Jonathan and told him of her upcoming move.

"That's a very brave move, not knowing anyone there," he said. "But I understand why you want to leave here. You will do well wherever you move, Catherine. I know you have not had a happy life here and I pray that God will watch over you and bless you and your children." Catherine also told him about Isabella and he said that it must have been God's will. Catherine gave him her new address and said she would stay in contact with him.

Catherine wanted to visit the cemetery before her departure so she rented a carriage and driver for the day. She had picked up four wreaths from the florist and asked the carriage driver to wait thirty minutes while she visited her family at the cemetery. The headstones had all been set; Minnie Wyman, John and Amelia Merit, and Anne Eastman. Minnie's grave was only a few feet away from her families, and Catherine put a wreath on Minnie's first. She placed a wreath that had the word "Beloved" on each of the other graves. It took her back to the little cemetery in Sandgate where the rest of her family was buried, and she could still picture the last image she had of it when her mother placed flowers on the graves before they left on their journey here. I miss you all, she said silently, and she felt the tears sting her cheeks. She knew she would be back at some point, but this was the hardest part of leaving Galveston; the memories of the ones she loved most and who also loved her. She silently said the Twenty-third Psalm and then looked over towards the tree that she had imagined John standing by. She wiped the tears from her face with her handkerchief. She had to cherish the memories and keep them alive in her heart. It was the only thing that had gotten her through these past few years. These four people had now been replaced with her four beautiful children and she knew they would give her new memories. Daniel had Catherine's mother's sweet smile and John's disposition. Adam had Catherine's father's strong will, Emma had Catherine's sister's sweet disposition, and Isabella had Alex's compassion and good looks. They would all be a reminder of who she was and the people who loved her, and she took comfort in the fact that God had blessed her.

The day before the move, Catherine picked up several mail-order catalogs from some local suppliers and medicine from the pharmacist that she would need in her work. She stopped at the post office and asked that they forward her mail to her new address, then stopped at William Monroe's office to get a copy of some of the papers he kept. Her last stop was the bank and she gave them instructions where to wire the funds in her account. Catherine opened her safe-deposit box and removed all the treasured items that had survived the flood. It was done, now. She had taken care of everything, except the fact that her past would still follow her and she prayed that Carla and Clay would never find her or her children.

Catherine carefully watched as the movers took the right pieces of furniture, trunks and boxes. After she took a quick walk through, Catherine joined Martha and the children in a carriage that would take them to the train station. The movers were to unload the next day in Rosenberg after lunch.

Michael had offered to meet Catherine and her family at the train station at 4:00 p.m. that afternoon and drive them to the house. Catherine wondered on her trip what she should tell Michael about Isabella. She hated lying. She had only told him that she had three children and it was impossible to hide the fact that Emma and Isabella were sisters. She decided that she would just introduce Isabella as a cousin to Emma and say no more. She had no plans to get involved with any men, and besides, Michael was already married and she planned to keep the relationship with him on a business level.

Michael was waiting as they got off the train and Catherine made the introductions. He did look at Isabella curiously, but said nothing. When they approached the house Catherine was overwhelmed. All of the vines and overgrowth that had taken over the front yard were gone and it was neatly manicured. The exterior had been totally painted a dark grey and the shutters painted white as she had asked.

The interior was equally as nice. It looked brand new. The floors had been redone and the old wallpaper had been replaced with a similar design.

"You have done a remarkable job on the improvements and I can't thank you enough," Catherine said. "You've managed to take care of every detail including new sheets on the bed. It's amazing."

Michael was proud of the job his men had done, and stood back as the children ran from room to room screaming.

"Sorry, they've been on their best behavior all day, and they are excited," Catherine said.

"I've got two of my own and I understand what you mean," he said.

Michael brought the luggage in and Catherine thanked him. "I'll come by your office tomorrow and settle up with you on the money," she said.

After Michael left, she showed Martha and the children the rest of the property. When they went into the back yard she saw three tree swings and a seesaw that wasn't there before. She assumed Michael had done that as a courtesy, and she had to remember to thank him. The children were getting hungry and they set out to walk to the café. It was hot and she hadn't thought about transportation until now. She apologized to Martha for the long walk. The waitress had to put two tables together for them, and Catherine asked her to bring water to the table as soon as possible. They ordered and the waitress brought some rolls for the children to eat while they waited. There was a bell that rang every time someone came in the door and Catherine happened to look up when she heard it ring. It was Alex and Meredith. Catherine looked away and began talking to Martha and didn't look up until Meredith stopped and introduced herself and Alex. Catherine introduced Martha and the children and said it was nice to meet them. She knew Alex recognized her and she could not help but notice Alex looking at Emma and Isabella. She felt like she had been caught, and it was an awkward moment for her.

Michael had come through the door and stopped at her table to say hello again. Catherine thanked him for the swings and seesaw and said the children couldn't wait to play on them.

"I need to put up another one for Isabella," he said, smiling as he walked over and joined Alex and Meredith.

Catherine looked up once and noticed Alex's back was to her and she was relieved. She would have died if she had to see his face again. She had no idea what she would say to him when he finally confronted her with her decision to move here. Maybe he would just let it go and pretend they had no knowledge of each other's pasts. A few minutes later, Meredith walked over to the table and asked Catherine when she would be open to see patients.

"I will have regular hours starting the first of the week," Catherine answered.

"Good, I'd like to be your first patient. I'm not really showing yet, but I think I'm about three months along," Meredith said.

"Uhh, that would be wonderful. How about 9:00 a.m.?" Catherine said.

"That will be perfect," Meredith said and walked back to her table.

Michael and Alex stood up when Meredith sat back down. Catherine noticed Alex look at her when he got up and she wanted to run. It had not crossed her mind that she might be the one to deliver Alex's third child. Several other people came over and introduced themselves and welcomed them. Catherine was glad when the children had finished and they could leave. She hardly touched her food and the waitress put it in a bag for her to take home.

When they walked back home, there were two people standing on the porch. A Negro man introduced himself as Lucas Miller and his wife's name was Celli. He was inquiring if there might be work for them. He said his wife was also a midwife and that he could cook and take care of the property. He said that they had two grown children who did not live with them

"Mr. Michael Atwood knows us very well, and would be a reference if you need one," Lucas said.

Martha took Catherine's children around the back to play, and

Catherine invited Lucas and Celli into the house.

"The property is quiet large, as you can see, and it would be a full-time job for whoever accepted the position," Catherine said. "I will also be getting a horse and wagon for transportation and that would be part of the job. I need some help with the laundry and I plan to hire someone to do that exclusively and I hope to find someone soon."

Catherine addressed the remainder of the questions to Celli. Celli's mother had been a midwife and taught Celli the little bit of medicine that she knew and she said she was eager to learn.

"I will also need someone to help out with the children from time to time," Catherine said and Celli said that was fine. They addressed wages, and Lucas said that if they could live in the carriage house and if she paid for their food, they would only need $3.00 a week. Catherine said that they would try it for three months and if it did not work out, they would have to leave. She also told him that she wanted to talk to Mr. Atwood the next day and if their reputations were as they said, they could move in after lunch.

Catherine showed them through the house and told Lucas that all the cooking would be done in the larger kitchen at the back of the house because the small inner kitchen would be used as her laboratory and she needed the access to the water. She showed them the carriage house, which was very modest. There were two bedrooms and a small water closet with a sink. The furnishings were modest, too, but the Millers assured her it was sufficient.

Everything was falling into place for Catherine. If the Millers were as good as she thought it would be a godsend to have the extra help. She just hoped that business would be good enough to feed two families and four children.

After Catherine and Martha put the children to bed, Catherine walked through the house again. She loved the old house and couldn't have been happier with her decision except for the fact that Alex lived in the same town. It was not what she had planned. She still thought about him a lot and she had hoped that moving to a new town would help her to forget. Now he is living several miles from her and his wife was expecting his baby. What had she gotten herself into she wondered. She was still in love with him, she finally admitted to herself. What a mess. It seemed she went from one hardship to another. The only difference was that Carla and Clay were vindictive and Alex wasn't. He was still a gentleman and he would always be one, she reminded herself.

Catherine had walked into town early the next morning intending to buy some groceries, but the only thing open was the café, so she ordered food to go and took it home and left it on the counter. They had sold her a box of cereal and two pints of milk and she also selected a coffee cake. She would get groceries later.

Catherine was at Michael Atwood's office at 8:30 a.m. and she walked up and down the porch until she saw him drive up in his automobile. She had not seen any other automobiles and wondered how much they cost. It was most likely far out of her reach, she thought.

"Good morning, Dr. Merit," Michael said. "I hope you haven't been waiting long."

"Not at all," she answered and smiled at him. "The Millers came by the house last night and they appear to be just what I need in the way of help," she said. "Do you know very much about them?"

"Lucas's father worked at the house for my uncle, and Lucas actually grew up in the apartment above the carriage house. He's a hard worker and he knows what he needs to do without being told. Celli, his wife, also grew up in this town, and her mother had been the town's midwife until she died last year. Celli picked up where she left off. You couldn't find better Christian people," Michael said. "Lucas has worked for my company for the past five years."

"You mean you would be willing to give him up?" Catherine asked.

"The old shack they live in is in need of a lot of repair and it's only one bedroom. The carriage house would be a step up for them. Now that you are the new doctor in town, Celli's services won't be needed. I'm doing it for them, too," he said.

"That's very generous of you and I greatly appreciate it," Catherine said. Catherine took out her check book and asked Michael how much she needed to write her check for and he gave her the amount.

"I've collected some parcels, and they are in the back room. Would you like me to have Lucas take them to your house? They've been anxiously waiting to hear from you," Michael said.

"Yes," Catherine smiled and said. "My movers will be here this afternoon and I could use their help. There is one more thing," she said. "I noticed that the telephone line stops at the end of town and I think it important to have a telephone. What do I need to do to get it extended to my house?" she asked.

"I'll bring it up at the next city council meeting," he replied.

Catherine thanked him and left. As she walked out the door, Eric Reynolds was coming up the steps. He stopped and introduced himself to Catherine and apologized that he was not able to meet her when she came in to look at the property.

"I know Michael has taken good care of you," he said. Catherine told him she was very pleased with the property and thanked him for his help in finding it. Eric watched as she walked over to the bank. He was kicking himself for not taking her seriously enough to stay in town and help her himself. Eric was twenty-five and had been working in the family business for a couple of years. He was a cousin of Michael's, and not married. He considered himself a ladies' man and went to Houston often to find girls and have a good time. Maybe he might be spending more time here, he thought. She was gorgeous.

Michael watched Catherine out his window as she walked across the street and he couldn't help but be smitten with her. His wife had been at the sanatorium for over eight months and he knew he was partly to blame. Michael had several mistresses and Helen had found out about one of them. With Helen at the sanatorium, Michael enjoyed his new found freedom and divided his leftover time between two widows. Michael found it hard to concentrate on his work so he decided to take Catherine's check to the bank and deposit it. He saw her sitting in the bank president's office when he went in. He smiled at her when their eyes made contact. He saw Catherine go into the safe-deposit area and wondered if he might be able to prolong his visit there. He walked over and spoke to the bank president. It seemed Dr. Catherine Merit was at the top of everyone's list to talk about.

The bank president was no different. He smiled at Michael and said Dr. Merit was a real catch for some young man. Michael was on the board of directors of the bank and the president pointed to a deposit slip Catherine had filled out. Michael was impressed, but didn't say anything. He turned to leave as Catherine came out and he asked if she needed a ride anywhere.

"What I really need is transportation," she said. "Do you know where I could buy a horse and a buggy?"

"I'll be happy to drive to the livery stable and see if they have something that could work for you," Michael said.

He helped her into his automobile and they drove to the livery stables a quarter of a mile away. There was an older buggy, but Catherine preferred something with a cover and the man showed her a picture of one he could order from Houston and have for her the next day. It was more like a carriage but it could carry six adults comfortably and the cover could be pulled back. Catherine paid for it and Michael said that he had a horse and tack that he would sell her for a reasonable price and would get it hitched up for her and delivered the next day. Michael didn't tell Catherine, but his family also owned the livery stable.

Catherine asked him to drop her off at the grocery store and she quickly picked out groceries so she could get home in time to meet her movers. When she set out walking with her arms full, Eric ran out the door and offered to carry the groceries for her. Michael watched and figured it wouldn't take Eric long to get his heart broken. Michael didn't think Eric would be her type, and he smiled when he thought about Catherine turning him down for a date. Yes, he thought, she will probably break a lot of hearts.

Lucas and Celli were already at the house, and Lucas had opened all the parcels he had brought from Michael's office and set them on the counter, waiting for Catherine to tell him where she wanted things put. When Lucas saw Catherine and Eric walking with groceries, he quickly went out to help. Catherine thanked Eric and Eric asked her if she would like to have dinner with him sometime.

"I have a lot of things I have to do, and I'm afraid there won't be much time for fun, but thank you anyway," she said.

Michael saw Eric come back with a long face and knew instantly that Eric had asked her out and she told him no.

"I wouldn't get my hopes up, if I were you," Michael said to Eric. "She's a beauty, but she has a fierce bite and she'll break your heart."

Michael knew he was saying the same thing to himself. He figured something happened in her past that made her resilient and untrusting. He decided he might do some checking on her background. He knew a few prominent people in Galveston, and he was curious.

CHAPTER 22

Catherine, along with Lucas and Celli, worked over the entire weekend setting everything up in the small clinic Catherine prepared in the downstairs front of the house. The dining room was going to be the waiting room. She had a small office in between two examination rooms, a lab, and she saved the large room at the back for a playroom and learning room for the children. She moved the large kitchen table into the middle of that room so they could eat their meals there and then the children would use it for their projects. There was one more small room which she closed off. She would eventually add a bed in it in the event someone had to stay overnight. When she finished, she had time left over to spend with the children. Lucas and Catherine prepared a grocery list and on Monday, Lucas would do the grocery shopping. Celli helped with the children and Martha was thankful for the help. Celli had a friend who came daily to do laundry, which would be a full-time job once the clinic opened.

Catherine was up early the next morning and was surprised that there were several townspeople outside waiting to see her. Alex and Meredith were also waiting. I can do this, Catherine said to herself as she opened the front door and showed people into the waiting room. She was pleased that Celli could read and write so she could take the patients' names down in the order they came in. Meredith had made an appointment so Catherine asked her to come in first. Alex stood up as she greeted them and Catherine explained that she would ask him to come into her office after she visited with Meredith.

She asked Meredith a number of questions before she completed the examination. After Catherine finished with the pelvic examination, she took the stethoscope and listened to the baby's heartbeat. She smiled and then let Meredith listen. The two smiled at each other.

"Do you think your husband would like to hear it?" she asked. Meredith said yes. Catherine called Alex in and showed him how to put the stethoscope in his ears and listen to the baby's heartbeat. He had a gleam in his eyes and he squeezed Meredith's hand and reached down and kissed her. He handed Catherine the stethoscope back and thanked her.

"You seem to be in good health and you might want to come back in the next two or three months so we can monitor the baby's progress," Catherine said. She felt overwhelmed and excused herself and left the room.

Catherine walked over to the small window in her office and looked outside at the trees. She had not had that experience with Alex when she was pregnant with Emma, and she felt betrayed. She couldn't help but notice the way Alex looked at Meredith. He used to look at her that way and it hurt. Celli knocked on the door and asked if it were all right if Mrs. Cooper got dressed now.

"Yes, I'll be out in a minute," Catherine said.

The fees had been posted on the wall, and when Catherine came back out into the waiting room, Alex handed her a dollar for the visit. She thanked them both and called the next patient. A young woman had a twelve-year-old boy who had a bad cut on his leg and Catherine cleaned the wound and sewed it up using twelve stitches. The mother said they had no money, but they grew vegetables and she gave a bag filled with potatoes, cabbage, and squash to Catherine as payment. Catherine wrote a paid-in-full receipt and handed it to her. There was nothing difficult about the rest of the patients who came through the clinic that day; a baby with colic, several bloody noses, another pregnancy and few more cuts. The waiting room was finally empty and all in all, Catherine earned three dollars and fifty cents that day, an assortment of fruits and vegetables, a chicken, and a peach pie. She was hoping to close early, but three men came in before she put the closed sign in the window and said they were from the paper mill.

She called the first man in and after asking a few questions, she realized that the men were trying to get the better of her. The first one told her that his pecker was enlarged and he wanted her to look at it. Catherine called Celli into the room and told the man he had to take his pants off and let Celli shave him so she could get a better look. His mouth dropped open and he said that he didn't think it was that bad and he left. When Catherine went out to call the next man in the waiting room, it was empty. She and Celli laughed and hugged each other.

"Good work, Celli," Catherine said. Celli turned the open sign to closed, and they locked the door.

Catherine went back to check on the children and found Isabella crying.

"Adam pulled the arm off of her doll," Martha told her.

Adam gave his mother a defiant look. It was one she had seen before from his father. Catherine knew Adam was going to be a challenge so she took his little hand and she made him sit on the steps on the back porch. She told him to stay there and she went back and consoled Isabella and said that the two of them would sew it back together after supper. Catherine went back to Adam and took his hand. He was two years old and still was not talking much, but Catherine knew he understood, so she asked Adam if he knew why he broke Isabella's doll. He shook his head no. She asked him if he was sorry he broke the doll and he shrugged his shoulders.

"Would you please go and give Isabella a hug?" Catherine asked him. He got up and ran back in the house and hugged Isabella and kissed her on the cheek. My little Adam, she thought, you are going to use up all my energy.

The next day, the gossip had spread all through town about the three men from the paper mill who tried to play a joke on the new lady doctor and how it had backfired in their faces. Michael chuckled when he heard, and it didn't surprise him that Catherine didn't fall for it. Her mystique only made Michael more interested in who she really was. She seemed too perfect.

Michael, Alex and Meredith had dinner together again that night and they all laughed when they heard about the joke. "Good for her," Meredith said. "That was not a proper way to introduce her to our town."

"I'm thinking about checking with some friends of mine in Galveston about her past. When I first talked to her, she said she only had three children and now she has four. Isabella looks like a half-breed, but Catherine said she was Emma's cousin. It doesn't make sense," Michael said.

"Her medical degree is framed on her wall and there is another award that says she graduated in the top fifteen percent of her class, what more do you need?" Meredith asked.

"Just curious," he answered.

Alex thought for a moment and said, "What difference does it make what her past is? If she is qualified to do the job, leave her be. Everyone seems to like her and I would hate to run her off."

"I'm not suggesting that we run her off. I was just curious," Michael said.

"Why don't we stop by on our way home tonight and invite her to come to dinner tomorrow night?" Meredith said.

They finished eating and Alex and Michael waited in the automobile while Meredith went up to the door and rang the bell. A few minutes later, Catherine answered the door. Meredith would not take no for an answer and finally Catherine said yes.

"Good, I'll have Alex pick you up at 6:00 p.m. tomorrow evening."

Catherine could hardly sleep that evening, knowing that Alex would be picking her up and she would be alone with him for the first time. She wished she had just moved to Houston and taken her chances there. That would be her backup plan if things backfired on her. She loved it here in Rosenberg. She felt safe and the people were really nice to her. She prayed that Alex would not be mad at her.

Catherine saw her last patient at 4:00 p.m. and after spending time with the children, she took a quick bath and put on one of her prettier dresses. She had left part of her hair hanging over her shoulders and put half of it on top of her head. She secured it with the ivory barrette Samuel had given her. She smiled when she thought of Samuel and their intimate times together. Her mind quickly went back to Alex and knots began forming in her stomach. She heard the doorbell at 6:00 p.m. and quickly kissed the children good-bye.

Alex was dressed in a suit and he looked extraordinarily handsome. He helped her into the automobile and they drove off. Before they got to the ranch, Alex pulled off the road and drove down a trail and parked behind some trees. He turned to Catherine.

"Why here, Catherine?" he asked. "The last time I saw you, you were with your fiancé and I assumed you were married by now."

Catherine didn't look at him. "He cheated on me and I broke off the engagement. I saw the ad that the city of Rosenberg had placed in the Houston paper, and I checked into it. After I signed the papers on the house and wrote the check, Michael told me about his sister and the man she was married to, and it was you. It was too late to back out. I'm sorry, Alex. No one has to know," she said.

"Michael seems to be infatuated with you and has decided he wants to find out more about your past," Alex said staring away.

"Is that why I'm here tonight?" she asked.

"That was Meredith's idea. She really likes you," Alex said.

"Even if he finds out about my past, there was no one except the attorney who even knew about you. They won't find out we were married," she said.

"What about Beaumont?" Alex asked.

"You remember that?" she asked.

"Just bits and pieces," Alex said. "And where did Isabella come from?"

"I think I need to tell you about her another time. Aren't we going to be late?" Catherine asked.

Alex started the car and asked, "Do you mind if I tell them you weren't ready when I picked you up?"

"No, that's fine," she said.

They rode the rest of the way in silence.

Alex slowed the automobile down as they made their turn through two large wrought-iron gates that had the name Atwood cut into the iron. It was impressive and Catherine wondered why a man like Michael felt it necessary to investigate her past. Was God punishing her again? she wondered. She had prayed and asked God to forgive her every day of her life. Was there no end to her anguish? For now, she just wanted the night to be over.

When they arrived, Catherine apologized for not being ready when Alex arrived. "We're just happy you could come at all," Michael said. "And by the way, you look stunning."

Catherine thanked him and accepted a glass of wine Meredith handed to her. "Let's toast to Rosenberg's new doctor," Michael said, and raised his glass.

"You have a beautiful home and it's my privilege to be here," Catherine answered.

The dinner was served in an elegant fashion. A Negro servant with gloves served soup first and then the main meal which was stuffed pheasant, red potatoes, and peas. The salad was served last and Catherine wondered if Michael was trying to impress her or just find out if her English upbringing was for real. Michael suggested they have dessert and after-dinner liquor in the living room. He helped pull out Catherine's chair and she rose and followed him into another room. So far, there were no pertinent questions asked about her past. She did say that she had gone to a boarding school in England, but did not comment further about her family history. The evening was almost over and Catherine announced that she really needed to get home and check on her children. Michael offered to drive her home and Catherine was relieved that she would not have to justify her motives again to Alex for moving to Rosenberg. Michael apologized to Catherine that he had seemed reluctant to accept her abilities when he first met her.

"You are just so different from any of the other women I have met. I mean that in a good way," he said. "I really respect you for leaving your home and moving to a new town not knowing anyone," he said.

Catherine thanked him and said that her strength had come from her mother and God. "I was lucky to have a strong, loving mother and I could only hope to be like her," she said.

When they got to Catherine' house, Michael asked her if she had any future plans other than opening the clinic. "My children are my future and their livelihood depends on me. That's all I can expect right now; raising healthy, intelligent, godly children."

That evening Catherine found it even more difficult to fall asleep and stay asleep. The dreams had begun to creep into her sleep again, and the worst one was always when David was raping her. She hated him for making her feel like she wasn't worthy of having a happy life. Tomorrow was Saturday and she hoped there would be no emergencies so she would not have to talk to anyone. The clinic was closed on Saturdays and Sundays except for emergencies. She did love her job and her children and she tried to tell herself that was enough.

Catherine had wanted to start going to the little church the pastor had invited her to, but it meant she would probably run into Michael or Alex and Meredith. She just decided she would stay home and tell the children stories out of the Bible. Out of sight and out of mind was probably better, anyway, she thought. The less she saw of

Michael and Alex, the better off she would be.

Several weeks had gone by, and Michael wondered why he hadn't seen Catherine going to the store or the bank. Lucas made frequent visits to the stores and the bank so he decided he would stop him one day and ask. It was a Friday afternoon just after lunch when Michael saw Lucas enter the bank. He walked over and casually waited for him to finish.

"Hello, Lucas," Michael said.

"Oh, Mr. Atwood, it's good to see you, sir," Lucas said.

"How do you like your new job working for Dr. Merit?" Michael asked.

"Dr. Merit is very good to us, sir. She is really nice to me and my family and I sure thank you for sending us to her," Lucas said.

"I'm curious," Michael said, "I never see her anymore. She used to go to the café and the bank."

"She always sends me, sir. She says she prefers staying home. It's good to see you, I gots to go," Lucas said.

When Michael got back to his office there were several letters on the floor that had been put through the mail slot in his door. He picked them up and one in particular caught his eye. It was from one of his banking friends in Galveston.

Michael tore it open and read it. The letter said that Catherine Merit had been married to a friend of his by the name of John Merit when she was sixteen. He said that Catherine had been living in an orphanage and John Merit married her so she would not have to stay in the orphanage. He went on to say that after they had been married a year, she disappeared and that John Merit had her declared dead when another year passed, and he married a Galveston socialite. He had heard that she came back to Galveston after being gone two years, and then went to medical school and that was about all he could tell him except that John Merit had died of natural causes a year or so ago.

Michael shook his head and wondered where her four children had come from. It was a mystery and he really wanted to solve it.

The next time Michael invited Alex and Meredith to his house for dinner, he told them about the letter. Alex felt Michael was crossing the line and told him so.

"What difference does it make what her past is? Maybe the children were orphans and she took them in. The townspeople seem to like her and she minds her own business," Alex said.

"Sorry if you think I'm crossing the line, Alex. I'm just curious, that's all," Michael said.

Meredith sensed there was tension and she changed the subject. She had never seen Alex so defensive about anything before. Maybe her brother was going too far, but it wasn't up to Alex to challenge him.

After dinner they went into the living room and Michael went to get after-dinner drinks. Meredith said something to Alex and it hit him the wrong way. He didn't answer, and told her he was going to take a walk. The words in the letter seemed to hit a nerve with him. He remembered Catherine telling him that she had been abducted and held captive for two years and that she had borne two sons. He thought hard, trying to remember Emma and he remembered that Catherine was pregnant when she came to see him in the sanatorium. Oh God, he thought, Emma is my child. Alex started sweating and wondered if he should tell Meredith the truth. He wondered what Michael would say. Would he try to run Catherine out of town? His head began to hurt and he felt light-headed. Meredith came outside and saw Alex leaning up against the tree with his hand on his head.

"Alex!" she screamed. "What is it? Michael, Michael," she screamed.

Michael came out and helped Alex get back in the house and into the guest bedroom.

"Go get Dr. Merit," Meredith said.

Michael left and drove his automobile faster than he had ever driven it before. Catherine was reading the children a bedtime story when she heard a hard pounding on the door. She knew it must be an emergency and told Martha she might have to leave. When Catherine opened the door and saw Michael's face she asked, "Is it Meredith?"

"No, Alex has taken ill," he said.

Catherine ran to her lab and picked up several things and put them in her medical bag. When she came back she said, "I'm ready."

Catherine asked Michael what had happened and he told her he wasn't sure. Alex had gone for a walk and they found him outside holding his head and he was delusional. Michael went on to tell Catherine that Alex had a bullet fragment in his head from a gunshot wound and that had caused memory loss. Catherine didn't comment.

"Did Alex have any alcoholic drinks?" she asked.

"Yes, we had a couple of scotches," Michael said.

When they got to the house, Michael took Catherine back to the guest bedroom. She took out her stethoscope and checked Alex's heart. He was unconscious, but he had a strong heartbeat. Catherine checked his temperature and it was 104 degrees.

"We need to get his temperature down. Help me get his clothes off," she said. Michael began taking Alex's clothes off. "Just his shirt and pants," Catherine said. "And I need a pail of ice water and some towels." Meredith brought them back to her and stood back. Catherine put a towel in the ice water and then squeezed it out, placing it over Alex's body. She took a small towel and squeezed it out and began wiping Alex's head. She checked his heartbeat again and put some smelling salts under Alex's nose. He began coming to and pushed Catherine's hand away.

"What happened?" he asked. "You had a heat stroke. This is probably one of the hottest days of the year. Do you mind if I look at your head?" she asked.

Alex lay still while Catherine examined his old wound. She tried to remember the x-ray and estimated that the fragment was about an inch and a half over his right ear.

"Are you hurting anywhere?" she asked.

"Just a bad headache," he said.

"Do you get them a lot?" she asked.

"More than I care to have," he said.

Catherine took his temperature again and it had come back down to 101 degrees. She took the towel off his chest and put it back into the cold water, squeezed it out again and laid it on his chest. He grimaced from the cold.

Catherine asked Meredith to bring some ice water so she could give Alex some pills. She held up his head as he swallowed two aspirin and drank the water. Catherine told Alex that he needed to lie still and he should plan on staying the night there. She left the room and Meredith and Michael followed her out.

"I'll stay for a while and make sure his temperature continues to come down before I leave," Catherine said.

"What do you think caused him to get sick?" Meredith asked.

"It could be a mixture of the alcohol and the heat. The brain is a complex organ and I suspect that the fragment is lying next to a main nerve in the cortex. Alcohol sometimes increases the flow of blood, and if he becomes tense the vessels might constrict, causing him to become light-headed. Was Alex upset about something?" Catherine asked.

Meredith and Michael looked at each other but didn't answer.

"Once Alex recovers from this, I suggest that you take him to the doctor who is treating him. He is seeing a specialist, isn't he?" Catherine asked.

"Yes," Meredith said. "Is he going to be all right?"

"I think once this passes he will be fine. Having his specialist see him is just a precaution to make sure that the fragment hasn't moved," Catherine said.

Catherine went back into Alex's room and he opened his eyes and smiled at her.

"You certainly had everyone scared," she said as she put the stethoscope to his heart and listened. She checked his temperature again and it was back to normal. She put everything back in her bag and told him to stay in bed. Catherine took the towels off of his body and asked him how he felt.

"Good as new," he said.

"Take it easy for a few days and let me know if your headache comes back," Catherine said. "I'll be at the clinic tomorrow, if you need me."

It was almost midnight when Michael took Catherine back to her house.

"Meredith and I can't thank you enough. Alex is everything to her," Michael said. When they got to the house Michael took out a twenty-dollar bill and handed it to Catherine.

"I don't have any change," she said. "You can pay me another time."

"I don't want any change," he said as he walked Catherine to the door.

They exchanged goodnights and Catherine went inside.

Michael was greatly impressed by Catherine and wondered what might have happened if she had not been there. He knew one thing. Her past was her business and it didn't matter if she had five kids out of wedlock, he wanted her to stay in Rosenberg.

CHAPTER 23

The next Sunday Catherine was trying to teach "Jesus Loves Me" to the children. The buzzer rang several times and Celli said she would get it. When she came back in, she said there was a Mr. Cooper who needed to see her. Catherine met Alex in the parlor and asked if he felt all right.

"I'm fine, Meredith and Michael went to Oakwood Sanatorium to see his wife, Helen, and they will be there for awhile. I wanted to talk to you, if you have time."

Catherine took Alex in her office and closed the door. She waited for him to speak first.

"I remembered you were pregnant when you came to see me at the sanatorium and I guess I forgot about it until Michael brought it up. Is Emma my daughter?" he asked.

"Yes, she is, but that is not why I moved here," Catherine said.

"Where did Isabella come from?" Alex asked.

Catherine was silent and Alex stared at her. "Do you remember when you first had your accident and they took you to an Indian reservation?" she asked.

Alex thought and concentrated on her question, and finally said, "Mary, Mary Windsong, she was pregnant, wasn't she? What happened to her?"

Catherine told him about Clarence calling her because he didn't know where Alex was. "She was Emma's sister and I didn't want her to go to an orphanage, so I went to Beaumont, picked her up, and took her back to Galveston with me. She and Emma are very close and I hope you won't take her away from us."

"I have two daughters and didn't even know it. How crazy is that?" Alex looked at Catherine and could see she was worried. "No, no, I think it best if Isabella stays with you."

"She calls me mommy," Catherine said, "and I love her."

"I've really messed up your life, haven't I?" Alex said.

"It's not your fault and I don't blame you. I left Galveston because too many people knew that Adam and Emma were not my first husband's children, but had his last name. They made it difficult for me. I was working at St. Mary's Hospital and they wrote a letter challenging my reputation and they terminated me. My house was egged numerous times and I felt I had to make a new life for me and my children somewhere else. Call it coincidence or fate, but I ended up here," she said. "I've spent a lot of the money I made off the sale of the farm in Beaumont to fix up this place and turn it into a clinic. I really don't want to leave, but I will, if you want me too."

Catherine was trying not to cry when Alex came around the desk and took her hand and pulled her up facing him.

"I know now why I fell in love with you. We'll just keep it our little secret," Alex said. He wanted to kiss her, but kissed her hand instead. "Would you mind if I stop sometimes and see the children?" he asked.

Catherine smiled and said he could. Alex said he had one more thing to ask her and Catherine listened as she watched him sit back down. She sat in her chair and listened. "Should I have the operation to remove the fragment?" he asked.

"When you left Galveston and ended up at the sanatorium, I had decided to go back to medical school. I began reading all the books in the library about head injury and functions of the brain. My thesis my senior year was on head trauma. No, absolutely not. Your chances of dying are too great. I don't know what your doctor in Houston is telling you, but you could end up deaf, blind, or have total memory loss again. The danger is too great," Catherine said.

"What about these headaches?" he asked.

"I think I can help you with that. You should limit your alcohol intake to one or two drinks, the fewer the better. I'll give you some herbs that you can make into a tonic that you should drink every day and that will also help with the headaches," she said, and continued, "You should try not to get overheated, also."

Alex thanked her and got up to leave and said, "By the way, Michael said he wasn't going to pursue your past anymore. He really likes you a lot."

It was awkward when Alex got up to leave. Catherine walked around the desk and he waited for her to go ahead of him and he grabbed her hand.

"Thank you, Catherine, I hope you'll be happy here and if the children need anything, would you let me know?" he asked.

Catherine said yes and handed him a large packet of herbs.

"Put a tablespoon of these herbs in some orange juice each day and drink it. It should help with your headaches."

She watched Alex leave and found it hard not to put her arms around him. When Alex had told her before they were married that he wanted to spend the rest of his life with her, she never dreamed it would be in separate houses. She watched him through the window until he and Pilgrim disappeared. Her body was aching with love for him, and he would never know.

Michael and Meredith's visit with Helen did not go well. Helen was belligerent and shouted obscenities at him. Meredith could usually calm her down, but today was not a good day. Helen had wanted Michael to bring the children, but when Michael had spoken with Dr. Seymour the day before, he told him Helen's obstinate behavior had escalated and that it might scare the children. They finally had to medicate Helen and she went back to her room. Meredith could see tears in Michael's eyes and she felt compassion for him. They both knew Helen would never leave the sanatorium and Meredith knew her brother longed for companionship and love. He would never divorce her, which meant he would be growing old alone. He loved his children, but someday they would be grown and then he would have no one. Meredith hugged him when they got in the car and she smiled at him.

"I'm not going anywhere. Alex and I will always be there for you," she said.

Several weeks had passed, and one morning when Catherine woke up she looked out her upstairs window and saw several men working outside her house in the street. She dressed quickly and went downstairs. Michael was standing in the street talking to one of the other men when Catherine approached them.

"Dr. Merit, I hope we didn't wake you up. The city council has agreed to extend the telephone line and you should be able to get a telephone by the end of the day tomorrow," Michael said.

Catherine gave him a big smile and thanked him. "That is worth getting out of bed early," she laughed.

Michael loved to hear her laugh. She looked fresh and beautiful and he tried not to stare at her. Catherine stood back as several men unloaded the long pole off a mule-driven wagon. It was amazing as she watched them put the pole in the ground and then used the mule to pull the pole up. It was fascinating, she thought.

"I'm going to have some hot tea and I think Lucas already has the coffee on, if you would like to join me," Catherine said to Michael.

"That would be nice," Michael said and he followed Catherine inside to the kitchen in the back of the house. "You've really transformed this old place and it looks wonderful," Michael said.

Lucas was in the kitchen and already had the tea pot heated. "I'll bring you a tray shortly, Dr. Merit, and coffee for you, Mr. Atwood," Lucas said.

"I'm afraid we don't have a formal dining room and we use

this room for everything," Catherine apologized as they walked into the room she used for their meals and a place for the children to play. Lucas brought in the tea and coffee and some muffins he had made earlier. "Thank you Lucas," Catherine said. "Celli and Lucas have been wonderful and I can't tell you how much I appreciate having them. You really should come over some evening with your children now that the weather has cooled down. They can play outside together. Lucas made the children a sandbox and I must warn you that they will get dirty," she laughed again.

Michael was totally infatuated with Catherine and said they were free Saturday afternoon. "Why don't I bring a picnic for everybody," he said.

"That would be great," Catherine replied. "Why don't you ask Meredith and Alex to come? How does 4:00 p.m. sound?"

"Sounds great, and I'll be looking forward to it. I guess I need to check and see how the men are doing with your telephone pole," he said, as he smiled at her and left.

After Michael was gone she wondered if she had made the right decision by asking that Meredith and Alex come. It would be a way for Alex to get to know the girls, she thought, and dismissed her worry about it not being a good idea.

CHAPTER 24

Over the next few days Catherine had Lucas prepare the back yard for the picnic. Lucas had taken an old door, made a table out of it, and put it on the back porch. After lunch on Saturday, Catherine, Martha, and Lucas took some of the kitchen chairs outside. The children had a smaller table with two benches in their family room and Lucas took that out on the porch too. The weather was really nice and several of her flowering plants were blooming. She was ready, Catherine thought. It would be the first time she had entertained at her new house and she was excited about it. Before everyone arrived, Catherine decided to take Adam aside and talk to him about his manners. The two sat on the back porch and Catherine told him she needed his help taking care of the guest. She told him that another little boy and girl were coming over to play and she wanted them to feel welcome and that he should be especially nice and play with them. Adam shook his head yes, kissed his mother, and went back to the sandbox.

Before her guests came there was an emergency and Catherine had to quickly set a broken arm. A twelve-year-old boy had fallen out of a tree and his father brought him to the clinic at 2:00 p.m.

She had just finished up when Michael and his two children, Meredith and Alex rang the bell. Catherine had Lucas take the basket of food to the kitchen and Catherine showed them to the back yard.

"This is wonderful," Meredith said as they walked out to the back porch. "This place never looked this nice when our uncle lived here," she said. Michael introduced Nicolas and Heather to Catherine's children. Emma and Isabella looked at Heather, who was three, and they took her hand and walked her over to a doll house on the porch. Daniel and Nicolas went to the swings and Adam went back to the sandbox. Catherine decided to walk over and see what Adam's interest in the sandbox was. She stood and watched and noticed he was burying something. She bent down and said, "Show mommy what you are doing."

He took a stick and moved the dirt back. "Oh!" Catherine said. Something was moving and it had feathers. Apparently a baby bird had fallen from a tree and Adam was trying to bury it. "Sweetie, let's find another place to take him. I'm afraid if you bury it here, it will scare the girls."

"No," Adam screeched out.

Everyone was looking and Catherine smiled at them.

"I think over by the fence would make a better place to bury it." She said softly. "Let me get a bag to put it in. She motioned to Lucas to come to the sandbox. She asked him to get a paper bag and put the bird in it and help Adam bury it by the fence. She took Adam's face in her hands and said, "Mommy loves you, now you go with Lucas."

Catherine went back to her guests and apologized and told them what Adam had done. "Nicolas used to be that way. He wanted to bury everything," Michael said.

The rest of the day was uneventful. Michael had brought fried chicken, potato salad, sliced tomatoes, and rolls. Lucas had set out a cheese tray and fruit, and had also made a peach cobbler. Everyone ate well.

Catherine tried to teach the younger children how to play Ring around the Rosy and Michael and Alex could hardly take their eyes off of her. Meredith joined in when she saw Catherine getting all the attention. They laughed and played with the children and after awhile Alex and Michael joined in too. When the sun went down Catherine brought out some canning jars and lids and she showed the children how to catch lightning bugs. She could hardly remember when she had had so much fun.

Catherine had noticed that Heather did not seem to feel well. She picked her up and took her over to the porch and looked at her closely. She was wheezing and seemed to be short of breath.

Michael saw Catherine looking at her and came over. "Is Heather all right?" he asked.

"Have you noticed her wheezing before?" Catherine asked.

"She just started a few weeks ago. I thought she was getting a cold at first, but after awhile, she seemed to get better. What is it?" Michael seemed concerned.

"I'm concerned that she seems to be having trouble breathing, and I would like to take her inside and look at her," Catherine said.

Catherine asked Celli and Martha to take the children in for their baths. Alex offered to take Meredith and Nicolas home and come back for Michael.

After Catherine examined Heather, she told Michael that the girl had early signs of asthma and that if it went untreated it could be serious.

"My younger sister died from complications of asthma. I think we have caught it early and there are things today that were not available six years ago when my sister died. I am going to recommend you to a doctor at Houston General by the name of Dr. Samuel Allen. If it's all right, I would like to keep Heather here overnight so I can keep an eye on her. She needs to be under a tent with humidity and I have a baby bed in one of my exam rooms. Would you help me bring it into my lab?" she asked Michael.

Catherine put several pots of water on to boil and went to the cabinet to get some herbs. Michael was holding Heather now, and watched Catherine get the tent ready.

"She is not going to like being under the tent and inhaling the steam, and I hope you don't mind her crying."

Catherine could see that Michael looked worried. Alex had come back and she asked Michael to let him in. Alex asked what he could do and Catherine told him to just take care of Michael. When the tent was ready, she took Heather's clothes off, leaving her pantalets on and then took her over to the tent. She began screaming and crying while Catherine held her under the herbed steam tent. Catherine began singing to her in French and after awhile she stopped crying. When she finally fell asleep Catherine put her in the crib and moved it closer to the steam, placing the tent over it. She put another pot of water on the stove and then she pulled a chair over by the bed and sat in it watching Heather sleep. It was almost midnight. Michael and Alex had been waiting in the parlor and Michael came into the kitchen.

"How's she doing?" he asked.

"She seems to be breathing much easier and I think she will be fine. I'll stay here with her during the night. You should go home and get some sleep," Catherine suggested.

"I'm not leaving either of you. You and I can take turns sitting with her," Michael said. Michael could see Catherine was hot and tired.

"It is hot in here. I'll tell Alex he can go," Catherine said, and left the room.

Catherine walked Alex out to the front porch and told him goodbye.

"The girls are beautiful," Alex said. "I'm glad you moved here. We had a good time today."

Catherine smiled and shook her head yes.

By the next morning, Heather was much better and Michael thanked Catherine for all she had done.

"I want to thank you for getting me the phone. I'll call Houston General and set up an appointment with Dr. Samuel Allen. If you'll leave me your phone number I'll call you and let you know what time you should have her there on Monday."

"I would love for you to come with us," Michael said.

"Mondays are usually full of patients and I hate not to be here. Dr. Allen and I worked together at St. Mary's Hospital in Galveston and he will take good care of Heather. They have inhalers with new medicine that you will be able to use for her to inhale that will keep her lungs open. I'll give him an update on her history. You'll like him a lot," she said.

Heather was with Celli in the kitchen eating some cereal and Michael followed Catherine into her office.

"How much are overnight visits?" he asked. Catherine told him he still had a credit from the twenty dollars he paid her last time. She had gotten up from her chair to walk Michael out, when he blocked the door and grabbed her, bringing her face up to his. It surprised her and before she could resist, Michael kissed her softly and then more passionately. She just stood there, not really sure how to react. He saw her surprised look and then apologized.

"I've been wanting to kiss you since the day I met you," he said. "I did not mean to offend you."

"I know your wife is not well, Michael, but I do not go out with married men. I would appreciate it if you would keep our relationship on a business level," Catherine explained. Michael seemed embarrassed and left to get Heather.

Later in the day Catherine called Samuel at Houston General and he was happy to hear from her. She told him briefly about moving to Rosenberg and opening up a clinic and then said, "I want to refer a patient to you and I would appreciate your seeing them first thing Monday morning if you have an opening."

"How about 10:00 a.m.?" Samuel asked. Catherine said that would work and she gave him the information about Heather's condition.

After they finished, Catherine had almost hung up the phone when Samuel said, "I need to see you, Catherine. I didn't like the way things were left the last time I saw you. May I come see you?"

"Rosenberg's a small town, Samuel, and it would probably be best if I came there," she said.

"I'll rearrange my schedule and be off next Saturday and Sunday. Will you come?"

"Yes," she answered, "but under the circumstances I think I'll stay at the Roosevelt Hotel if you will make me a reservation."

"I understand and I guess I deserve that. I really miss you and I'm looking forward to seeing you," Samuel said.

Catherine gave him her phone number at the clinic and Samuel gave her his home number. She hung up the phone and smiled as she put the receiver in the cradle. She needed a small vacation, she thought. Catherine wrote a note and posted it on the front door of the clinic. "Clinic will be closed next Saturday and Sunday".

Meredith accompanied Michael and Heather to Houston for their appointment on Monday. They were there thirty minutes early, but so was Samuel. He usually did his hospital rounds early and then saw patients at 11:00 a.m. This appointment was an exception and he did it because of Catherine. Meredith was expecting to see an older man with glasses and was surprised at Dr. Allen's incredible good looks. After examining Heather and taking an x-ray of her lungs, Samuel told Michael that catching her symptoms early was a good thing and that a new breath inhaler would probably reduce her symptoms dramatically. He said he would like to see her again in three months but that they should do follow up visits with Dr. Merit every two weeks.

"What can you tell us about Dr. Merit?" Michael asked.

"I worked with her at St. Mary's and she is very capable. I would gladly have her on my team if it were possible," he said.

"What about her family? Where did all her children come from?" he asked.

"Why don't you ask Dr. Merit? I'm sure she knows the answers better than I," Samuel said and excused himself.

Catherine had begun her usual Monday morning by getting up

at 6:30 AM and checking on the children. She liked to watch them sleeping and it validated her reasons for coming here. She would protect them with her life. She walked over to Adam's bed and smiled at him. She adored Adam and his strong will. She knew he would be fearless, and a challenge, but she vowed he would not get the best of her. Daylight had begun shedding light through the curtains and she looked out and saw Alex approaching her house on Pilgrim. She left quickly and went down the stairs to the door. She was on the porch when he approached.

He tipped his hat and she smiled at him. "Come in for coffee?" she asked. Alex got off his horse and went inside.

"Michael and Meredith took Heather to Houston and I thought if you didn't mind, I would bring Nicolas over to play with the children later. I offered to look after him today. He had such a good time the other day I thought he might enjoy coming over again," Alex said.

"Of course, Martha would love the help with the boys," Catherine said.

Alex stopped and read the sign she had put up. "Taking a trip next weekend?" he asked.

"I have some business in Houston and I just needed a couple of days away from everything," she answered.

"Your fiancé still in Houston?" he asked.

"He's not my fiancé anymore and yes, he is still in Houston, but that's not why I'm going," she lied.

Alex smiled at her and followed her into the kitchen. Lucas poured Alex some coffee and prepared a cup of hot tea for Catherine. Lucas asked if Alex would eat some scrambled eggs and Alex said he would if it were not too much trouble. Catherine and Alex talked about the children and that he was looking forward to becoming a father. With Lucas in the kitchen with them, they had to be careful what they said. When Lucas left the room Alex said, "I keep having a recurring dream and I wondered if it might mean anything to you."

Catherine listened but didn't say anything.

"Did I deliver Adam at the farm?" he asked.

"Yes, you did. What else do you remember?" she asked.

"You," he said softly, looking at her closely.

Catherine looked away. "Maybe it would better if you didn't try to remember," she said. "Meredith is a lovely woman and I know you love her. What we had is over, Alex."

"You are probably right, but I just wanted you to know that I'm really glad you moved here and allow me to see the girls," Alex said as he finished his last sip of coffee and got up to leave. "I'm here for you if you need anything, Catherine."

Catherine had wanted to tell Alex that Michael had kissed her but thought better of it. She did not want to cause any more friction between them.

Alex walked to the front door and Catherine followed several steps behind him. When he got out on the porch, he turned and looked at her, saying nothing. He saw tears in her eyes and took a step towards her, but she stepped back and closed the door.

When the clinic opened, Catherine was glad the waiting room was full. She needed to keep her mind occupied. Alex's visit upset her. If he was beginning to remember their life together, it was too late. He had a wife and she was going to have his child. Catherine liked Meredith and she would never consider trying to woo Alex away from her, no matter how much she loved him. Alex would never leave her either. That was the kind of man he was. If only it didn't hurt so much, she thought.

Catherine walked back to the kitchen at noon to take a break and get something to eat. She saw the children playing in the back yard and Alex was up on the porch with Emma and Isabella, looking at their doll house. She couldn't help but feel badly for him. Alex was their father and they would never be able to call him daddy.

On Tuesday, it seemed to be a normal day with patients who had problems with either their stomachs or a rash that would not heal. Her last patient was a woman, who gave her name as Agnes Whiting.

She told Catherine she had some female problems and needed to see her. Catherine looked at the patient form she had filled out and it indicated she was a widow with two teenagers and she was thirty-three years old. Catherine asked her several other questions and then the woman finally admitted that she had a lover and that each time they were intimate, it was painful. Catherine explained to the woman that it was not unusual for sex to be uncomfortable, especially if the man rushed their intimacy. Agnes kept her head down and appeared to be embarrassed. They talked some more and Agnes finally admitted that the man was married but that his wife was ill and lived at a sanatorium.

For some reason it did not surprise Catherine when she realized that the widow's lover was Michael. It did not sit well with her, though, because she felt Michael was taking advantage of the woman.

"He only comes over to my house after the children go to sleep and lately he only comes once a week. I'm afraid I've fallen in love with him," she said, crying.

"Mrs. Whiting, if your friend is married, you realize that there is not a future with him, don't you?" Catherine asked.

"Yes, but he was a friend of my husband's and the first time it happened, I tried to stop him, but he assured me that he had affections for me and that he would help me get over the death of my husband. Back then, he was sweet and attentive and I enjoyed being intimate with him, but lately, when he comes over, he takes me and he leaves quickly. I feel so ashamed. I know he does not love me and I can't seem to end it. I don't know what to do," she said with tears in her eyes.

"Mrs. Whiting, nothing I could say would ease the pain you are feeling, but I will tell you one thing," Catherine said sternly. "You need to be strong and the next time he wants to take you to bed, tell him you no longer want to be his mistress. You don't owe him anything and you have nothing to be afraid of. I would assume this man is a gentleman?" Catherine asked.

"Yes, very much so," she answered. "I know you are right, but I love him and I don't want to lose him."

"Then, you must know that you are headed for heartache. Not many men leave their wives, especially if they are ill. I'm sorry for your plight, but until you recognize where you stand with him, you will continue to feel violated. If you want to continue your relationship with him, then you must tell him that you want him to spend more time with you, so you will be able to enjoy your sexual encounters with him, too," Catherine coached her.

"I'm not sure how to do that. It makes me feel uncomfortable to talk about our intimacies," she said.

"You are giving him more than he is giving you, and you need to speak up for yourself. Trust me; he will respect you more if you tell him how you feel. I'm sure you can figure out something to tell him that will not make you embarrassed. Most men are takers and as long as women give in to their desires, they will always take advantage of us," Catherine said.

"I never thought of it that way," Agnes said. "I know you are right and I will give it a try. I appreciate your advice."

After Agnes left, Catherine shook her head and hoped that the woman would at least try and take up for herself. It was sad that she was so unhappy, Catherine thought.

The remainder of the week went by quickly and Catherine was glad when her last patient left at 2:30 p.m. She was hoping she could go to the general store and get a new dress to wear on Saturday. She had no idea what Samuel had planned, and decided on a simple peach dress with a lace collar. It hugged her slender figure and made her look taller than her five-foot-four-inch frame. She noticed a beautiful, soft, pale ecru shawl as she started to pay at the counter and she put it around her shoulders. Perfect, she thought. Catherine paid for her purchases and hurried home to spend the rest of the day with the children. She was already feeling guilty about leaving them for two days. They were outside playing when Alex, Meredith and Michael drove by with Michael's children and stopped.

Catherine waved them to get out and come into the back yard and they did. Michael thanked Catherine again for sending them to Dr. Allen in Houston, and Heather seemed to be as good as new. They stayed awhile and the children played. Alex was quiet and Catherine wondered if one of his headaches had come back. She offered them a drink, but they said they were not staying very long, and had only come by to thank her.

Catherine was up early on Saturday morning. She had packed the night before. She went into the children's rooms and leaned over and lightly kissed them, not wanting to wake them up.

Celli usually had Saturday and Sunday off, so Catherine had asked if she would work and help Martha with the children. Celli could also help if there were any light emergencies in the clinic. Catherine had showed her how to sew up stitches and set small breaks. Celli already knew how to deliver babies, so Catherine felt everything was covered. She left the Roosevelt Hotel number and also Samuel's phone number, although she didn't write Samuel's name by it.

CHAPTER 25

Catherine picked up her small bag and walked the short distance to the depot. She had difficulty sleeping the night before, not sure what her weekend would be like. She had not seen Samuel since she walked in on him with another woman a few months ago. She had mixed feelings about that day. They had been engaged for a short while and she wouldn't make the same mistake of letting him talk her into it again. She loved being with him, but she was not sure she was in love with him.

The train ride took less than an hour. There was a short stop in a small town, but Catherine paid no attention to the name. Her mind was on Alex and she tried hard to put him out of her mind. He had been in and out of her mind all week and she knew she needed to try and erase all memories of him. She was going to spend the weekend with Samuel and she felt a slight hint of excitement when she thought about it. Samuel was fun and easy to be with. Maybe that was why she said yes when he asked her to come. She liked teasing him and she had to admit he was an incredible lover and she longed to be special to someone.

As she got off the train, Samuel was standing by the tracks with a huge smile on his face and flowers in his arms. Oh my, he looked so handsome she thought, as she got off the train. He picked her up and swung her around and kissed her. She kissed him back and it was as though they were never apart. He handed her the flowers and she thanked him. Samuel picked up her bag and took her hand as they walked to a waiting carriage.

"We can't check you into the hotel until after lunch, so is it all right if we take your bag back to my place?" he asked.

"Of course," Catherine answered.

The city was bustling with activity even though it was early. There were street vendors everywhere selling all kinds of vegetables, and there were wagons filled with pots and pans and trinkets.

"It's the second Saturday of the month and the farmers and trades people come into town to sell their wares. I thought we might check it out later on today, if you would like," Samuel said.

When they got to Samuel's brownstone, he unlocked the door and let Catherine walk in first. Samuel put Catherine's bag down and began to say something, but Catherine put her hand over his mouth and he stopped. She pulled his face to hers and gently kissed him on the mouth. Samuel kissed her back and they both wanted more. Samuel wasn't sure how far to take this and decided to let Catherine take the lead.

"I must admit, I wasn't sure how I was going to feel when I kissed you. I know you have had other women besides me, but I haven't been with a man since I was with you. Would you make love to me now?" she asked.

Samuel didn't have to say anything. He took the shawl off her shoulders and took the ivory clip from her hair, allowing her hair to fall over her shoulders and breasts. He pulled her hair back and kissed her on the back of her neck and she moaned.

"I've missed you Catherine," he whispered.

"I've missed you, too," she whispered back.

Samuel unbuttoned the front of her dress and his breathing quickened as her dress fell to the floor. Catherine unbuttoned Samuel's shirt and slid it off his muscular arms. He picked her up and carried her to the bed. While they kissed, they slowly began peeling the undergarments off each other, all the while kissing and wanting more.

Samuel moved his hand between her legs and she gasped as he touched and fondled her. When she was ready she pulled him inside her and they both erupted in pleasure. They lay silent for awhile, enjoying the aftermath of their erotic acts.

"You're right, Catherine. I have been with other women, but none of them compare to you. It's just sex with them. It's more than that with you. I really love you, Catherine. I've tried to forget about you, but I wake up every day thinking of you and I go to bed thinking of you. I think of you even when I'm having sex with other women," Samuel said.

Catherine turned over on her stomach and lifted her head, placing her hand underneath her chin so she could look into his eyes. "If you are going to ask me to marry you again, the answer is no," she said, teasing him.

"That's to be debated," he said and tickled her. She squealed and tickled him back. They were tossing and rolling with laughter in bed and then they kissed. They made love again. This time it was slow and sweet and tender. It was as though they were slipping into a ritualistic rhythm, cherishing each other's bodies as though they never wanted to stop. They gave their all to each other and neither held back. Pleasure was their ultimate outcome and they felt the electricity flow through each other's body. They collapsed and lay still for awhile and then finally drifted into a peaceful sleep, wrapped in the warmth of each other's bodies.

When they woke up, Samuel was watching Catherine as she opened her eyes and smiled at him. "Do I need to cancel the reservation at the Roosevelt?" he asked.

Catherine chuckled and said, "I'll have to think about that. Hmmm, yes."

Samuel was smiling at her as he watched her and gently moved some of her hair from her face with his finger. His fingers moved down to her breasts and he circled her nipple with his finger. She watched, saying nothing.

"I think we need to get up and get something to eat," Samuel said softly, "or we may never get out here."

Catherine didn't answer, but began stretching, and Samuel watched as she extended her arms up over her head and licked her lips. God, she was gorgeous, he thought. He reached over to grab her and she jumped out of bed laughing, and ran to the bathroom. Samuel shook his head and got up looking for his clothes. He liked that she was playful and fun. He was always relaxed around her. She made him feel exhilarated and on top of the world. No one would ever know the tragedy she had suffered and he admired her for her courage. He knew she probably would never marry him, but he was not going to give up. She was here now and she was his for two days.

It was an absolutely beautiful fall day and they held hands as they walked to the restaurant. There was seating outside under a canopy, so they chose to sit and watch the people in the streets while they ate. Samuel ordered wine and then sandwiches for both of them. They were like two young lovers without a care in the world.

"And how are the children?" Samuel asked.

Catherine thought for a few minutes and looked away. "They are all right, aren't they?" he asked, concerned.

"Yes, they're wonderful, except Emma has a sister," she finally said.

"A sister?" Samuel asked.

Catherine told him how Isabella came to live with them and Samuel rolled his eyes. "You are unbelievable, Catherine," he said. "You are barely twenty-one years old, and now you have four children."

"That's why you and I will never marry, Samuel," Catherine protested. "I love all my children, including Isabella, and they will always come first. What you and I have right now is not reality. I came here to forget about everything for two days. I feel carefree and like I can absolutely do anything when I'm with you. Please don't spoil that for me."

Samuel looked at her. "So I'm your weekend entertainment?" he asked.

"I didn't mean it like that, Samuel. You and I have different ideas about our future and want different things out of life. You like the big city and you have to admit you like a variety of women. I want a monogamous relationship and someone who wants lots of children," Catherine said.

"You underestimate me, Catherine," Samuel said, and looked away.

Catherine took a deep breath and put her hand on Samuel's. "Think about it, Samuel. You still have to finish out your year at the hospital. I live forty miles away and have spent a lot of my money building a clinic. The children love being outdoors and I'm at home with them every day, even though I'm working."

"What about Alex?" Samuel asked.

"I've always been honest with you, Samuel. I found out after I moved to Rosenberg that Alex lives in the same town. He knows Emma and Isabella are his children. His wife, Meredith, is pregnant with their first child and he loves her very much," Catherine explained.

"So I guess you run into him a lot?" Samuel asked.

"He comes over periodically to see the girls," she answered.

Samuel took a deep breath and looked away. "Do you still love him?" he asked.

"No, at first I thought I did, but after seeing how much he loves Meredith and realizing that he is not the same man I fell in love with, I, we just have remained friends," Catherine said.

"Is that all?" Samuel asked.

"That's everything," Catherine answered.

There were musicians playing instruments in the streets and they began walking over to their table while they played a lively turn. Several of the gypsy dancers began dancing around the table Catherine and Samuel were sitting at. One of the gypsies grabbed Catherine's hand and encouraged her to dance. Catherine got up, moving to the music, and she took her shawl and held it above her head and began dancing in the street. She was smiling and she never took her eyes off Samuel. Her moves became sexy and tantalizing. She twirled and laughed as Samuel watched in admiration. When the music stopped, Catherine walked over to the table and Samuel grabbed her, pulling her onto his lap and kissing her. Everyone cheered and clapped.

"It's still early, shall we check out the street vendors?" Samuel asked.

Catherine shook her head yes. Samuel took her hand and led her through the crowd to the shopping area. They looked at trinkets, clothing, and jewelry, and picked out a few gifts for Catherine to take home. Samuel took Catherine over to a small wagon that had hair accessories and he picked out a barrette with flowers and ribbon on it and bought it for her. He clipped it in her hair.

"Remember me when you wear it," he said, smiling at her.

There was an empty table outside a saloon and they sat at a small table. Samuel ordered two glasses of wine and they sipped it while they watched the dancing. Samuel pulled his chair close to Catherine and he put his arm around her. Catherine looked at him and couldn't remember when she had been so happy. She was always relaxed around Samuel and he made her feel so special. She loved a lot of things about him and the more she thought about it, she decided she liked everything about him. If things were different she would marry him today.

On their way back to Samuel's house, they stopped and bought presents for the children. Catherine told Samuel she wanted to check on the children and asked if she could use his phone to make a long distance call. She only spoke for a few minutes, as the children were outside playing and Lucas answered the phone.

"Everything is fine here," he said.

Catherine told him to let Martha know she would be coming in on the 1:00 p.m. train the next day. After she hung up she walked over and put her arms around Samuel and told him how happy she was. He smiled and asked if she wanted to go out somewhere special. She stepped back and began unbuttoning Samuel's shirt.

"I'd rather keep you to myself," she said.

The two became immersed in an erotic frenzy of passionate love. The evening was one neither would forget and it went by quickly. They slept until 10:00 a.m. on Sunday morning and when Catherine woke up she had started her period. She had failed to bring anything, so Samuel dressed and went to the drug store. He also stopped and picked up some scones and pastries. Catherine had bathed and her hair was still wet when Samuel got home. He had put a kettle of water on the stove and got out two cups for their tea. After she dressed she walked over to the table where Samuel was waiting for her to sit down.

"I'm going to miss you," she said as she played with a piece of scone she had broken off.

Samuel was watching her, and he took her hand that was holding the piece of scone. He lifted it up to his open mouth and then licked her fingers.

"I'm going to miss you, too," he said.

After they finished eating, Catherine began packing her bag and walked over to where Samuel was washing the cups in the kitchen.

"Thank you for a wonderful weekend," she said.

Samuel dried his hands and pulled her to him and they hugged. "Maybe we can do it again someday," he said. "Are you ready to go?"

They took the trolley to the train depot in silence. They were both a bit melancholy and neither wanted to say goodbye. Samuel gave her a sweet kiss and she boarded the train. He stood and watched, waiting for her to find a seat by the window. Catherine looked out and saw him staring toward her with an empty look on his face. Their eyes searched each other for some kind of answer but there was none. It took all her will not to get off the train and run after him. But it was a life she knew she could never have.

Samuel put his hands in his pockets and looked down at the ground as the train began chugging forward. He looked up just as her car moved past him and Catherine thought she saw tears in his eyes. He continued to watch the train as the caboose passed by him and then he turned and slowly walked away.

CHAPTER 26

The train ride back to Rosenberg seemed to take forever. Catherine knew Samuel was in love with her and when she was with him she felt the same way. She had to be the one to stay strong. She would never forgive herself if anything happened to Samuel. It was better this way, she tried to convince herself. In time he would forget her and find someone more suitable. The only thing she had to look forward to now was seeing her children. They were her life and that had to be enough, she thought.

Lucas heard the train whistle and walked quickly to meet Catherine's train. She was already walking towards the house when he caught up with her. Catherine saw something in his face that gave her concern.

"Is something wrong?" she asked.

"Mr. Atwood's wife, Helen, committed suicide last night. She made a noose out of her torn sheets and hung herself after she tied it around the bars in the door. When they went to her room this morning it was too late. Mr. Atwood and Mrs. Cooper are on their way to pick up her body. Mr. Cooper stayed here to make arrangements for the funeral."

"Oh no," Catherine said. "That's horrible."

The children were in the back yard when they got to the house and Catherine went around back to see them. She hugged and kissed them and then sat on the porch and watched them play. Her thoughts went to Michael and his children and how awful it was that the children would have to grow up without a mother.

Alex tied Pilgrim to the fence at the front of the house and then walked around back. He could hear the children playing and he wondered if Catherine was home. When she saw him she stood up and waited for him to hug the girls. Adam and Daniel were playing in the sandbox and Lucas was helping them make a sand house.

"I'm so sorry. Lucas told me about Helen," Catherine said to Alex.

"It wasn't the first time she had done something like this. But this time she waited until after the last check to put the sheets through the bars. Michael is taking it pretty hard," Alex said. "There will be a church service in the morning at 11:00a.m.and burial will follow that."

"How are you and Meredith doing?" she asked.

"We're doing all right. We're just concerned about Michael. He feels guilty and, of course, he's worried about the children," he answered. "I expect they'll be home before dark."

"How was Houston?" he asked. Alex noticed that she looked exceptionally beautiful and had a glow about her. He wondered if she had seen her old fiancé, but didn't feel he had the right to ask.

"It was nice. I enjoyed having a little time to myself," she answered.

Alex looked at her and thought it interesting that every time he was with her he wanted to put his arms around her and hold her. She was so beautiful and caring and he felt as if he were falling in love with her again. He had to fight his feelings for her and knew that she would never allow him to become her lover. He was married to Meredith now and he would never betray her no matter how much he might care about Catherine. He would just have to keep his distance, he told himself.

The funeral was on Monday morning and Catherine had placed a note on the front door that they would open at 1:00 p.m. She rode in the wagon with Lucas and Celli to the outskirts of town where the small Christian Church would hold the service. Before they went in, Lucas told Catherine that he and Celli would wait outside for her.

"Negro folk ain't allowed in this church," he declared to Catherine.

Catherine went in alone and saw Agnes Whiting, so she walked towards her pew and took a seat. The ladies exchanged smiles but said nothing. She felt badly that Celli and Lucas could not come in. It looked like half of the townspeople were there. It wasn't surprising, because Michael was from an old family and many of the people worked for him. The preacher got up and nodded towards the side door, where a man was standing. When he opened the door Michael and his family walked in and took their seats on the front row in front of Helen's coffin. The church choir sang several old hymns and then the preacher walked over to the pulpit and said that everyone was there to celebrate the life of Helen Ingram Atwood.

Catherine had noticed an older man with his head down, and she wondered if he was Helen's father. Catherine listened as the preacher gave a background of Helen's upbringing and that she had lost her mother two years earlier. The service lasted about thirty minutes and after the family left out the side door they had come in, the remainder of the people left through the front door.

Lucas and Celli were waiting in the wagon and Lucas helped Catherine get into it. The cemetery was only a mile from the little church and even though the sky was cloudy, the temperature was tolerable. They waited off to the side for the pallbearers to carry Helen's coffin to the grave. Alex was a pallbearer, but he was the only one Catherine knew. Several people stopped and acknowledged Catherine and walked past her to get closer. Catherine's thoughts went to her first husband and Daniel's father. She missed John, and she knew Michael was in as much pain as she had been in when John had passed. Losing a loved one was never easy and she had compassion for him.

After the graveside service she walked up and hugged Michael and Meredith. Meredith invited her to the house for a family gathering after the funeral, but Catherine said she had patients waiting and needed to get back to the clinic.

When she got back to the clinic, several people were on the front porch waiting.

"I'll make you a quick sandwich and put it in your office, Dr. Merit," Lucas said.

Catherine and Celli put on their lab coats and Celli called the first patient. Johnny Simmons was the man from the paper mill whom she had seen a week earlier. He had come to the clinic because he had a bad cut on his arm. Catherine had warned him to keep the wound clean, but when she removed Mr. Simmons' bandage it was obvious he had not heeded her warning. The smell was overwhelming. She looked at it carefully and asked him if he had gone back to work right away, and he said yes. The wound was not clean and had sawdust in it. Infection had already set in and his chances of survival were about fifty-fifty. She cleaned the wound and removed the old stitches. Mr. Simmons grimaced in pain as she began putting new stitches over his infected wound.

"You need to be in a hospital. I'm afraid the tetanus virus is setting in. Do you have someone who can help you get to Houston?" she asked. Mr. Simmons nodded his head yes. Catherine knew he was probably not telling the truth and asked if he had a wife or loved one who could help him.

"I've got family," he said and left.

Another young woman by the name of Paula Schmidt Brady came in and Catherine noticed she spoke very little English, so Catherine spoke to her in German. Paula looked pleased that Catherine could speak in her native tongue. She told Catherine she was seventeen and that her parents answered an ad in the Houston paper from a man who would pay for a mail-order bride. Her family sold her for fifty dollars and the man picked her up at the train station. She had been in Rosenberg for four months and she thought she might be pregnant. Catherine explained that she needed to have her undress and that she would need to allow Catherine to examine her lower extremities. Paula gave Catherine permission, and Celli showed her behind a curtain where she could undress. She came out with a sheet around her and lay down on the table. When Catherine pulled the sheet up she noticed bruising and some red slash marks on the girl's abdomen and legs. Catherine and Celli looked at each other. After Catherine examined Paula, she had her sit up and she checked her breasts and found bite marks and more bruising.

It made Catherine angry that this sweet young girl was being taken advantage of and she told Paula in German that she did not have to stay with the man if he was hurting her.

"My parents told me it was my duty to do what he said and not to try and come back home," she cried.

"Would you like for me to talk to your husband?" Catherine asked.

"No," she cried. "He will hurt me more."

After Paula left, Catherine knew how Alex must have felt when he knew she was being brutalized and that she had refused his help. She had tried to reason with Paula, but she of all people understood what Paula was going through. Fear was a powerful tool for a man to use when he wanted his way with a woman and it was just one more indignity for them to endure. Catherine didn't know what she was going to do about it, but she wasn't going to ignore it.

A week later Catherine read in the small weekly newspaper that Johnny Simmons, the man she had treated from the paper mill, had died of natural causes. Nothing was mentioned about his injury. It was a shame that his life ended so soon. He was only forty-one years old.

Catherine knew that unless people were willing to help themselves, there was nothing she could do. Death was just as much a part of her job as was healing. She hated losing a patient, but until medicine became more advanced, all she could do was try and save the ones she could. Even if Mr. Simmons had taken precautions to keep the wound clean it was not uncommon for one to get infected. There were no drugs to counteract it.

The weekend was almost here and Samuel had not called her. She missed him terribly. Catherine had seen Alex stop several times to see the girls but he always left shortly after she would stop and say hello. She wondered just how much he remembered and felt he was trying to put some distance between them.

She had not seen Michael or Meredith at all since the funeral and decided they must be in mourning. The days were not so bad, but the nights were long and lonely. Catherine wanted to call Samuel and each time she stood by the phone she would stop herself from picking it up. She wondered if he were working or with someone else. She couldn't blame him if he were. She had rejected him and she knew it must have hurt terribly. To escape her loneliness, Catherine began reading her Bible every evening before bedtime and while it brought her peace, her dreams were not so kind. She was continually tormented by her treacherous nightmares and she often woke up during the night and paced the room. She felt like she was still trying to run from something, but she didn't know what. Maybe she had taken on too much; four children, the clinic, Alex, and now Samuel. She wished Galveston were closer so she could visit with Father Jonathan. He always seemed to help her sort through her fears. Maybe when things settled down she would plan a one-day trip and go see him.

CHAPTER 27

Samuel decided to pick up an extra shift over the weekend. It had been hard for him when Catherine left. She occupied his mind night and day. He had several of his usual girls come by and ask he if wanted company, but he declined. One night when he got home late, there was a knock on the door. When he opened it, his neighbor, Sherry, came in and put her arms around Samuel and rubbed up against him. He really didn't want her to stay but thought some company might cheer him up. He poured two glasses of wine and offered one to Sherry.

"I've missed you, Samuel. You are always working at the hospital and you need to have more fun," she said.

Sherry had a simple dress on and when she stood up she untied the two sashes on top and her dress fell to the floor. She was standing naked. She began kissing Samuel and started unbuttoning his pants. Samuel watched her and she put her hands inside his pants.

"Come on Samuel," she pleaded, "It'll relax you."

She pushed Samuel back on the sofa and straddled him. They started kissing and Sherry unbuttoned his shirt and was kissing his chest. Samuel took her by the shoulders and rolled her off of him.

"Not tonight, Sherry," he said and stood up, buttoning up his pants.

"Wow, what's wrong with you?" she asked.

Samuel walked over to the door and opened it. Sherry stepped into her dress and tied the sashes. "Let me know if you change your mind," she said.

After she left, Samuel lay in his bed, angry with himself that he didn't make her go home when she first got there. Sherry meant nothing to him and he was tired of being a playboy doctor. He was ready to settle down, and he wanted Catherine more than ever. He finally drifted off to sleep, contemplating how he could convince her to marry him.

On Friday, Catherine was seeing her last patient when Celli came in and told her that Mr. Atwood wanted to see her when she had finished. Catherine was waiting in her small office when Michael came in.

"I'm so sorry about Helen and I extend my sincere condolences," she told him. "How are you doing?" she asked.

"It really hit me hard," Michael said. "I know we haven't been living together for a while, but it hasn't been easy. Nicolas understands, but Heather is too young. I loved Helen a lot and I can't help but feel guilty that I may have been part of her problem," he said.

"You shouldn't blame yourself, Michael. Mental illness and depression are difficult to diagnose and cure. I lost my first husband and I understand that you want to blame yourself, but you shouldn't. Is there anything I can do for you?" she asked.

"I'm really having trouble sleeping and when I do fall asleep, I wake up in the middle of the night and can't go back to sleep," he said.

"I can give you some tablets that might help, but you need to cut back on coffee and try not to drink more than two cups a day. The coffee is a stimulant and will often cause insomnia," she told him.

Catherine wanted to see what else Michael had on his mind so she waited.

"I don't plan to get out and start dating for a few months, but I was wondering if you might come over to dinner at my house sometime, just as a friend. You are easy to talk to and you seem to have a calming effect on my nerves," he said.

"I would be happy to, but only if Alex and Meredith are there. Since you are in mourning, I think we should not be alone," she commented.

"Of course," he said. "I wouldn't want you to be uncomfortable either."

"I'm always available here at my office, if you need me," Catherine said.

Michael left and Catherine couldn't help but be apprehensive about his wanting to have her over to dinner. He was the last man she would want to get involved with. He was much too curious about her previous life and he seemed to always want to be in control of everything. She valued her friendship with him, but other than that, she preferred not to be put in a situation where they would be alone together. It was especially hard now that she knew he was carrying on a relationship with one of her patients. She knew she could never tell him about Agnes' visit, but she also knew it had been wrong. She had to keep her distance and she had to be careful.

After Catherine put the children to bed she went to her dressing table and picked up the barrette that Samuel had bought her. She clipped it in her hair and smiled at her image. She longed to hold him in her arms. She wasn't sleepy and thought she might take a walk. It wasn't totally dark but the fall weather was beginning to set in, so she took her shawl.

Catherine walked out the front door and stood out on the porch for a few minutes, then sat in one of the rocking chairs. She clutched her shawl around her and she began thinking of Samuel and their nights of love-making. It was almost 8:00 p.m. and she couldn't hold back anymore; she had to talk to him. She went back inside and stared at the phone for a few minutes trying to get her nerve up. As she was standing there, it rang and she jumped. She picked it up on the second ring and said, "This is Dr. Merit."

"I think my wife is having a miscarriage," the man said on the other end.

"Who is this?" She asked.

"Joe Brady, my wife is Paula Brady," he said.

"Can you bring her here?" Catherine asked.

"No, I need to come get you. She is bleeding a lot," he said. "I'll come get you."

Catherine went upstairs to Martha's room and tapped lightly on the door. "I have to leave and go to Joe Brady's house. His wife, Paula, is having a miscarriage," Catherine said.

"You should probably have Celli go with you. It's late," she said

"I'll be all right. I should be back in a couple of hours," she said.

Catherine was waiting on the front porch when Joe Brady rode up in his buckboard. When he got down off the buckboard, Catherine couldn't help but notice he was carrying a gun in his holster.

"How long has Paula been bleeding?" she asked. She could smell liquor on Joe Brady, but didn't comment.

"An hour or two," he said.

Catherine decided not to antagonize him. She could recognize his anger and displeasure. She had seen it before when she was with Brooks. It seemed to be a trademark of the beasts, she thought.

Joe Brady lived in a nice, large house about a mile outside of town and she wondered if he made Paula take care of it by herself. When they walked inside, Brady took her to a small bedroom in the back of the house which was down a dark corridor.

Paula was lying on a small cot and she had her back to them. Catherine went over and knelt beside her on the floor and took out her stethoscope. Paula had a faint heartbeat and Catherine turned her over on her back. She moaned slightly, but did not wake up. There was a towel between her legs and Catherine asked Brady to bring the lantern closer so she could have more light. She asked for more clean towels and he put the lantern down on the bedside table and went to fetch them. Catherine was able to stop the bleeding, but she knew from the amount of blood that was on the towels that Paula might not make it.

"She's lost a great amount of blood, and I'm not sure she is going to make it through the night, Mr. Brady," Catherine said. "I couldn't help but notice a lot of bruises."

"She falls a lot," he said.

"I don't think so," Catherine said. "I know brutality when I see it. Tell me, did you beat her up before she miscarried?"

Joe pulled out his Colt .44 revolver from his holster and grabbed Catherine's hair, pulling her toward him. He put the gun to her head.

"I heard you were too big for your britches and I got news for you. I ain't above killing you or her if you say anything. Accidents happen in this town, and I know where you and your little ones live, so I expect you to keep your mouth shut. If she dies, she dies," he said.

He pushed Catherine to the floor and undid his pants. He pulled Catherine's dress up and she kicked him hard in the groin and he collapsed to the floor. She got up to run but he caught her leg and she fell. She kicked his face with her foot and he released her.

She got up and ran as fast as she could out the front door and over to a grove of trees. There was barely any light and she had no idea where the road was. She was hiding behind a tree trying to catch her breath when she heard him calling her name. She stood frozen. She looked around the tree and saw he had a lantern with him and he was walking in her other direction. She took off running away from the house and didn't stop. Surely she would find a house or someplace she could get help, she thought. She heard him calling her name and he seemed to be getting closer. The memory of her running away from David Brooks in Galveston flashed before her and then she tripped. She fell and hit the ground hard. It knocked the wind out of her and she tried to get her breath. She heard him calling her name again, "Catherine, where are you?"

She lay still, hoping he would go past her, afraid he might find her. She tried not to panic and she could hear her own heartbeat. She slowly turned over on her back and she felt a rock beside her hand. She carefully tried to pull it out of the dirt and it seemed to be stuck. She dug her hand and fingers deeper and finally wedged it loose. If he was going to take her, she was going to fight for her life. She saw the light coming closer and she pretended to be unconscious.

"Well, looky here," he said. "The little doc is lying here just waiting for me."

He put the lantern on the ground and bent down to pull up her dress. She lunged forward and hit him in the head with the rock. He fell over, dropping his gun in front of him, and he was dazed.

Catherine got up quickly, picked up his gun and aimed it at him. "Don't make me shoot you," she said.

"You don't have the nerve," he said as he pushed himself up. He started walking towards her and she ordered him to stop. He was grinning as he came within five feet of her and reached for the gun. Catherine squeezed the trigger. The blast knocked her back and she fell on the ground. She watched as the glow from the lantern revealed the shock on his face. Blood was spilling from his chest where he took a direct hit. Catherine began sobbing and then she heard someone calling her name.

She was on the ground still holding the gun when Lucas, Alex, and Michael came up. Michael walked over to Brady and saw he was dead. Alex took the gun from Catherine and helped her get up and she grabbed him, shaking.

"It's all right, you're safe now," Alex comforted her.

"How did you know to come?" she finally asked.

"When you didn't come home, Martha woke Lucas and told him where you had gone. He called Michael and Michael called me," Alex said. "Brady has always been known for his drinking and battering of his woman. We heard him calling your name when we got out of the car. Are you hurt?" he asked Catherine. "You're bleeding."

Catherine touched her hand to her head and said, "It's just a small cut. I need to get back to the house and see about Paula. She had a miscarriage after Brady beat her up."

They walked back to the house and Michael called the sheriff's home and woke him up. He told him what happened and the sheriff said he would be coming shortly.

Catherine was still shaking when they got to the house. Alex made her sit down and went to get a cup of water.

"I'll be all right. I just need a minute," she said. Lucas and Michael went to find Paula. A few minutes later Michael returned and said, "I'm afraid she didn't make it."

"I should have done something when she first came to see me. I knew she was being abused, but she begged me not to say anything. She was afraid he would hurt her worse," Catherine said.

Lucas brought Catherine's doctor's bag and opened it up. He took out a piece of gauze and some medicine to clean her wound. She grimaced as he cleaned the blood from her forehead.

"I've never killed anyone before. What will they do to me?" she asked.

"It was clearly self-dense," Michael said.

After the sheriff arrived and spoke to everyone, he told Catherine she was free to go. It was well after midnight when they got to the house. Michael jumped out of the car and told Alex he would take Catherine in. Lucas followed and took Catherine's bag into the house. Martha had fallen asleep and was sitting in a chair in the front room. She jumped up when they came in. Michael said he would check on Catherine the next day, and left.

Catherine told Martha that she was all right and that she should go to bed. Catherine went to her room and closed the door. She was still dazed and upset and she fell into her pillow and cried.

The light was coming through the window when she woke up and she had a headache. She looked at her watch and it was 9:30 on Sunday morning. She was still dressed in her clothes from the night before and there were spots of blood covering the front of her dress. She went into the bathroom and turned on the shower. She took off her clothes and stood under it for a long time. She felt dirty and she wasn't sure she would ever get over killing a man. She had committed a sin and she wondered if God would ever forgive her. There was a knock on the door after Catherine got out of the shower, and she put on her robe.

"I brought you some hot tea," Martha said. Catherine opened the door and thanked her.

"I'm going back to bed. I'm not feeling well. Could you please see if Celli could help you with the children today?" she asked.

Catherine crawled back in bed and relived the night before. She knew she had no choice but to protect herself. Why did he force her to shoot him, she wondered. No matter how bad he was, he didn't deserve to die, she thought. Martha knocked on the door and went in. Catherine was lying on the bed staring out toward the window.

"I've brought you something to eat, and Mr. Atwood is downstairs. He would like to see you," Martha said.

"Tell him I'm not up to visitors. I really don't want to talk to anyone," she said.

Catherine finally fell back to sleep. She woke up when the phone rang an hour later and she suspected it was Michael or Meredith calling. She just needed to be left alone, she thought. She sipped on her cold tea and picked at the scone Martha had brought her earlier, but put it back down. Her mind felt muddled and she kept seeing Brady's face after she shot him. She felt like her own life had drained from her.

Catherine had awakened from another bad dream after a few hours and she began crying again. She hated that she had killed someone and she dreaded getting out of bed. It was 3:20 in the afternoon when she heard the door open. She didn't turn around, and assumed it was Celli or Martha coming to check on her. How was she ever going to face anyone, she wondered.

She felt someone sit on the bed beside her. She slowly turned over and Samuel smiled down at her. She reached up and grabbed him and cried into his chest. Samuel stroked her hair and held her.

"This will pass, Catherine. You had every right to shoot that man. You've got to stop punishing yourself. Everyone is worried about you. I'm worried about you," Samuel said tenderly.

"How did you find out?" Catherine finally asked.

I hadn't talked to you in a while so I called this morning. Something was just nagging at me and I just needed to talk to you. Martha told me what happened and that you wouldn't come out of your room. I was worried about you," he said. "I had two days off and I wanted to come see you."

"I'm glad you did. Thank you," she said. Samuel felt her trembling and he told her he was going to give her a sedative and he wanted her to rest. "I'll take care of your patients tomorrow."

Samuel picked up his bag and retrieved a needle and some medicine. After he gave her the shot, she clutched him and held him until she began to feel faint. Samuel put her head down on her pillow and watched as she closed her eyes. He leaned over and kissed her on her forehead. He hated that Catherine always seem to be right. She told him that bad things always happened to her and now this was just one more thing she could use to protest his marriage proposal. He wasn't going to give up, even if it took a lifetime. He watched her sleep for a while and then left her room and went downstairs.

He had not seen the children in a while and he wanted to visit with them. Celli stopped him and asked how Catherine was, and he introduced himself to her and told her that he had given Catherine a sedative.

"I'll be helping you with her patients tomorrow, if that's all right with you. Maybe after I say hello to the children, you can show me around." Celli said that she would be happy to.

Samuel made his way to the back of the house and found Lucas in the kitchen. They greeted each other and Samuel introduced himself.

"I'm making Dr. Merit some soup and its ready if you would care to have some," Lucas said more as a statement than a question.

"That sounds wonderful. It's been awhile since I've eaten and I must admit I'm really hungry." Samuel sat down at a small table in the kitchen and Lucas put a large bowl of soup in front of him along with some cornbread and butter.

"You're a great cook, Lucas. Catherine is fortunate to have you," Samuel said. "I've given her a sedative and she will be out for a few hours. I'll make sure she eats some of your soup when she wakes up," Samuel said.

He watched the children through the window as they played in the back yard. Daniel and Adam were on the swings and Emma and Isabelle were playing on the back porch. After he finished eating, he went outside to see them. The boys ran to him when they saw him. He bent down and picked up both of them, one in each arm, and walked over to where Emma and Isabella were.

"Hi Emma," he said, and she smiled at him. "You must be Isabella," he said.

"Issy," Daniel said.

The boys wiggled out of Samuel's arms and ran back to the swings. Samuel watched both girls as they picked up their dolls and showed them to him. He looked over at Martha and told her he had given Catherine something and that she would be asleep for a while.

"I should have never let her go out alone with that man. I tried to stop her," Martha said.

"When Catherine makes her mind up about something, it's difficult to change her mind. You shouldn't blame yourself, Martha," Samuel told her. He walked over and touched her shoulder. "Thanks for telling me this morning, when I called, that she was hurting. She thinks she committed a sin when she shot the man. It's going to be a challenge to convince her otherwise," he said as he looked off across the street. He saw a man getting off a horse and he instinctively knew it was Alex.

Martha introduced the two men and told Alex that Dr. Allen was an old friend. "Catherine's told me about you," Alex said.

"She's told me about you, too," Samuel said. The two men sized each other up for a moment and then Alex walked over and knelt down beside Emma and Isabella.

After he watched the girls playing for a few minutes, he walked back over to Samuel and asked in a low voice, "Is Catherine going to be all right?"

"In time she will. I've never killed anyone, so I can't imagine how she feels. Doctors are supposed to save lives and she took her vow seriously," Samuel said.

"It's good you came," Alex said. "Take good care of her."

He told the girls goodbye and waved at the boys as he got on his horse and left. Alex felt out of place with Samuel there. He knew Catherine would be glad to see Samuel and she needed someone in her life right now. Someone who would be able to comfort her and tell her everything would be all right. Alex knew he had lost that opportunity when he had asked Catherine for an annulment. Clarence was right when he told Alex that someday he might wake up and regret letting Catherine go. At the time he told Alex that, Alex never dreamed they would be living in the same town. He did love Meredith, but he also had regrets.

Samuel went back upstairs to check on Catherine. She looked so peaceful, he thought. Samuel had only slept about thirty minutes on the train and he had been up for over twenty-four hours. He lay down beside Catherine and put his arms around her. He breathed in the smell of her clean hair and closed his eyes, feeling the warmth of her body next to his. He wanted more than anything to kiss her and make love to her and assure her that things would get better in time, but he knew she needed to sleep so he closed his eyes, too.

It was 5:00 in the morning when Samuel woke up. Catherine was still asleep and he quietly got out of bed. He washed up in the bathroom and took a clean shirt out of his bag and put it on.

"Good morning," Samuel said to Lucas when he walked into the kitchen.

Lucas greeted him and asked how Dr. Merit was.

"I'm sure she will feel better after one of your great breakfasts," Samuel said smiling at Lucas.

Lucas poured Samuel some coffee and gave him a plate of eggs, toast and bacon. Samuel devoured all of his breakfast and was delighted when Lucas put a large piece of coffee cake in front of him.

"Do you cook like this all the time?" Samuel asked.

"Yes sir. I enjoy cooking for Dr. Merit and her family," Lucas assured him.

Lucas had put a single rose from the garden in a small vase and placed it on Catherine's tray. After he put Catherine's food on it, Samuel took it upstairs and set it on the bedside table. He sat down on the bed beside her and kissed her on the cheek. Catherine opened her eyes and smiled at Samuel. He smiled back at her.

"Let me help you sit up so you can eat something," he told Catherine. She sat up and Samuel placed the pillows behind her back. He lifted the bed tray and put it in front of her.

"I'm not leaving until you eat it all. Someone told me you had not eaten in twenty-four hours, so you must be hungry," Samuel said.

Catherine sipped her tea and ate the eggs, bacon, and a few bites of toast. She wasn't that hungry, but knew she would feel better if she ate something. She stopped after she had eaten most of it. She left a piece of the toast and ate a few bites of coffee cake. Samuel watched her and asked if she was feeling better.

"Yes, getting a good night's sleep and having you next to me was really comforting," she said.

Samuel knew she was still depressed and said, "Why don't you just take it easy today. Rest, play with the children, or do nothing. I'm going to look after your patients and you, if you need me." He smiled at her and picked up the tray to leave.

"Samuel," she called and he turned to look at her. "Thank you for coming. I don't think I could get through this without you."

He put the tray on a nearby table and walked back over the bed. She reached up and pulled him down so she could kiss him. Samuel put his arms around her, and their embrace lingered for a few more minutes.

"I don't know why I'm so tired. Did you put something in my tea?" she asked.

Samuel didn't answer, but smiled back at her as he got up. "Rest, just rest," he said.

Catherine watched as he left the room. He really was a wonderful man, she thought, and he was easy to love. Catherine did not know that Samuel had put a sedative in her tea and she felt drowsy. She felt comforted that Samuel was there and after a few minutes she went back to sleep.

When the clinic opened, Samuel had Celli introduce him as a visiting doctor from Houston. He enjoyed playing country doctor. They all had a story, he thought. It was different from the hospital. A lot of the patients had brought Catherine gifts and flowers. They all said the same thing. "Old man Brady was a force to be reckoned with." One lady told Samuel that she always thought Brady had killed his first wife. He had forgotten what it was like to be in a small town. When anything happened that was out of the ordinary, the chain of gossip didn't stop until the last person was told. He thought it interesting.

When there was a break between patients, Samuel went upstairs and checked on Catherine. He knew she would scold him for giving her another sedative, but he felt strongly that she needed to have some time to regain her strength. She would have insisted on being in the clinic with him if he hadn't given her one. He quietly opened the door and walked over to her. She was peacefully sleeping and he ached to hold her.

Samuel was seeing his last patient when Catherine walked in

with her lab coat on.

"I know what you did, and I'll need to discuss that with you later," she said as she looked at his notes on the patient. "I see from Dr. Allen's notes that you are feeling better today, Mrs. Anderson," Catherine said smiling at her.

After Mrs. Anderson left, Samuel waited to hear what Catherine was going to say about the sedative. He had leaned back on one of the exam tables and folded his arms, waiting for Catherine to scold him. She walked over to him and bit her lip. She took his face in her hands and leaned over and kissed him.

"Thank you for making me feel safe again. I wish you didn't have to leave," she said. "Are you on at midnight?"

"Yes, but I probably need to leave soon. I need to go back to my place and shower," he answered.

"How did you like playing small town doctor?" Catherine asked, standing just a few inches away from him.

"It was interesting. I could probably play the role, if the opportunity were there," he said as he put his arms around her.

"I've missed you, a lot," Catherine said softly.

They kissed and held each other for a while. When they released each other, Samuel said he needed to grab his small bag that he left upstairs and try and make the next train at 5:00.

Catherine waited for him to come downstairs. She was surprised when Samuel came out of her office.

"Sorry, I entered through the wrong door and ended up in your office," he said and smiled at her.

Catherine walked him to the front door and they kissed. She watched him as he started walking toward the depot. Watching him leave was harder than she thought it would be, so she went into her office, feeling down and alone again. She saw a sealed envelope on her desk with her name, Catherine, written on the front. She opened it quickly, wondering if Samuel had written it.

My dearest Catherine,

I drown in your presence and seek to have you near me, Your beauty overwhelms my soul and pours life into my being. Be mine, my darling and let no one keep us apart, I am your infinity and you have my heart.

I love you, Catherine. Please marry me.

Forever yours,
Samuel

Catherine clutched the letter to her breast and ran out the door. She could see Samuel as he approached the depot and she began running.

"Samuel!" she screamed. "Samuel!"

Samuel turned and began walking towards Catherine. As they got closer, Samuel thought he heard Catherine said yes. He grinned and ran to her.

"Did I just hear you say, yes?" he asked.

"Yes!" she screamed. "Oh yes!"

CPSIA information can be obtained at www.ICGtesting.com
Printed in the USA
LVOW07s1609170815

450458LV00001B/14/P